Two-Dollar Bill

Also by Stuart Woods in Large Print:

Blood Orchid
Capital Crimes
Cold Paradise
Dirty Work
Orchid Blues
The Prince of Beverly Hills
Reckless Abandon
Chiefs
Dead Eyes

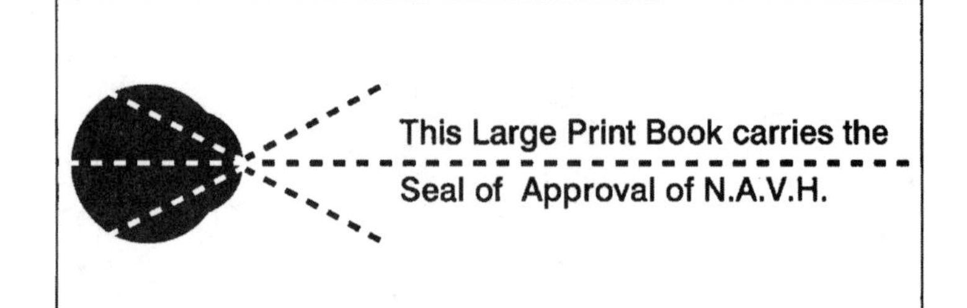

Two-Dollar Bill

Stuart Woods

Waterville, Maine

A Stone Barrington Novel

Published in 2006 by arrangement with G. P. Putnam's Sons, a division of Penguin Group (USA) Inc.

The text of this Large Print edition is unabridged.
Other aspects of the book may vary from the original edition.

Set in 16 pt. Plantin by Christina S. Huff.

Printed in the United States on permanent paper.

The Library of Congress has cataloged the Thorndike Press® edition as follows:

Woods, Stuart.
Two-dollar bill / by Stuart Woods.
p. cm.
ISBN 0-7862-7367-4 (lg. print : hc : alk. paper)
ISBN 1-59413-137-6 (lg. print : sc : alk. paper)
1. Barrington, Stone (Fictitious character) — Fiction.
2. Private investigators — New York (State) — New York — Fiction. 3. New York (N.Y.) — Fiction. 4. Large type books. I. Title.
PS3573.O642T88 2005b
813′.54—dc22 2005000105

This book is for Emma Sweeney.

As the Founder/CEO of NAVH, the only national health agency solely devoted to those who, although not totally blind, have an eye disease which could lead to serious visual impairment, I am pleased to recognize Thorndike Press* as one of the leading publishers in the large print field.

Founded in 1954 in San Francisco to prepare large print textbooks for partially seeing children, NAVH became the pioneer and standard setting agency in the preparation of large type.

Today, those publishers who meet our standards carry the prestigious "Seal of Approval" indicating high quality large print. We are delighted that Thorndike Press is one of the publishers whose titles meet these standards. We are also pleased to recognize the significant contribution Thorndike Press is making in this important and growing field.

Lorraine H. Marchi, L.H.D.
Founder/CEO
NAVH

* Thorndike Press encompasses the following imprints: Thorndike, Wheeler, Walker and Large Print Press

1

Elaine's, late. For some reason no one could remember, Thursday nights were always the busiest at Elaine's. Stone Barrington reflected that it may have had something to do with the old custom of Thursday being Writer's Night, an informal designation that began to repeat itself when a lot of the writers who were regular customers gathered on Thursdays at the big table, number four, to bitch about their publishers, their agents, the size of their printings and promotion budgets, their wives, ex-wives, children, ex-children, dogs and ex-dogs.

The custom had withered with the imposition of smoking rules, when Elaine figured that number four needed to be in the smoking section, and since the new, no-smoking-at-all law came into effect, Writer's Night had never been revived. Anyway, Stone figured, every night was Writer's Night at Elaine's, and that was all right with him.

On this particular night, every table in the main dining room was jammed, and the overflow of tourists and nonregulars had filled most of the tables in Deepest Siberia, which was the other dining room. The only times Stone had ever sat in that room were either when Elaine had sold the main dining room for a private party, or when he was in deep shit with Elaine, something he tried to avoid.

Tonight, however, Elaine was fixing him with that gaze that could remove varnish. He had been to a black tie dinner party and had stopped by for a drink afterward, just in time to secure his usual table, the last available. Now he was sitting there, sipping a brandy, and not eating dinner. Elaine strongly preferred it if, when one sat down at a table, especially on a night as busy as this, one ordered dinner. She didn't much care if you ate it or not, as long as it got onto the bill.

To make matters worse, Dino had wandered in, having also dined elsewhere, and had sat down and also ordered only a brandy.

Suddenly, Elaine loomed over the table. "You fucking rich guys," she said.

"Huh?" Stone asked, as if he didn't know what she meant.

She explained it to him. "You go out and eat somewhere else in your fucking tuxedos, then you come in here and take up a table and nurse a drink."

"Wait a minute," Dino said, "I'm not wearing a tuxedo."

"And I'm not nursing this drink," Stone said, downing the rest of his brandy and holding up his glass, signaling a waiter for another. "And you may recall, we were in here last night, eating with both hands."

"A new night begins at sunset," Elaine said. "Now get hungry or get to the bar." She wandered off and sat down at another table.

"You feeling hungry?" Stone asked.

"Yeah, a little," Dino replied.

Stone handed the waiter his glass. "Bring us an order of the fried calamari," he said, "and get some silver and napkins on the table, so it'll look like we're ordering."

"You think that'll work?" Dino asked, looking sidelong at Elaine.

"Maybe she'll get distracted," Stone said. "Bring us a bottle of the Frascati, too, instead of the brandy," he said to the waiter. "And some bread."

"The bread is a good move," Dino said. "You don't think she really meant that about going to the bar, do you?"

The bar crowd and the restaurant crowd at Elaine's were occupied by different tribes, each of whom acknowledged the presence of the other only when eyeing their women.

Neither Stone nor Dino had ever had a drink at the bar.

"Nah," Stone replied. "It's just her sense of humor." He looked up and was elated to see Bill Eggers, the managing partner of Woodman & Weld, the law firm to whom Stone was of counsel, coming in the front door. Stone waved him over and pumped his hand.

"Sit down and order dinner," Stone said.

Eggers sat down. "I already ate," he said.

"Shhh, Elaine will hear you. Order *something* for Christ's sake." Stone shoved a menu at him.

"Why?"

"You want to drink at the bar?"

Eggers opened the menu. "I guess I could eat some dessert."

"Good."

"I've been out with a new client," Eggers said. "He'll be here in a minute; he went to get his limo washed."

"Huh?"

"He wants to make sure it's *hand* washed," Eggers explained, "and he doesn't trust his driver to do it right."

"And you want this guy for a client?"

"Actually, *you* want this guy for a client, because he wants you for his lawyer."

"You mean he asked for me?"

Eggers nodded. “Go figure.”

A new client did not usually ask for Stone; he first came to Eggers with some embarrassing, awful problem: a private detective in the employ of his wife had photographed him in bed with a bad woman; his son had been accused of the date-rape of his headmaster’s daughter; his wife, drunk, had driven his Mercedes through a liquor-store window. Like that. Eggers then hunted down Stone, whose lot it was to handle the sort of thing that Woodman & Weld did not want to be seen handling. In return for this service, the firm would occasionally hand him a nice personal-injury suit that could be settled quickly.

“What’s his problem?”

“He doesn’t have one, that I know of,” Eggers said. “He’s a rich Texan, which may be redundant; he’s a good-looking guy who attracts women like blackflies on a May day in Maine; and he’s unmarried.”

“What kind of problems could he possibly have?” Dino asked. “Has he killed somebody, maybe?”

“Not that he mentioned.”

“How’d you come by him?” Stone asked.

“He was recommended by another Texan client, a very valuable one, a client you are not to go anywhere near.”

"And he just asked for me, out of the blue?"

"Out of the clear blue. He said, and I quote," and here Eggers lapsed into a broad drawl, " 'I hear you got a feller, name of Barrington, does some stuff for you. I want him to handle my little ol' account.' "

"He must be *planning* to kill somebody," Dino said. "Maybe drum up some business for me?" Dino was the NYPD lieutenant in charge of the detective squad at the 19th Precinct, sometimes called the Silk Stocking Precinct because it covered the Upper East Side of New York City. He had been Stone's partner, back when Stone had been a police detective.

"Here he is now," Eggers said, nodding toward the front door.

A man of about six-four and two hundred and twenty pounds, broad of shoulder and narrow of hip, wearing a western-cut suit and a broad-brimmed Stetson, filled the front door.

"He looks like one of the Sons of the Pioneers," Dino said.

Stone hated him on sight. "Make sure he orders dinner," he said to Eggers.

2

The Texan had a bone-crushing handshake. "Hey," he said to the table, then he started crushing bones. "I'm Billy Bob Barnstormer."

"That's Lieutenant Dino Bacchetti of the New York Police Department," Eggers said, "and that's Stone Barrington."

"Did you say 'Barnstormer'?" Stone asked incredulously.

"Yep," Billy Bob replied. "My grandaddy was a pilot in World War One, and after that he barnstormed around the country for a while, before he started up Southwest Airlines."

"I thought Herb Kelleher and Rollin King started Southwest," Stone said.

"Them, too," Billy Bob replied blithely. "Like I said, he was barnstorming, and his name was originally Barnstetter, so it made sense to make the change while he was doing that work. He got used to it, I guess, so he had it changed, legal-like."

Dino looked nervously at Elaine and slid a menu across the table. "Have some dinner."

"Thanks, me and ol' Bill, here, already ate."

"Bill is having dessert," Dino said.

"I think I'll have some bourbon for dessert," Billy Bob replied. He turned to the waiter. "What you got?"

"We've got Jack Daniel's and Wild Turkey and Knob Creek, but Stone is the only one who drinks that, except for that writer."

"I'll have me a double Wild Turkey straight up," Billy Bob said, then turned his attention to Stone, giving him a broad, pearly smile. "I heard some good things about you," he said.

"What did you hear?" Dino asked. "We never hear anything good about him."

Stone shot Dino what he hoped was a withering glance.

"Well, even back in Texas we get some news from the East ever now and then. Can I buy you fellers a drink?"

"We've got one already," Stone said. "What sort of problem have you got, Billy Bob?"

Billy Bob looked puzzled. "Problem?"

"Why do you need a lawyer?"

"Well, shoot, everybody needs a lawyer don't they?"

"Hard to argue with that," Eggers agreed.

"You planning to murder anybody?" Dino asked hopefully.

"Not this evenin'," Billy Bob replied, flashing his big grin again. "They got a pissing place around here?"

"Through the door, first on your left," Stone said, pointing.

Billy Bob got up and followed directions.

"That ol' boy has either the best teeth or the best dental work I've ever seen," Dino said.

"How did you come up with this guy again?" Stone asked Eggers.

"I told you, he came recommended by a good client in Texas. Stone, just talk to the man, will you?"

Billy Bob arrived back at the table simultaneously with his bourbon. He peeled a bill off a fat roll and handed it to the waiter.

The waiter looked at it. "A two-dollar bill? I haven't seen one of these in years."

"Coin of the realm, my friend," Billy Bob said.

"The Wild Turkey is eight dollars," the waiter said.

"That's on my bill," Eggers said.

"And the Jefferson is for you," Billy Bob told the waiter.

The waiter pocketed the money and went away shaking his head.

"Jefferson?" Dino asked.

"Thomas Jefferson is on the two-dollar bill," Stone said.

"I thought he was worth more than that," Dino said.

"Me, too," Eggers interjected. "Madison is on the five-thousand-dollar bill, except there isn't one anymore. I don't know who's on the ten-thousand-dollar bill."

"Chase," Stone said.

"There's no president named Chase," Eggers replied.

"Salymon Portland Chase," Stone said. "Secretary of the Treasury and Chief Justice of the Supreme Court."

"How do you know that?" Dino asked doubtfully.

"I know a lot of stuff," Stone replied.

"So, Billy Bob," Dino said, "is that whole wad in your pocket two-dollar bills?"

"Naw," Billy Bob said. "I got some hundreds in there, too."

Stone's calamari and Eggers's dessert arrived. Billy Bob tossed down his Wild Turkey and ordered another.

"When did you get into town?" Stone asked, trying to keep a conversation going.

"This evenin'," Billy Bob replied. "My GIV sucked a bird in a engine out at Teterboro, so I'm going to be here a few days while they stick a new one on it."

"I always wanted a Gulfstream Four," Eggers said wistfully.

"Sell you mine when my Gee Five gets here," Billy Bob said. "I got one on order."

"What's the difference?" Dino asked.

"The Five is bigger, faster, got more range. Shoot, I can go from Dallas to Moscow on that thing, not that you'd want to. Don't know why anybody would want to go to Moscow. Freeze your balls off."

Everybody nodded gravely. Conducting a conversation with Billy Bob Barnstormer was not going to be easy.

"What business are you in, Billy Bob?" Stone asked.

"Why, whatever turns a two-dollar bill," Billy Bob replied. "You name it, I'm in it. Me and Warren Buffett got a little start-up goin', but I cain't talk about that, yet."

Stone tried again. "What's your *main* interest?"

"Money."

"Can you be more specific?"

"American dollars."

Stone sighed.

Eggers jumped into the breach. "Stone, most of our clients are in more than one business. Sounds like Billy Bob, here, is an investor."

"I like that," Billy Bob said. "An investor. Yeah."

"Where you staying while you're in town?" Dino asked.

"Well, usually I take the presidential suite at the Four Seasons," Billy Bob said, "but all their suites are booked up for some kind of convention, so I guess I got to scare up some other accommodation."

"New York hotels are tight this time of year," Dino said. "Stone, why don't you put up Billy Bob at your house? You've got a lot of room."

Stone aimed a kick under the table at Dino, but Dino was too quick for him. "Well, I think Billy Bob is looking for a higher level of service than I'm able to offer," Stone said.

"It would be very kind of you, Stone," Eggers chimed in. "After all, it's very late, and Billy Bob is a client."

Stone looked desperately for an out.

"Why, thank you, Stone," Billy Bob said, sounding truly grateful. "That's the nicest thing anybody ever did for me. And I thought all New Yorkers was tight-assed sons of bitches." He shook his head in wonder.

"Oh, not all New Yorkers," Dino said. "Stone is a prince of a fellow."

"He certainly is," Eggers agreed, pursing his lips to suppress a laugh. "A king, even."

"If I were a king," Stone said, "neither of you two would have a head."

"Now, Stone," Dino said, "that's unkind. And just when Billy Bob was thinking well of you."

"I still think well of him," Billy Bob said, tossing back another Wild Turkey. "Well, I think I'm about ready to hit the bunkhouse. You ready, Stone?"

"Yes, I guess I am," Stone said, rising. "You get the bill," he said to Eggers.

"Sure thing, Stone."

"C'mon, boy, I'll give you a ride in my limousine," Billy Bob said.

Stone followed him toward the door, stopping at a table to give Elaine a peck on the cheek. "Good night, Elaine."

"Good riddance," she said.

3

Stone stepped out into the bitterly cold night and turned up his overcoat collar. Billy Bob joined him, overcoatless, and pointed at an absurdly long white limousine at the curb.

"Just hop in there, boy," he said.

As he climbed into the enormous car, Stone tried to remember the last time someone had called him "boy." Probably when he was a boy, he concluded.

Billy Bob climbed into the car and settled in beside him, then, simultaneously with the slamming of the door, the window beside Stone suddenly crazed over, apparently because of a bullet hole in its center. This was followed quickly by two more bullets, and this time, Stone could hear the gun. He had not even had time to duck. He looked out the now-absent window in time to see a black Lincoln Town Car turn left onto Eighty-eighth Street, against the light, and disappear down the block.

He turned to speak to Billy Bob and found him no longer there. Stone hipped his way across the seat and got out of the curbside door, looking for Billy Bob. The Texan stood in the street, holding an old-fashioned Colt Single-Action Army six-shooter with a pearl handle, looking for a target.

"Are you nuts?" Stone yelled at him.

"Huh?" Billy Bob asked, noticing Stone for the first time.

Stone snatched the pistol out of his hand. "Give me that!"

"Hey, what are you doin'?" Billy Bob demanded.

Stone stuck the weapon into his inside overcoat pocket. "You can get three years at Riker's Island just for holding that thing in this town."

"You mean New York won't support a man's Second Amendment right to bear arms?"

"Let's just say that the New York Police Department has a different interpretation of the Second Amendment than you do."

Stone walked back toward Elaine's.

"Where are you going?"

"To get the police," Stone called over his shoulder. "Somebody has just tried to kill you, and if I were you, I'd get out of the street before they come back." He went back into the restaurant and walked back to the table he had just left. "You'd better get some people over here," he said to Dino.

"Somebody just took a few shots at Woodman & Weld's newest client."

"What!!!" Bill Eggers shouted.

"Yeah, you can really pick 'em, Bill."

Dino got on his cell phone and called the cavalry.

Fifteen minutes later, Dino's detectives were conducting their preliminary investigation of the incident, and a criminalist was searching the car for bullet fragments.

One of the detectives walked over to Billy Bob, notebook in hand. "You're Mr. Barnstormer, is that right?" the detective asked.

"That sure is right," Billy Bob said.

"You got any identification, sir?"

Billy Bob produced a Texas driver's license.

"Is this your current address?" the detective asked, checking the license.

"It sure is."

"Are you armed, Mr. Barnstormer?" the detective asked.

"Hold it, Billy Bob," Stone said, placing a hand on his arm. "My name is Barrington. I'm Mr. Barnstormer's attorney," he said to the detective. "I'd like to point out that your question is inappropriate, in the circumstances, since Mr. Barnstormer is the intended victim here, and I instruct him not to answer. I will tell you, though, that Mr. Barnstormer is not carrying a weapon."

"Okay," the detective said, making a note. "Anybody see the car?"

"I did," Stone replied. "I was sitting next to the shot-out window, and I saw a black Lincoln Town Car make a hard left onto Eighty-eighth Street, running the light. It had New York plates, but I couldn't get the number."

"Okay," the detective said. "Mr. Barnstormer, can you think of anyone in New York City who might want to cause you harm?"

Billy Bob looked at Stone.

"You can answer that one," Stone said.

"Nope."

"No one at all?"

Billy Bob looked at Stone again, and he nodded.

"Nope."

"Do you know anybody in New York, Mr. Barnstormer?"

"Sure, I know lots of folks. I know Lieutenant Bacchetti over there, and I know a feller named Mr. Michael Bloomberg."

"You know the mayor?" Stone asked, surprised.

"Yep, we're real tight, Mike and me."

"I think that's all I need to know for the

moment, Mr. Barnstormer," the cop said. "Where are you staying?"

"You can reach him through me," Stone said, handing the detective his card. "Can we go now? You through with the car?"

The criminalist walked over.

"You find anything?" the detective asked him.

"No bullet fragments," the young man said, "but I found some residue on the broken glass."

"What kind of residue?"

"Whoever did the shooting used frangible ammo, the kind of stuff you use at the firing range. The slugs disintegrated on impact with the glass, which is why the window on the opposite side of the car didn't take any hits. Looks like you've got an environmentally conscious shooter."

"A real citizen," Stone said. "Is the car released?"

"Sure," the criminalist said.

"Are you through with Mr. Barnstormer?" Stone asked the detective.

"For the moment."

"Thank you and good night," Stone said, climbing into the car. "Let's go, Billy Bob."

The car pulled away from the curb, and Stone gave the driver the address before turning to his new client. "All right, Billy Bob," he said, "what the fuck was that all about?"

"How the hell should I know?" Billy Bob responded.

"You don't know who your enemies are?"

"I don't have no enemies, to speak of."

"What about the ones not to speak of?"

"Well, you know, you do business, you piss off a few people along the way."

"You do much business in New York?"

"Now and again."

"You do business with anybody of a criminal nature?"

"Well, you never know what folks do in their spare time."

"You know anybody with connections to organized crime?"

"I do business with businesspeople, that's all," Billy Bob said, sounding defensive.

"You piss off anybody in New York?"

"Not that I know of," Billy Bob said.

Stone was having trouble speaking, now, since he was sitting next to the blown-out window and the icy air was blowing in his face at thirty miles an hour, and his lips didn't want to move. He put his gloved hands over his face and waited for the car to reach its destination.

* * *

The car pulled up in front of Stone's town house in Turtle Bay, and everybody got out. The driver went to the trunk and began unloading luggage, while Stone, in amazement, counted. Eight pieces of black alligator luggage with brass corners were disgorged. Stone reckoned there was fifty thousand dollars' worth of reptilian baggage there. It took all three of them to get it up the front steps of the house and into the entrance hall.

"Pick me up at nine o'clock in the morning," Billy Bob said to the driver, "and get me a car with a back window."

"I'd advise you to travel in something less conspicuous," Stone said, "since people are shooting at you. Try a black Lincoln, like the shooter; there are thousands of them in the city."

"Okay," Billy Bob said to the driver, "something shorter and blacker." He tipped the man and sent him on his way.

Stone and Billy Bob humped the luggage into the elevator, and Stone pushed the button for the third floor. "Left out of the elevator, first door on your right," he said. "I'll walk up; we wouldn't want to break the cable."

"What time do you get up?" Billy Bob asked. "I fix a mean breakfast."

“Not early,” Stone said. “Kitchen’s on the ground floor; help yourself.” He let the elevator door close and headed for his own room, thinking only of how to get the man out of his house at the earliest possible moment the following morning.

4

Stone was wakened by the smell of seared meat. He rolled over and checked the bedside clock: 8:30 A.M. He had overslept. He struggled out of bed, got into a robe and walked downstairs to the kitchen.

Billy Bob Barnstormer was standing before the Viking range, turning over a thick strip steak on the integral gas grill, while stirring something in a saucepan on an adjacent burner. He looked over at Stone. "Hey! G'mornin'! I didn't wake you up, did I?"

"You did. What are you doing?" Stone looked at the steaks; he had bought them at Grace's Marketplace, at hideous expense, with the idea of cooking them in the company of a woman he knew.

"Why, I'm just rustlin' up some grub for us," Billy Bob said. "I had to go with what I could find in the icebox, 'cept for the grits. I brought those with me."

"You travel with grits?" Stone asked.

"Only when I go north," Billy Bob explained. "You cain't get 'em up here. How you like your beef cooked?"

"Medium to medium rare," Stone said, annoyed with himself for cooperating in this endeavor. "I'm not sure I can eat a steak at this hour of the day."

"Don't worry, you'll have the grits and some eggs to cut the grease. Breakfast is the most important meal of the day, y'know." Billy Bob picked up a bowl of what looked like a dozen eggs, whisked them briefly with a fork and dumped them into a skillet holding a quarter pound of melted butter. "Have a seat," he said. "Oughta be two minutes, now." He turned the steaks again.

Stone got a container of fresh orange juice out of the Sub-Zero and poured two glasses, put some coffee on, then set the table and sat down. Reconsidering, he got up and found two steak knives, then sat down again.

Billy Bob forked the steaks onto the two plates, then scooped out some grits, then filled the unoccupied portion of the plates with scrambled eggs. He took a bottle of Tabasco sauce and sprinkled it liberally over his eggs, but when he tried for Stone's plate, Stone snatched it away.

"Hold the Tabasco," Stone said. "You're trying to put me in the hospital, aren't you?"

"Aw, it's good for you." Billy Bob sat down and sawed his steak in half. It was blood rare, blue in the middle.

So was Stone's. He got up and put it back on the grill, then sat down and started on his eggs and grits.

"You like your meat burnt, then?" Billy Bob asked through a mouthful of food.

"I like it medium to medium rare," Stone said, getting up and flipping the steak. He waited another couple of minutes, then removed the meat to his plate.

"Real nice morning out there," Billy Bob said. "I brought in your paper."

"The forecast for this morning was six degrees Fahrenheit," Stone said.

"Yeah, I guess it's about that," Billy Bob agreed.

"You call that a real nice morning?"

"Well, the sun's shining bright," Billy Bob said. "That's good enough for me."

"Did you come to New York without an overcoat?" Stone asked.

"I never really needed one," Billy Bob said. "I spent a week in Nome, Alaska, on an oil deal once, in the middle of the winter, and I got by all right without one. What'd you do with my gun?"

"I locked it in my safe," Stone said. "You can have it back when you're on your way out of town."

"You folks sure are fussy about what a man carries," Billy Bob said.

"It's not us folks; it's the NYPD."

"You're my lawyer; get me a license for the thing."

"You have no idea what you're asking," Stone said. "The process is so long and drawn out that most people stop when they see the forms. And in the end, you only get it if you can prove you carry diamonds or large amounts of cash."

"How large is a large amount of cash?"

"I don't know, fifty grand, maybe."

"Well, shoot, I'm carrying that right now. I mean, it's in my briefcase. That's pocket money where I come from."

"In New York it's an invitation to get hit over the head. You think that had anything to do with your getting shot at last night?"

"You know, I've been thinking on that, and you know what? Them bullets was fired at *your* side of the car."

Stone stopped eating. "They were *not* fired at me."

"Well, we just don't know that, do we? You made any enemies lately?"

"I'm a lawyer," Stone said. "People don't shoot at lawyers."

"Why, shucks," Billy Bob said, "in Texas, every lawyer I know is packin'. Don't you ever pack?"

"Sometimes, when it's called for."

"Well, there you go."

"They weren't shooting at me. Nobody has ever shot at me, except when I was a cop."

"Maybe there's bad people you put in the pokey; maybe they're all pissed off about it."

There had, in fact, been such a case in Stone's past, but only one, and he was not about to admit it to Billy Bob Barnstormer. "Nope."

"Well, how 'bout that feller with the German name that got after you and Dino that time?" Billy Bob asked.

"How'd you hear about that?" Stone asked.

"I got my sources. You think I'd hire you without checking you out?"

"You haven't hired me, Billy Bob, and it's my considered opinion that there's no reason why you should."

"I don't see how you figure that," Billy Bob replied. "I needed a lawyer last night."

"Not really; all you needed was somebody to disarm you. I just made the investigation go a little faster."

"Funny, I thought it was when I mentioned Mike Bloomberg that things got to going faster."

"Right, you see? You don't need a lawyer."

"Well, I think I'm going to be the judge of that," Billy Bob said, taking an envelope from a pocket and laying it on the table.

"What's that?"

"Your retainer," Billy Bob said.

"My retainer for what?"

"For representing me as my lawyer. It's a check for fifty grand."

Stone gulped and washed down some eggs with some orange juice. "What are you involved in, Billy Bob?"

"Why, I don't know what you mean."

"I mean, you got shot at last night, and you seem real anxious to have a lawyer."

"Just in case."

"Just in case of *what?*"

"You know what I mean."

"No, I *don't* know what you mean."

"Everybody ought to have a lawyer. I have a lawyer ever' place I do business."

"And how many lawyers is that?"

"A whole mess of 'em."

"At fifty grand a pop?"

"Well, I pay less in the boondocks, but when you're in a place like New York, you got to go first class."

"I appreciate that, Billy Bob, but if I'm going to be your lawyer, you're going to have to level with me."

"Stone, I promise you, the second there's

something to level with you about, I'll level with you."

Stone eyed the envelope with the check. He had been prepared to instruct his secretary to sell some stock this morning, since he was cash poor.

"Well, all right, I'll represent you, but you've got to keep me up-to-date on what you're doing, if I'm going to be effective."

"Why, sure I will," Billy Bob said soothingly.

Stone didn't feel soothed. He felt stuffed like a pig, having just eaten the biggest breakfast of his life. All he needed now was an apple in his mouth. He read the *Times* and tried to forget his stomach.

The phone rang, and Stone picked up the kitchen extension. "Hello?"

"Good morning," a man said. "May I speak with Billy Bob Barnstormer, please? This is Warren Buffett calling." Stone was stunned into silence for a moment.

"Hello?" Buffett said.

"Sorry, just a moment." Stone held out the phone to Billy Bob. "It's for you."

Billy Bob took the phone. "Hello? Hey, Warren, how you doin'? Just fine thanks. We ready to go? Shoot, I been ready for a month. You want some money? How much? Thirty? That gonna be enough to give us a decent cash reserve? You sure you don't need more? Well, it's there if you need it. I'll get it to you this morning. Nah, I got your account number from last time. Great, you take care now." Billy Bob hung up. "Mind if I make a long-distance call on your phone? I'll pay, of course."

"As long as it's not to Hong Kong, be my guest."

Billy Bob dialed a number. "Hey, Ralph. You up yet? Okay, when you get to the office wire Warren Buffett thirty million dollars. Yeah, same account as last time and the time before that. You know the drill. Okay, talk to you later." Billy Bob hung up. "Well, we're off!"

Stone stared at him, wondering. Well, he'd seen Buffett on television lately, and it had *sounded* like him.

5

Stone worked in his office most of the day, clearing his desk of papers that had piled up over the past couple of weeks. It went like that, usually — he neglected things, then got them done in a rush. He had his secretary, Joan Robertson, deposit Billy Bob's check, and she looked relieved to have the money in the bank.

Late in the afternoon he went upstairs and looked for Billy Bob, but he had, apparently, checked out of the Stone Hotel. For a moment, Stone was confused by the pile of alligator luggage still in the guest bedroom. Then he found a note: "Thanks for the sack, Stone. Keep the luggage as a house present. I got some more. Billy Bob B."

Stone gazed at the cases in disbelief, pushing at them with a toe as if they might bite. They felt empty. He'd leave them there and argue with Billy Bob about it later.

He had a big event, starting at six o'clock — Woodman & Weld's annual firm party at the Four Seasons restaurant. He got out a fresh tuxedo, shirt, shoes, jewelry and a bow tie, then shaved and got into a shower. He had just finished and turned off the water when he heard a noise from the direction of his bedroom and the murmur of voices.

He grabbed a terry-cloth robe and walked toward the sounds. Two men in suits were having a look around his bedroom. "Who the hell are you?" Stone demanded.

The two men turned and looked at him, unsurprised. "FBI," one of them said, and they both flashed IDs.

"What are you doing in my bedroom?"

"Your secretary let us in and told us to wait."

"She didn't tell you to wait in my bedroom."

"She wasn't specific."

"What do you want?"

"The United States Attorney wants to see you."

"Well, tell him to call and make an appointment."

"Wants to speak with you *now*."

Stone checked the bedside clock. "At this hour of the day?"

"Get dressed," the man said.

What the hell could the U.S. Attorney want with him? Stone wondered. He went back into the bathroom, dried and combed his hair, then went back into the bedroom.

The two FBI agents were still standing there, looking bored. He went into his dressing room and got his clothes on.

"The occasion isn't formal," an agent said, when Stone reappeared.

"I always dress for the U.S. Attorney," Stone said. "Let's go." They went downstairs, and Stone grabbed a heavy, black cashmere topcoat, a white silk scarf, a black hat and some warm gloves. New York was in the midst of its coldest winter in years. They went outside and got into a black Lincoln that was idling at the curb, apparently driven by another agent.

"We have to go all the way downtown?" Stone asked. "It's rush hour; it'll take at least an hour, and I have to be somewhere."

"Relax, we're not going far," an agent said.

Ten minutes later they stopped at the Waldorf-Astoria, at the Towers entrance. The agents led him to an elevator, and they went up many floors, stopping near the top of the building. The elevator opened into a large vestibule, and Stone could hear the sound of many voices beyond a set of large double doors. An agent opened a side door and showed him into a small study.

"Be right with you," the agent said, closing the door behind him.

Stone shucked off his overcoat and tossed it onto a sofa, next to somebody's mink coat. He looked around the room: It didn't appear to have been done by a hotel decorator but seemed actually to be used as a study. Behind him, a door opened and closed, and Stone turned around. A tall, blond woman in a tight black cocktail dress walked toward him, her hand extended.

"Good evening, Mr. Barrington. I'm Tiffany Baldwin, the U.S. Attorney for New York."

Stone shook her hand. "The last time I saw you," he said, "you had a different name and were six feet six and wearing a double-breasted suit."

"I believe you're referring to my predecessor," she said.

The change was news to Stone. "When did he predecess?"

"He handed over the reins an hour ago. He's the new Deputy Attorney General; I'm replacing him tomorrow morning at nine. Those voices you hear through there are a welcome-aboard party for me." She waved him toward a chair and took one, herself.

"U.S. Attorneys are not named Tiffany," Stone said, "and they don't look in the least like you."

"Thank you, I think," she replied. "Sorry

about the name, but by the time I graduated from Harvard Law, it was too late to change it. I'll never forgive my parents, of course, but what are you going to do?"

"Well, now we know why *you're* here," Stone said. "But what am *I* doing here? Are you going to offer me a job as your deputy?"

She smiled sardonically. "Hardly."

"What do you mean, 'hardly'?" Stone said, sounding wounded. "I went to law school, too, you know, though not at Harvard."

"Well, that immediately disqualifies you, doesn't it?"

"Watch it. I'll spread the word, and you'll spend all your time in New York being given a hard time by old NYU Law grads."

"I'll look forward to it. Now to business. I want to talk with you about a client of yours."

Not Billy Bob Barnstormer, Stone thought. Not already. "What client is that?"

"Rodney Peeples."

"Rodney who?"

"Peeples."

"Never heard of him."

"Come now, Stone; confirming that you represent him is not a breach of attorney-client confidentiality."

"I'm not being confidential, I'm being baffled," Stone replied.

Tiffany Baldwin sighed. “It’s going to be like that, is it?”

“Like what, baffled? I am genuinely baffled. I have never heard of Rodney Peeples, and I suspect neither has anyone else, name like that.”

“It does seem improbable, doesn’t it?”

“My whole evening, so far, seems improbable,” Stone said. “Whose apartment is this?”

“It belongs to the Ambassador to the United Nations; the Attorney General borrowed it for the event.”

“The Attorney General is in there?” Stone asked, pointing at a door.

“He is.”

“I’d like to leave now; I don’t want to catch anything.”

“What?”

“I’m afraid that if I breathe the air I might leave here as a tight-assed, right-wing, fundamentalist, anti–civil libertarian with a propensity for singing gospel music. And I don’t think that’s treatable.”

She laughed in spite of herself. “Come on,” she said, rising. “Let’s get out of here.”

Stone stood up. “You’re afraid of catching it, too, aren’t you?”

“Not a chance.”

"Where are we going?" he asked, helping her into the mink coat from the sofa.

"To the same party," she said.

"No kidding?"

"No kidding. I may as well give you a lift."

"You're just a party animal, aren't you. Do you have another one after Woodman and Weld's?"

"My last party of the evening."

Stone grabbed his coat and followed her into the vestibule, where an FBI agent had the elevator door held open. They rode down in the elevator in silence, then got back into a waiting Lincoln, which was longer than the other one, while the two agents accompanying them got into a black SUV behind them.

"I don't think I've ever had this many chaperones on a date," Stone said. "And armed, too."

"This isn't a date," she said. "It's a coincidence."

6

Tiffany Baldwin pressed a button, and a glass partition between them and the driver slid up. "Okay," she said, "it's not a coincidence."

"Oh?"

"Nope. I'm new in town, and I needed a date for this party, and I once saw you across a crowded room, and I figured, what the hell?"

"I'm flattered. And is this Rodney Peeples fiction?"

"Nope, he's real, but elusive. We heard a rumor that you were involved with him, so it was a good excuse to call you."

They pulled up in front of the Four Seasons, and the doorman got the door.

"Let's leave our coats in the car," Tiffany said. "Then we won't have to stand in line for the coat-check room when we leave."

Stone tossed both coats and his hat into the rear seat and hustled her into the building, his teeth chattering. They climbed the big staircase and emerged into the Grill Room, which had been mostly cleared of tables so those present could drink and pump each other's hands without bumping into the furniture. A string quartet was sawing away at some Mozart in a corner, and great quantities of food and drink were being consumed.

Stone snagged two glasses of champagne from a passing waiter, and they waded into the crowd.

"Well," Tiffany said, "this is a good introduction to New York City. I recognize a lot of faces here; how many of them do you know?"

"Hardly any, except for the lawyers I run into in the hallowed halls of Woodman and Weld, but I recognize the same faces you do." They were former cabinet members, politicians, a couple of United States senators, the mayor, the police commissioner and enough city councilmen, CEOs and movers and shakers that if laid end to end would reach somewhere into the northern regions of Central Park.

Bill Eggers elbowed his way through the mob and, ignoring Stone, gave Tiffany a big hug and kiss. "Welcome home, kiddo," he said.

"Home?" Stone asked.

"I interned at Woodman and Weld for two summers during law school," she said.

Eggers took her by the hand and led her

up some stairs to a level overlooking the party. Somebody rang a silver bell, and the crowed quieted a bit.

"Good evening, everyone," Eggers said. "On behalf of Woodman and Weld I want to welcome you all here to our annual profit-draining salute to our clients and friends. I will keep you long enough only to introduce you to the newest member of the New York legal fraternity, who has just been appointed the United States Attorney for the Southern District of New York. Formerly, as a law student, she worked summers at Woodman and Weld, and I firmly intend to use that connection every chance I get on behalf of our clients. May I introduce Ms. Tiffany Baldwin!" There was loud applause. Tiffany raised a glass to the crowd and mouthed a thank you, but said nothing. She descended the stairs with Eggers, and Stone could not get near her for an hour, such was the press to meet her.

It was not until he had been swept into the main dining room for dinner that he found her again, his place card opposite hers.

"I assume you met everyone in the place," he said, sitting down.

"Twice," she said, fanning herself with her hands. "What happened to you?"

"I was flotsam in the tide, but you were

right, this event is an excellent introduction for you. Now half the movers and shakers in the city can say they know you when their friends say, 'Who the hell is Tiffany Baldwin?' "

"Call me Tiff," she said. "It takes some of the sting away."

"What were your parents thinking?"

"Louis Comfort Tiffany was a distant relative by marriage," she said, "and giving me his name gave my mother an excuse to tell people about the kinship every time she introduced me to someone. Never mind that trailer trash from Maine to California were naming their daughters Tiffany, even if they didn't always spell it correctly. You'd be astonished at the number of ways the name can be misspelled."

"What were you doing before your new appointment?"

"Well, until this morning I was an assistant attorney general."

"So, you're a Republican?"

"No, but the AG doesn't know that, and my father is a major contributor to the party and a friend of the First Family, and that passes for political credentials."

"You must have won a lot of cases for the Justice Department," Stone said.

"Yes, indeed, and always the tough ones

that the boys didn't want to try. They were mostly during the Clinton years, though. The boys began to catch on that the tough cases got them noticed."

"So, now you're the one who's going to try to put that nice Martha Stewart in jail?"

She raised her hands as if fending off the remark. "Nope, that one belongs to my predecessor and his chosen people. I wouldn't touch it with a very long pole. I take it, from your view of the AG, that you're a Democrat?"

"A Yellow Dog Democrat."

"What's that?"

"That's somebody who would vote for a Yellow Dog before he'd vote for a Republican."

"I wouldn't say that too loudly," she said, looking around. "This is a very Republican-looking crowd to me."

"Nah, they're mostly rich Democrats, though in a setting like this it can be hard to tell the difference."

Her eyes were fixed on the entrance. "Well, it's real hard to tell what *that* is."

Stone looked over his shoulder to see Billy Bob entering the room. He was wearing a western-cut tuxedo that seemed to be sprinkled with stardust, and on his arm was a six-foot-tall woman who looked like a stripper who had been redone by Frédéric Fekkai and Versace. "Oh, that's my newest client, one Billy Bob Barnstormer."

"You're kidding," she said.

"I am not."

"Where did he get that suit? It looks like he's playing Vegas."

"Texans have places to get things like that," Stone said. "They keep them from the rest of us."

"Thank God for that. Who is he? What does he do?"

"It's hard to say, exactly. He goes out into the world and gathers money from trees. He flew into Teterboro in a GIV last night and stayed at my house, leaving many pieces of alligator luggage behind as a house gift. And he got a phone call this morning from Warren Buffett."

"I should have such house guests," she said.

"Do you have a house, yet?"

"They're putting me up in a government suite at the Waldorf Towers until either I find a place or they need it for somebody more important, whichever comes first."

"I would extend your residence there as long as possible."

She shook her head. "No, I have to pay my own room service and laundry bills. Do you have any idea what they charge for dry cleaning a silk blouse?"

"A week's pay?"

"Very nearly, and breakfast this morning was forty-five bucks."

"I hope you ate well."

"Better than I intended to. I felt I *had* to finish it."

"I know how you feel. Billy Bob cooked me breakfast this morning — a strip steak and half a dozen eggs. I couldn't eat lunch, and I'm not very hungry now."

He looked back at Billy Bob and his date, posing for a photograph with the mayor, whose head hovered at about the height of the date's nipples, which were threatening to become visible. They all seemed the best of friends.

Stone was still thinking about that phone call that morning. "Excuse me a second," he said. He walked out of the dining room and into the hallway, next to the huge Picasso weaving and called Bob Cantor, who did all sorts of technical investigations for him.

"Hello?"

"Bob, it's Stone; are you near your computer?"

"Always."

"Can you do your magic and tell me the origin of a phone call that came to my house about nine-fifteen this morning?" Stone could hear the tapping noises from Bob's keyboard.

"Did you get a lot of calls this morning?"

"That was the only long-distance call before about ten."

"Here we go: It came from the residence of somebody named Warren Buffett, in Omaha, Nebraska. Holy shit, are you getting calls from Warren Buffett?"

"It would appear so. Thanks, Bob." He hung up and returned to his table.

"Everything all right?" Tiff asked.

"Seems to be," Stone replied. He was going to have to start taking Billy Bob Barnstormer seriously.

When the dinner was over, they went back to her waiting car.

"I'll give you a lift home," she said. She lowered the partition window slightly and gave the driver the address.

"You know my address?"

"You'd be amazed at what I know about you."

Shortly, they stopped in front of his house. "How about dinner tomorrow night?"

"Let me call you when I see how my first day is going," she said. "Will you take me to Elaine's? I've never been."

"Sure." He gave her his card. "The cell-phone number is on there, too, if I'm not in my office. But then, you probably already know my cell-phone number."

"Of course I do," she said, pecking him on the cheek. "Thanks for squiring me tonight; I'd have felt awkward alone."

"I doubt if you've ever felt awkward in your life," Stone said. He slid out of the car and ran up the front steps, carrying his coat.

7

When Stone got to his bedroom, Billy Bob's house present was stacked up at the foot of his bed, and Stone was confused. Maybe Joan had worked late and moved the luggage, but how had she even known about it?

The following morning, Stone woke at his usual seven o'clock, and this time, to the smell of frying bacon. He got into a robe and went down to the kitchen. Billy Bob was at the stove again, and his date of the night before was perched on a stool at the counter. Stone wondered if they had the mayor tucked away somewhere.

"Hey, Stone," Billy Bob said. "You're out of steak."

"Sorry about that," Stone said.

"This here is Tiffany," he said, nodding at the young woman.

She extended a hand. "Charmed, I'm sure."

Stone wasn't sure he could stand another Tiffany in his life. "I thought you'd gone to a hotel," he said to Billy Bob.

"Well, I thought so, too, but the Four Seasons won't have my suite until tomorrow night. I still had your key; I hope it ain't too much of a imposition."

"Oh, no," Stone said. "Make yourself at home. You, too," he said to the new Tiffany.

"I already did," she said. "I fucked Billy Bob's brains out last night in your guest room."

Billy Bob laughed loudly.

"I'm so pleased for you both," Stone said. "Billy Bob, I'll eat two of those eggs and two strips of bacon, and no more. I still have indigestion from yesterday."

The phone rang, and Stone answered it. "It's for you," he said. "Warren Buffett again."

Tiffany Two held the phone to Billy Bob's ear, so he could talk and cook at the same time. "You got it, Warren? Good. Everthing all right, then? Good. We got to talk about that other deal pretty soon. Yeah, I'll be at this number until tomorrow, then at the Four Seasons. Watch your ass, Warren; bye-bye."

Stone hung up the phone, feeling this was all wrong. One didn't tell Warren Buffett to watch his ass. Or did one? He didn't really know.

* * *

Stone was reading in his study when Tiff called. "How's your first day going?" he asked.

"Meeting after meeting, mostly just to get introduced to everybody. I've been brought up-to-date on a couple of cases."

"You sent up Martha Stewart, yet?"

"I told you, I'm keeping my distance from that. I didn't even ask about it."

"My guess is, you're going to get your ass kicked."

"Not *my* ass, sweetheart; I've got full deniability on that one. Looks like I'm okay for dinner, though. What time?"

"Pick you up at eight-thirty?"

"Why don't I pick you up? The car goes with the job."

"Do we really have to arrive at Elaine's with a security detail? I've got my reputation to think about."

"Tell you what, I'll ditch the Suburban, if the FBI will let me, but the driver will still be an agent. The office has had some threats, and the AG doesn't want me smeared all over a New York sidewalk. Like a lot of yokels, he thinks the city is a very dangerous place."

"I hope your office doesn't record your calls," Stone said, "or you're going to find yourself on the sidewalk job hunting."

"Good point. How does one dress at Elaine's?"

"Any way you like. I probably won't wear a necktie, if that helps."

"Okay, see you at eight-thirty; I'll dress sloppy."

Sloppy turned out to be a sheepskin coat over a cashmere sweater and tan slacks that showed off her ass beautifully.

They settled at a table and ordered a drink, then Elaine came over.

"Elaine," Stone said, "this is Tiff Baldwin, the new U.S. Attorney."

"I heard," Elaine said, shaking her hand. "You leave Martha Stewart alone, you hear?"

"Not my case! Before my time!"

"Fuckin' Attorney General!" Elaine said. "Next, he'll be after me!" She got up and went to greet some friends.

"You know," Tiff said, "practically everybody I've met so far in this city, including everybody last night, has hit me with that?"

"It's a good thing you're not running for office," Stone said.

"Thank God for small favors. You sleep well last night?"

"Well, I tossed and turned for a while, thinking of you, but I finally got a few hours.

Woke up this morning to find the Texan in my kitchen again, this time with his date. Oh, guess what her name is."

"Oh, God, don't tell me."

"I'm afraid so."

"You see the cross I bear."

"I do."

"What do you eat here?"

"Try the osso buco, unless you're dieting."

"I never diet; I exercise instead. The Waldorf has a very nice gym. Do you work out?" she asked, poking him in the belly with a finger.

"I hate it, but I do. I've got some equipment in the basement."

"It looks like a nice house; you had it long?"

"I inherited it from a great-aunt a few years ago and did most of the renovation myself."

"Nice to have a great-aunt, isn't it?"

"Yep. I'll show you the place sometime; my father did all the cabinetwork and millwork."

"Your father was a builder?"

"A cabinet and furniture maker. His father was a textile mill owner in Massachusetts, but they parted company over politics."

"What was the disagreement?"

"My grandfather was a Republican; my father was a Communist."

"No kidding?"

"Don't tell the AG; he'll come after me."

"Don't worry, his time is taken up with Islamists these days. Where'd your first name come from?"

"My mother's name was Matilda Stone."

"The painter?"

"Yes. You know her work?"

"I saw an exhibit of hers at the Morgan Library once, years ago. She's dead, isn't she?"

"They both are. Your folks still alive?"

"Very much so. Daddy is a Washington lawyer, and Mother is, well, a hostess and a great beauty. For a living."

"Baldwin and Peet?"

"The very same."

"So your daddy's rich, and your ma is good-lookin'?"

"That's about the size of it."

"Tough."

"Yes, it's been a hard life."

"You ready to order?"

"The osso buco sounds great."

Stone ordered it for both of them, along with a bottle of Amerone.

Dino came in, hung up his coat and sat down at their table.

"What are you doing here?" Stone asked. "Can't you see I'm trying to seduce this woman?"

"Introduce me," Dino said.

"Tiff, this is Lieutenant Dino Bacchetti, commander of the detective squad at the Nineteenth Precinct. Dino, this is Tiff Baldwin, the new U.S. Attorney."

"I heard about you on TV," Dino said. "Why are you trying to crucify Martha Stewart?"

Tiff buried her face in her hands and pretended to weep.

"It's not her fault, Dino," Stone said, "now go find another table."

"Okay, okay, I know when I'm not wanted," Dino said, getting up. "By the way, I talked to my guy who's heading the investigation of the shooting the other night. He thinks you were the target, not Billy Bob. See ya." And with a wave, he went and sat down with somebody else.

"Somebody's shooting at you?" Tiff asked.

"Ignore Dino," Stone said. "He's making it up."

"Are you really trying to seduce me?"

"Not yet."

Tiff dropped Stone off at his house at midnight.

"You going to be around this weekend?" he asked.

"Yep, I'm apartment-hunting all day Saturday."

"You'll be tired when you're done; why don't I cook you some dinner that night?"

"Sounds great; I want to see your house."

"And I want to show it to you."

8

Stone woke to the smell of absolutely nothing — no steak, no bacon. Maybe Billy Bob and his girl were sleeping in. Then, as he got out of bed, he noticed a sheet of his stationery on top of the pile of luggage at the foot of his bed. He picked it up.

"Hey, Stone," it read. "I got to go to Omaha right away to set up a deal. Tiffany is going to her place. I'll be back at the Four Seasons tomorrow night. Let me buy you some dinner. Billy B."

There was no date or time on it. He got himself together and went down to the kitchen for some breakfast, this time, his usual bran cereal. Helene, his Greek housekeeper, was tidying up.

"Good morning, Mr. Stone," she said, in her heavily accented English.

"Good morning, Helene. You can clean the big guest room; the occupants have checked out."

"Yes, sir," Helene said, and she went about her work.

Stone was halfway through his cereal

when he heard her scream. He ran toward the back stairs and met her halfway up, coming down.

Helene seemed unable to speak, but she was pointing up the stairs.

Stone ran all the way up to the top floor, which was more exercise than he had planned on that morning, and into the guest room. Tiffany was lying on her back in the bed, and he didn't have to look for a pulse to know she was dead. Her eyes and mouth were open, and there were big bruises on her throat. When he felt for a pulse she was cold.

Stone stepped back and looked at her, then around the room. Nothing was in disarray; her clothes were hanging neatly in the closet, and the guest bathrobe she had worn at breakfast the day before was thrown over a chair. He found her handbag under the robe but didn't touch it. He went back to his own bedroom and called Dino.

"Bacchetti."

"It's Stone."

"Whatsamatter? You sound funny."

"Billy Bob's girlfriend is dead in my guest room; looks like she was strangled."

"Did you screw with the scene?"

"Of course not."

"I'll be there with troops."

★ ★ ★

Fifteen minutes later, there were cops, crime-scene analysts and EMTs all over his house. Stone sat in his study, answering questions from two cops, Morton and Weiss, while Dino watched and listened.

"Where is the note?" Morton asked.

"In the trash basket next to my bed, where I threw it after I read it."

"Where is this Billy Bob guy?"

"The note said he had gone to Omaha. He's doing some kind of deal with Warren Buffett."

"How do you know that?" Dino asked.

"First, he told me so; second, he's had two phone calls from Buffett, on successive days. I checked out the first one, and it originated from Buffett's residence in Omaha."

"You check it out, too," Dino said to the two detectives. "And talk to Buffett. We got a time of death, yet?"

"The ME is upstairs working on it," Weiss said.

As if on cue, the ME came into the room, and he didn't waste any time. "Preliminary conclusions, death by strangulation, between nine and eleven, last night."

Stone breathed a sigh of relief.

"Where were you between nine and eleven?" Morton asked.

"At Elaine's." He pointed at Dino. "He can confirm."

"I can confirm," Dino said. "I got there a little before nine, and he was already there; I left a little before eleven, and he was still there."

"I didn't leave until about eleven forty-five," Stone said. "Elaine or the headwater, Gianni, can confirm that."

Weiss had left the room, and he came back with Billy Bob's note, holding it by a corner in his rubber-gloved fingers. "It's on your stationery," he said to Stone.

"I keep it on my desk in the bedroom, and in a pigeonhole over there." He pointed at a bookcase in the corner. "I guess Billy Bob found it when he was looking for something to write the note on."

A young man came into the room. "No prints," he said.

"Whadaya mean, no prints?" Dino demanded.

"No prints anywhere in the bedroom or bathroom, not even the corpse's. It's been wiped clean, the whole area."

"I like your purse," Dino said, nodding at the bag hanging on the young man's arm.

"It's the corpse's. Her name is Hilda Marlene Beckenheim, lives in Chelsea. There's credit cards, a Pennsylvania driver's license, a thing of birth-control pills and enough condoms to start a whorehouse."

"Hooker," Dino said.

"I'm so glad her name isn't Tiffany," Stone said.

"What?"

"Billy Bob introduced her to me at breakfast, yesterday, as Tiffany. One Tiffany in my life is enough."

"Had you ever met her before that?"

"No, but I saw her at a party at the Four Seasons the night before last. Somewhere there's a photograph of her with Billy Bob. Oh, yes, and with the mayor."

"The *mayor?*" Weiss asked.

"Don't worry, it's not a scandal; it's just a party photograph."

"Where else in the house might Billy Bob have left his fingerprints?" Morton asked.

"On that note," Stone said, pointing, "and in the kitchen. No, forget the kitchen, my housekeeper has already been in there this morning, wiping everything down. She's very thorough. By the way, she discovered the body. She's lying down in the second-floor guest room. Maybe she's recovered enough to talk to you by now."

Weiss headed for the stairs.

Joan Robertson, Stone's secretary, came into the room. "What's going on?" she asked.

"Joan," Stone said, "when did you last see Billy Bob?"

"Yesterday morning around ten, when he was on his way out. He said he had to go to Omaha, and he'd be back in the city tonight, at the Four Seasons."

"Do you have any idea why he didn't come see me before he left?"

"I thought you had gone out. Were you in the house?"

"I was here, in the study, reading, all day."

"When you didn't come down to the office, and when Mr. Barnstormer came down, I just assumed you had gone out."

Dino spoke up. "Did you see him leave the house?"

"Yes; a driver put his luggage into a black Lincoln and they drove away."

"How did you meet this Billy Bob?" Morton asked Stone.

"The head of the law firm I work for introduced him to me as a new client." He gave the man Eggers's name and number.

"I was there for that, too," Dino said. "Make a note; somebody took a shot at Billy Bob's limo the other night. DiAngelo caught the case; he'll give you details."

"Billy Bob's original name was Barnstetter," Stone said. "He says his grandfather changed it to Barnstormer, but it might help in running down his background. He came into Teterboro on a Gulfstream Four corporate jet, and he said an engine had to be replaced because of a bird strike."

"Where in Texas is he from?"

"I don't know."

"Anything else about him you can tell us?"

"He leaves a trail of two-dollar bills wherever he goes," Stone said. "Tips, mostly."

Weiss came back. "I called the Four Seasons Hotel. They know Barnstormer, and they have a reservation for him tonight, for a week."

"Be there when he arrives," Dino said.

Two hours later, the corpse was gone, and people were trickling out of the house. Stone took Dino aside.

"You'll notice I didn't bring Tiffany Baldwin into this."

"I noticed."

"Can we keep it that way?"

"I don't see why not; we can confirm your alibi without her."

"Good; the press would be all over it, if her name came into play."

"I'm not going to be able to keep your name out of the papers," Dino said. "They're already outside your door."

"Think you could give them a statement,

exonerating me and saying I've left on a Caribbean vacation?"

"I'll see what I can do," Dino said.

"I want to be there when your people question Billy Bob."

"Let's have dinner; they'll call me when he gets in, and we'll go over there."

"Tell them they're not to ask him any questions until I get there."

"You think he needs to lawyer up?"

"Wouldn't you lawyer up, in the circumstances?"

9

Stone got to Elaine's first and made a show of asking for menus. Dino got there ten minutes later.

"Anything new?"

"Nah. Morton and Weiss are at the Four Seasons, waiting. You have a number for Billy Bob's airplane or his cell phone?"

"No, neither."

"How about a home or office address?"

"Neither. Eggers doesn't have them, either; I called him."

"You lawyers really keep track of your clients, don't you?"

"He's new, okay? Don't give me a hard time."

"Somebody's got to do it."

"Shut up and order a drink." Stone nodded toward the approaching waiter. They ordered.

"Let's jump ahead in time," Dino said. "Suppose Billy Bob can prove he was in Omaha. What does that do for you?"

"For me?"

"You were alone in the house all day

with the girl."

"The ME said she died between nine and eleven last night. I was here, remember?"

"That was a preliminary estimate," Dino said, "before the autopsy. What if he comes back and says she died earlier or later?"

"You're just winding me up, aren't you Dino?"

"I'm just telling you to be prepared to answer some questions. If it turns out that the girl died at a different time, and you spent the whole day as the only two people in the house, well . . ."

"Well, what?"

"Was Helene there yesterday?"

"It was her day off."

"Swell, you just might end up fucked."

"Dino, I met the girl once, at breakfast yesterday. What motive would I have to kill her?"

"Well, let me put my detective hat on, here," Dino said, scratching his head. "You fucked her; it went wrong; she pissed you off; you strangled her."

"Get out of here."

"Or maybe you were playing that game where you *almost* strangle somebody to enhance the orgasm, and you were just a tad heavy-handed."

"Will you stop it?"

"Of course, maybe he hadn't checked the girl's neck for prints; maybe he'll find Billy Bob's there."

Stone gulped. "Oh, shit."

"What?"

"I touched her neck, feeling for a pulse."

"How many fingers?"

"Two or three."

"Well, I don't think we need to bother Billy Bob; I can just arrest you now and save everybody a lot of time and trouble. You want to cop to, say, man one? I'll speak to the DA."

"Go fuck yourself."

"Aw, come on, with good behavior — and you always behave well, Stone — you'd be out before it was time to collect Social Security. I mean, there was no malice aforethought. You didn't mean to kill her, right?"

Elaine came over and sat down. "What's up?"

Dino grinned. "We found a dead hooker in Stone's bed, and I'm going to arrest him as soon as we finish dinner."

"*I* found her and called you," Stone said, "and she wasn't in my bed, she was in the guest room."

"Well, that's certainly daintier, isn't it?" Elaine said. "I'd never think Stone would have a hooker in his bed, but in the guest room . . . ?"

"All right, you two."

"You think you know somebody," Elaine said, warming to the idea, "but you never know about their secret perversions, do you?"

"Not until the guy does a hooker in the guest room," Dino said.

Dino's cell phone rang, and he flipped it open. "Bacchetti. Yeah, I'm on my way, and don't question him until I get there." He closed the cell phone. "Billy Bob's back."

"But we haven't even had dinner," Stone said.

"You don't have to come; I can go over to the Four Seasons and help my guys question Billy Bob. Come to think of it, you might be better off if you don't protect him too much. I'd just as soon bust him as you; I just want to clear the case."

Stone threw down his napkin. "Let's go."

"Did you get the check?" Elaine asked.

Stone threw some money on the table.

"American dollars! How nice!" She tucked the money into the top of her dress.

"Watch it, Elaine," Dino said. "Stone knows people at the IRS."

"Get outta here, both of you," she growled.

* * *

Billy Bob was sitting on the sofa of his large suite, watching a shopping channel, which was selling awful jewelry. "Hey, Stone, Dino," he said. "What are these cops doing here? They wouldn't say anything until you got here."

Stone crooked a finger. "Come with me," he said. He led Billy Bob into the bedroom.

"What is going on?" the Texan demanded.

"Account for your movements yesterday," Stone said.

"What? What for?"

"Billy Bob, we don't have much time. Tell me what you did and where you went after I saw you at breakfast yesterday."

"You sound serious, Stone."

"There are three cops waiting in the other room. Is that serious enough?"

"Awright, we ate breakfast and me and Tiffany went upstairs. Then I . . ."

"Did you have sex with her?"

"What?"

"Did you fuck her, Billy Bob? Let's have it."

"As a matter of fact, I did. Then I got myself together, packed my stuff and left."

"Why didn't you take her with you?"

"Well, she was kind of tuckered out when

we finished, and she wanted to take a shower."

"Was she in the shower when you left?"

"No, she was still in bed, but she was thinkin' about it."

"Where did you go, then?"

"I went down to your office, but your secretary said you wasn't there, so I got in a car and went to Teterboro and flew to Omaha, to see Warren."

"I thought you had an engine down."

"Gulfstream service is real good; they flew one up and got it on there yesterday."

"All right, we're going back in there, now. Tell them what you told me. Have you left anything out?"

"What the fuck is going on, Stone?"

"It's better if they tell you. Have you left anything out?"

"No, that's it."

"All right, come on." He led the way back into the living room.

"Have you rehearsed your client enough, Stone?" Dino asked.

"Ask him your questions."

They asked their questions, and he gave the same answers he had given Stone.

"Can you prove you were in Omaha?" Detective Morton asked.

Billy Bob dug into a pocket and came out

with a card. "Warren Buffett's office number is on here," he said. "You can get him tomorrow morning. I happen to know he's out tonight."

"Berkshire Hathaway," Morton read from the card. "What's that?"

"It's just about the biggest investment company in the world," Billy Bob said. "Now, I ain't sayin' another word until somebody tells me what the fuck is goin' on."

"You didn't tell him?" Dino asked Stone.

"I wanted to give you that privilege," Stone said.

"Billy Bob," Dino said, "Tiffany was murdered in Stone's guest room some time yesterday. She was strangled. Did you have rough sex with the girl?"

"Hell, no, I was tender as a lamb!" Billy Bob said. "Who the hell killed her?"

"We were thinking you might tell us," Dino said.

"Well, I sure as hell didn't kill her, and I don't have no idea who did! Why would I want to kill her?"

"Did you give her any money before you left her?"

"Yep, I gave her six thousand bucks, in hundreds."

"There was no money in the room or in her purse," Morton said.

"Well, there you go," Stone chipped in. "You've got robbery for a motive. Somebody got into the house, robbed and murdered her."

Morton took a packet from his pocket. "We're going to need a DNA sample," he said.

"We'll stipulate that Mr. Barnstormer and the girl had sex yesterday morning, before he left."

"We still need the sample. If a robber had sex with her, we'll need to differentiate the sperm."

"Give them the sample, Billy Bob," Stone said.

Billy Bob opened his mouth and let the detective run a swab inside his cheek.

"Is that it, gentlemen?" Stone asked.

"For the moment," Morton said. "Don't leave town, Mr. Barnstormer."

"Is he under arrest?"

"Not at the moment."

"Billy Bob, you can go wherever the hell you want to, but keep in touch with me."

"I'm gon' be in New York for at least four or five more days," Billy Bob said, "maybe a week."

Stone stood up. "Good. Get some sleep, and we'll talk tomorrow."

Morton gave Billy Bob and Stone his

card. "Call me if you think of anything else."

Stone took Billy Bob aside. "Give me the key to my house."

Billy Bob dug into a pocket and forked it over.

"Now get a sheet of hotel stationery from the desk and write down your office and home addresses and phone numbers, your cell-phone number, the number of the phone on the airplane and your Social Security number."

"Why?"

"Because I like to be able to contact my clients when the police come looking for them."

Billy Bob went to the desk, wrote for a couple of minutes, put the paper in an envelope and handed it to Stone.

"Mind if we have a copy of that?" Dino asked.

"You can contact him through me," Stone said.

They left Billy Bob to get some sleep, and Dino dropped him off at home.

"What did you think?" Stone asked.

"He was plausible," Dino said. "But I wish I liked him more for the murder."

"Why?"

"Then I wouldn't have to think about arresting you."

10

Stone was having breakfast the following morning when Helene came into the kitchen.

"Good morning, Mr. Stone," she said.

"Good morning, Helene."

"That was a terrible business yesterday with that girl."

"Yes, it was; I'm sorry you had to be involved."

"She must have been very cold natured," Helene said.

"How's that?"

"I mean, the house is heated pretty warm, and there was a down comforter on the bed."

"I'm sorry, Helene, I don't understand."

"So why would she want to use an electric blanket?"

"Helene, I don't own an electric blanket."

"Oh, yes," she said. "You told me to buy one last year, when you had a guest who was cold in that room, remember?"

That stopped Stone in his tracks. "Yes, I think I do, now that you mention it."

"Well, she had it on, and it was turned all

the way up. How do you think she could stand that?"

"I don't know," Stone said, and his mind was racing. He reached for the phone to call Dino, then stopped. What was his obligation, here? If the girl had been under an electric blanket after she was murdered, her body would have cooled more slowly, and the ME's estimate of time of death, which would have been based on liver temperature, could have been off by hours. Reporting this fact to the police could tend to incriminate both his client and himself. The phone rang, and Stone picked it up.

"Hello?"

"It's Dino."

"Good morning."

"Not really, not for you and your client, anyway."

Stone's heart sank. "What do you mean?"

"The ME called this morning; when he gave us the time of death yesterday, he didn't know that the girl's body was under an electric blanket. Apparently, one of his techs moved the blanket and didn't remember to tell him until later."

"Helene told me about the electric blanket just a minute ago. I was about to call you."

"Yeah, sure you were. We got a whole new ball game here, you know."

"Well, neither Billy Bob's story nor mine is going to change."

"Actually, Billy Bob's ass is covered."

"Yeah?"

"Yeah. One of my people just talked to Warren Buffett's office; they confirmed that Billy Bob was there in time for a two o'clock meeting yesterday and didn't leave until four. That gives him time to leave your house when he said he did, drive to Teterboro and fly to Omaha in time for his meeting."

"Good for Billy Bob."

"Unfortunately, while his ass is covered, yours is not."

"Oh, come on, Dino."

"I don't really think you killed the girl, Stone, not even accidentally, but the consensus around here is that you're looking like the only suspect, and I can't squelch that. You know as well as I do that investigations follow the path of least resistance until some new fact stops them. Right now, the path to you is free and clear and well oiled. You better come up with some new facts."

Stone was about to reply, when the phone made a noise that indicated someone was at the front door. "Hang on a minute, Dino." He punched the hold button, then the button for the front door intercom. "Yes?"

"Mr. Barrington, it's Detectives Morton and Weiss; please open the door."

"I'm buzzing you in," Stone said. "I'm in the kitchen." He pressed the button for the buzzer, then went back to Dino. "I'm back."

"That was Morton and Weiss at your front door, wasn't it?"

"Yes. What do they want?"

Morton and Weiss appeared in the kitchen, and Morton held up a document. "We've got a warrant to search your house," he said. There were four uniformed officers standing behind them.

"Anything in particular?" Stone asked.

"We'll need the combination to your safe," Morton said.

"There are two of them; give me a second, and I'll open them for you." He turned back to the phone. "I guess you know about this."

"Yeah. Sorry I couldn't tell you sooner. Call me when they're done."

"Right." Stone hung up and pressed the intercom button for his secretary's office.

"Yes, Stone?" Joan said.

"The police are here to search the house; open your safe, but lock the filing cabinets containing clients' files."

"Okay," she said.

Stone turned back to the two detectives. "My secretary is opening the big safe in her office, but not the clients' files. Those are privileged, and your warrant doesn't cover them."

"Let's get it done," Morton said.

"Come upstairs, and I'll open my personal safe in my dressing room." He led them up to his bedroom and opened the safe. "Help yourself," he said, standing back.

Morton and Weiss shone a flashlight into the safe and began removing items, beginning with the handguns stored there.

"You have a permit to keep these weapons?" Morton asked. He held up Billy Bob's Colt sixgun.

Stone got out his wallet and handed them his permit. "The serial numbers are listed on the back of the license," he said, hoping they wouldn't check and find out that the Colt wasn't on his license.

"And you have a license because you're a retired cop?"

"That's right. Retired cops are entitled to them, just as you will be when you retire."

"I've got cash here," Weiss said, rummaging in the safe.

"I keep some cash in there," Stone said. "Never more than a few thousand dollars."

Weiss was holding a stack of hundred-dollar bills in his rubber-gloved fingers, dropping them into a plastic envelope. "I've got what looks like about five, six thousand dollars, in hundreds."

"That's what Barnstormer said he gave the girl, isn't it?"

"A coincidence," Stone said. "There are a lot of fifties, twenties and tens in there, too. I cashed a check for ten thousand dollars a couple of weeks ago; there's at least eight of it in that safe." He took his personal checkbook from his desk and handed it to Morton.

Morton looked through the register. "Yeah, here it is. Only problem is, it's the last check you wrote."

"That's why I got the cash — so I wouldn't have to write checks."

"Still, you could have dated it earlier, couldn't you?"

"Check with my bank; I'll call them for you, if you like."

"After we've run the bills for prints," Morton said. "Let's go see the downstairs safe."

Stone led them downstairs and showed them the safe in Joan's office. "Help yourself. This is my secretary, Joan Robertson, Detectives Morton and Weiss. Oh, Joan cashed the ten-thousand-dollar check for me; she can confirm the date."

Joan did so, and Morton handed Stone back his checkbook.

"We've got cash in here, too," Weiss said.

"There are times when we have a fair amount of cash in the safe," Joan said. "Occasionally, a client prefers to pay in cash."

"And it's always reported as income," Stone said.

"I can confirm that," Joan said. "I get the tax stuff together for the accountant."

"We're not the IRS." Weiss bagged the hundreds in the safe and wrote out a receipt.

Two hours later, when the police had gone, Stone called Dino. "Your guys are done," he said.

"I heard. I heard they found about six grand in hundreds in your upstairs safe, too."

"And they won't find Billy Bob's fingerprints on them," Stone said, "and not the girl's either."

"I hope you're right," Dino said.

"No, you don't; you're enjoying this."

"Dinner tonight? We never got around to it last night."

"See you at nine."

11

Stone and Dino arrived at Elaine's simultaneously, Stone in a cab and Dino in his umarked police car with driver. They walked in, and the first thing Stone saw was Billy Bob, sitting at Stone's regular table.

"Shit," he muttered under his breath.

"You mean you're not thrilled to see your client?" Dino asked.

"Shut up."

"Hey, y'all," Billy Bob said, delighted to see them. "Well, I'm glad I don't have to eat by myself. Y'all have a drink."

"So, Billy Bob," Dino said, "did your lawyer tell you you've been eliminated as a suspect in the girl's murder? We checked with Buffett's office, and they confirmed that you were in Omaha."

"Naw, Stone didn't mention that," Billy Bob said, looking askance at Stone.

"First time I've seen you," Stone said.

"Stone isn't off the hook, though," Dino said. "In fact, he's our prime suspect."

"Now why would ol' Stone want to kill Tiffany? You wouldn't do that, would you,

Stone?"

Stone sipped his bourbon and ignored the question.

"Well, what we look for in a suspect," Dino said, "is motive, means and opportunity. Stone had the means — his hands — and the opportunity — he was alone in the house with the girl all day — and as for motive, well, two out of three is often enough for a jury."

Stone ended his silence. "Dino forgot to mention that he needs physical evidence or an eyewitness," Stone said. "And, of course, he has neither."

"No, no physical evidence, though we did find his fingerprints on her throat."

"I felt her throat for a pulse," Stone said to Billy Bob.

"And the DNA from the sperm inside her," Dino added.

"Whose DNA?" Stone asked.

"His," Dino said, pointing at Billy Bob.

"He told you he had sex with her before leaving for Omaha," Stone pointed out.

"And that room was completely wiped clean of prints," Dino said.

"And why would either Billy Bob or I bother to do that? It's my house — perfectly normal for my prints to be found there, and Billy Bob was a guest, living in that room.

Normal for his prints to be there, too. Would I bother to do that in my own house?"

"Right," Billy Bob said.

"Dino," Stone said, "has it occurred to you that the murderer took his time? He wasn't in a rush, what with wiping down the room and putting an electric blanket over the body."

"That's kinda weird, ain't it?" Billy Bob asked. "Why would somebody want to keep her warm?"

"To screw up our estimate of when she was murdered," Dino said. "For instance, if you had killed her before you left for Omaha that morning, the blanket would have made it seem that she died much later, because the body wouldn't have cooled as quickly. What have you got to say about that, Billy Bob?"

"Don't answer that," Stone said.

"Oh, we're completely off the record here," Dino said, smiling.

"Don't say a word, Billy Bob."

Billy Bob was looking worried, now.

"So, Dino, what's the ME's new stab at time of death, now that he knows about the electric blanket?"

"Earlier than before," Dino said.

"Earlier? That's it? No ballpark?"

"Turns out the ME has never had a case where somebody tried to keep a body warm with an electric blanket," Dino said. "He's working on it, though, doing some tests."

"What kind of tests?" Stone asked. "Is he going to strangle somebody, then put a blanket over the body and take its temperature every ten minutes?"

"Something like that," Dino said, "except for the strangling part. He'll nail it down; don't worry." Dino excused himself and went into the men's room.

"Billy Bob," Stone said, "the police turned up at my house this morning with a search warrant, and they found your gun in my safe."

Billy Bob grinned. "Good thing I didn't *shoot* that girl."

"Don't even joke about it," Stone said, "and be careful what you say around Dino. Don't forget, he's the police."

"But Dino's your buddy, right?"

"Right, but he's still a cop. He's not going to let either of us off the hook, unless he has to, and if the medical examiner comes up with a supportable estimate of time of death that includes the time before you left for Omaha, then Dino is going to come calling on you. And by the way, the next time you leave town, come get that cannon of yours.

My secretary will give it to you. It's a good thing Dino's detectives didn't check the serial number against my license, or we'd have both been in trouble."

Dino came back from the men's room and began rummaging in his overcoat pockets. He came up with a clear plastic bag full of hundred-dollar bills and tossed it on the table. "Almost forgot," he said. "You can have your money back. We didn't find Billy Bob's or the girl's prints on any of it."

Before Stone could remove the money, Elaine came and sat down. "Hey," she said, "you're getting to be a pretty good tipper."

Stone stuffed the money into his own overcoat. "I've always been a good tipper," he said, "but not *that* good."

"Strangled anybody else lately?" she asked Stone.

"Stop it, you're worse than Dino."

"I think a woman did it," Elaine said.

"How come?" Dino asked.

"Stands to reason, doesn't it? Some woman Stone dumped probably did it."

Dino nodded. "Women are born killers, like cats. Who've you dumped lately, Stone?"

"I haven't dumped anybody; I *get* dumped, not the other way around."

"That's true," Dino said, nodding vigorously. "Stone gets dumped a lot."

"Well, not a *lot,*" Stone said, "but once in a while."

"More than that," Dino said.

"Just once in a while."

"Okay, who're you seeing at the moment?"

"The U.S. Attorney," Elaine said, "but she hasn't had time to dump him, yet."

"Why don't you two just get dumping off your minds?" Stone asked.

"What's-her-name dumped him," Dino said. "You know, the one that married the billionaire from Palm Beach."

"Right," Elaine said. "And there was Arrington, she dumped him. You know, Dino, Stone *does* get dumped a lot.

"Let's order dinner," Stone said, picking up a menu.

"About time," Elaine said, getting up and wandering over to another table.

After dinner, Billy Bob grabbed the check, tossed a wad of two-dollar bills on the table and stood up. "Y'all got to excuse me," he said. "Got a late date." He put on his coat and left.

"More two-dollar bills," Dino said, poking at them with a finger. "Where does he get them?"

"I have no idea," Stone said, "but there

never seems to be a shortage." He took a bill from the pile, stuck it in his pocket and replaced it with a pair of ones. "Souvenir," he said.

"Oh," Dino said, digging into his coat pocket. "I meant to give Billy Bob back Warren Buffett's card." He handed it to Stone. "You can give it to him next time you consult with him."

Stone glanced at the card and put it in his pocket. "Will do."

12

On Saturday night, Tiff arrived at Stone's house at seven, bearing an armload of shopping bags and looking a little frazzled.

"Whew!" she said, giving Stone a kiss. "I'm beat!"

"You need a drink," Stone said, steering her toward the kitchen. They passed through the living room and the library.

"This is a beautiful house," Tiff said. "Is this the cabinetwork your father did?"

"It is, all of it. The doors, too."

In the kitchen, she dropped her bags. He deposited her on the sofa tucked into a corner and took a green-tinted bottle of vodka from the freezer.

"What's that?" she asked.

"A specialty of the house," Stone replied. He found two thin crystal martini glasses, poured the liquid into each and returned the bottle to the freezer. He handed her a glass. "Try that."

Tiff sipped and smiled. "That's wonderful! What is it?"

"It's a very special vodka gimlet."

"Sounds powerful. What's in it?"

"Not as powerful as a martini. It's three parts of vodka and one part of Rose's Sweetened Lime Juice. What's special about it is the intensity. Normally, you'd pour the ingredients into a cocktail shaker, shake it until your fingers freeze to the shaker, then strain it into a glass. What I do is take a full fifth of vodka, pour six ounces of it into another bottle and replace that with the lime juice. Then I put it into the freezer for a few hours. That way, when it's poured, it's colder than ice, because the vodka doesn't freeze, and it hasn't been watered down by the melting ice in the shaker."

"Heaven." She sighed, sinking into the sofa.

"Did you have a good day?"

"Spectacular. I found an apartment."

"Tell me about it."

"It's what you New Yorkers call a classic six, on Park Avenue in the sixties, and it's already been renovated, so it's in move-in condition. It had been sold, and the owners moved out, but the co-op board turned down the buyer, so it's sitting there, empty, ready for me."

"Sounds great, but how long will it take for you to get board approval?"

"The board meets at the end of next week,

so if I can get all the paperwork together in a hurry, I'll know then. My real-estate agent says the board will like the idea of a U.S. Attorney living in the building, so there shouldn't be a problem."

"Co-op boards can be tricky," Stone said.

"I'll get the AG to write a letter of recommendation — the president, if I have to. Say, can I borrow your shower? I've been apartment-hunting and shopping all day, and I haven't had time to change."

"Sure, follow me." He led her up the back stairs into his bedroom, carrying her shopping bags. "There's a robe on the back of the bathroom door," he said.

"I won't be long," she replied, setting her gimlet on his desk.

Stone went back to the kitchen and began organizing dinner.

Soon, she came down the stairs, her hair wet, wearing tan leather pants and a tight sweater.

"New clothes?" he asked.

"Fresh from Madison Avenue's finest shops."

He poured her another gimlet. "I'm going to start dinner, now," he said. "I'm making risotto, so I may need some help stirring."

He emptied a packet of arborio rice into a

copper pan, with half a stick of butter and some olive oil, and cooked it until it was glossy, then began adding hot chicken stock to the pan, a little at a time. Halfway through the process, he tossed a pair of thick veal chops onto the grill of the Viking range and let them brown for a few minutes on each side.

When the risotto had absorbed all the chicken stock and the rice was tender, he added half a cup of crème fraîche and a considerable amount of freshly grated Parmigiano Reggiano cheese and stirred them in, then set the pan on a trivet on the kitchen dining table, forked the veal chops on two plates and added haricots verts that he had cooked earlier. He opened a bottle of Far Niente cabernet and held a chair for her to sit down.

"It looks wonderful," she said.

"We'll see."

She tasted the risotto. "Marvelous!"

They dined slowly, enjoying the food and wine. When they had finished, he took away the dishes and served them each a tiny slice of Italian cheesecake from a deli he knew.

He made espresso and poured them each a brandy.

"I feel so much better," she said. "You heard anything from Rodney Peeples?"

That brought Stone up short.

"We going to talk shop?"

"Just for a minute."

"This is only the second time I've heard that name — both from you. I am not acquainted with the gentleman."

"And he is not your client?"

"I would have to be acquainted with him for him to be my client."

"Good point."

"But, as long as we're talking shop, could I ask a favor of you?"

"Maybe."

"Your office handles cases with the Treasury Department, doesn't it?"

"Yes."

"You know anybody in the Secret Service you could have a word with?"

"Probably."

Stone dug into a pocket and came out with Billy Bob's two-dollar bill. "Could you ask someone there to run the serial number on this bill and see if anything pops up?"

She took the bill and looked at it. "Why?"

"Just a favor."

"I don't know about that."

Stone took back the bill. "Never mind."

"That was a very odd request. Do you think the bill might have been stolen?"

"No, I'm just curious to see what I can learn about it. You don't see a lot of two-dollar bills."

"I'm going to have to have a better explanation than that if you want me to have it run."

"I'm afraid I don't have a better explanation than that," Stone said. "Let's just forget it."

She grabbed the bill back. "Oh, all right," she said. "I'll call in a favor and have it run on an informal basis."

"That would be great."

"You're sure you don't know Rodney Peeples?"

"Will you stop with that name, Tiff? I've told you repeatedly that I don't."

"Okay, okay."

"How long will it take to run the two-dollar bill?"

"I'll make the call on Monday; a day or two, I guess. This isn't going to get me into trouble, is it?"

"If I thought it were, I wouldn't ask you to run it. It's just that I'm curious, and I don't have any contacts in the Secret Service. I'm only looking for information; I'm not asking anybody to intercede on behalf of a client."

"You have contacts in other federal agencies?"

"One or two," Stone said. "I recently had dinner with the United States Attorney for New York."

She laughed. "Yes, you did, didn't you? Now what?"

He leaned over and kissed her. "I'm open to suggestions."

"So am I," she said, kissing him back.

13

Stone was wakened by a ringing cell phone, and he knew it wasn't his. He opened an eye and found it filled with a naked breast, a pleasing sight. He reached across Tiff and grabbed her handbag from her bedside table, then he laid the handbag on her belly.

"Your belly is ringing," he said into her ear.

She made a noise and turned onto her side, away from him.

"Tiff, it's your cell phone."

"Shhhhhh," she said.

The cell phone stopped ringing.

Stone turned and snuggled up next to her back, enjoying the feeling of her buttocks against his belly.

Tiff made another, more approving noise and pushed against him.

Stone responded, and in a moment, they were both awake, working together to guide him inside her. That accomplished, they moved in concert, faster and faster, until they both came loudly.

"That was good," she said, when their breathing had returned to normal.

"It was better than good," Stone murmured, resting his cheek on her moist back.

She rolled over, threw a leg over him and put her head on his shoulder. "You're right," she said.

"I'm never wrong about these things."

She laughed, then seemed to fall asleep. Stone was nearly asleep, himself, when she jerked awake.

"Is that my cell phone ringing?" she asked.

"About fifteen minutes ago," he said. "Maybe they left a message."

"I don't want it," she replied. "What are our plans for the day?"

"Eggs Benedict, mimosas and the *New York Times*."

"I get the crossword."

"I'll make you a copy and race you to the finish."

"You wouldn't have a chance."

"Big talk."

"I'll finish it in half an hour."

"On Sunday? I'll finish it . . . quickly."

"I'm hungry," she said.

"You're saying you want me to leave you and make breakfast?"

"No, I'll leave you and make breakfast."

"Do I have to watch?"

"No, you can sleep, and I'll bring it up here."

"There's a dumbwaiter," he said. "Just press the button." Then he fell asleep.

Stone was awakened by the clanging of the dumbwaiter bell, and by the time Tiff had climbed the stairs, he had the trays arranged on the bed. He was surprised to see that she was still naked.

"You always walk around naked?" he asked as she climbed into bed and arranged her pillows.

"Always," she said. "Except at the office."

They dug into their food.

"Wonderful hollandaise," he said. "Just the right amount of lemon."

"Thank you, sir. Your risotto last night was wonderful, too. Lovely flavor."

"*You* were wonderful last night. This morning, too."

"I'm going to be wonderful again, as soon as I finish breakfast."

"You have an optimistic view of my capabilities," he said.

"I have an optimistic view of my capability to excite your capabilities."

"It's hard to argue with that."

"Then don't; just get rid of these trays."

He put the trays on the dumbwaiter and sent it downstairs, then returned to bed.

She was reaching for him again when her cell phone rang.

"Shit!" she said.

"Let it ring."

"Nobody has that number but my office," she said. "If they're calling on a Sunday morning . . ." She dug into her handbag and came out with the phone. "Hello? Yes, I'm awake, but I wasn't when you called earlier. What's up? That's good. You're kidding — on a Sunday morning? An hour, then, in his suite." She hung up. "You're not going to believe this."

"What?"

"The AG has got a bug up his ass about a case, and he flew to New York this morning."

"Why wouldn't I believe that?" Stone asked.

"Well, you wouldn't, if you knew the case and the AG. The whole business is crazy."

"Tell me about it."

"I can't," she said, "I have to get into a shower right now. I can't show up for a meeting, smelling of sex, with a religious fundamentalist."

"You never know, it might make his day."

"I very much doubt it." She struggled out of bed and he watched her backside appreciatively as she ran to the bathroom. A moment later, he heard the shower come on.

Stone fell back on the bed, a little relieved at not having to perform again so soon.

* * *

Stone had finished the *Times* and was struggling with the *Times* crossword puzzle when the phone rang. He glanced at the instrument and saw the doorbell light illuminated. He looked at his watch: two-thirty P.M. Who the hell would be calling on a Sunday afternoon? He picked up the phone. "Hello?"

"Mr. Stone Barrington?"

"That's right."

"This is Agents Williams and Marconi of the United States Secret Service. We'd like to speak with you."

"On a Sunday afternoon?"

"That's correct."

Stone sighed. "I'll buzz you in; find the living room and have a seat while I get dressed. I'll be down in a couple of minutes."

"Very good."

He buzzed them in, then got up, brushed his hair, put on some clothes and walked downstairs.

Two men in business suits rose as he entered the living room. They flashed their badges and introduced themselves, then everybody sat down.

"What can I do for you?" Stone asked.

Agent Williams produced a plastic bag

containing a two-dollar bill and handed it to Stone. "I believe you wanted some information on this two-dollar bill?"

Stone looked at it and handed it back. "I wanted information on *a* two-dollar bill; I can't guarantee it was this one.

Williams nodded. "Here's your information," he said. "It is one of a very large number of two-dollar bills stolen from Fort Dix army base in New Jersey in 1955."

Stone blinked. "You keep track of fifty-year-old robberies?"

"When the robbery is of four hundred thousand dollars and change."

"I commend you on your record keeping," Stone said.

"Thank you. Where did you get the two-dollar bill?"

"I'm afraid I can't say."

"What?"

Stone searched for the right words. "I'm sorry, but answering your question would violate the canon of legal ethics."

"Which part of the canon?" Williams asked.

"I'm afraid I can't tell you that, either."

"I was told you'd be cooperative."

"Who told you that?"

"The United States Attorney for New York."

"Well, she was right, in the sense that I *wish* to be cooperative, within the bounds of professional ethics, but, as I've said, revealing the source of the two-dollar bill would entail compromising legal ethics, and any court would back me on that."

The two agents stared at him in silence.

"Perhaps you can tell me why you are so interested in solving a crime, the statute of limitations on which expired decades ago?"

"Two army officers were murdered during the course of the robbery. There's no statute of limitations on that."

"I see. Well, gentlemen, I'm afraid the only thing I can do is to make inquiries of my own into the origins of the bill and, if I'm able to, let you know what I find out."

Williams handed Stone a card. "Please do so, and call me. You can always reach me on the cell number."

Stone shook the two men's hands and let them out of the house. Then he went to the phone and called the Four Seasons Hotel. Billy Bob's suite didn't answer, and Stone left a message for him to call back.

14

On Monday morning, when he still hadn't heard from Billy Bob, Stone called the Four Seasons again and was told that Billy Bob had checked out early that morning. Stone called Bill Eggers.

"Good morning, Stone."

"Good morning, Bill; we have a problem."

"What sort of problem?"

"You know our client Billy Bob?"

"I believe he's *your* client, Stone."

"He's a client of the firm, is he not?"

"To whom did he make out his retainer check?"

"Well, to me, I guess."

"Good guess. Now, whose client is he?"

"All right, my client. Would you like to hear about the problem?"

"Not really."

"There are ethical problems that might reflect badly on the firm."

"Since Mr. Billy Bob is not now nor has he ever been a client of the firm, I don't see how any of his problems could reflect on the firm in any manner whatever."

"His photograph in the company of the mayor, taken at the firm party, has appeared in the newspapers."

"We didn't tell the mayor who he could or could not bring to our party."

"You mean, he came with the *mayor.*"

"I believe he did."

"Are you aware that, the day after the party, Billy Bob's date was found murdered in his bed?"

"Good God! The Four Seasons must have gone nuts!"

"They weren't at the Four Seasons; they were in my guest room."

Eggers managed a vocal shrug. "Well, Stone, I don't see how that relates to the firm."

"It was at your request that Billy Bob was a guest in my home."

"It was just a suggestion."

"So, I'm stuck with Billy Bob, is that it?"

"Looks that way."

"Then perhaps you would give me some advice on the ethical ramifications of representing him."

"Would this entail your sharing details of your relationship with Billy Bob?"

"It might."

"Then my advice is don't violate

attorney-client confidentiality. I've got a meeting; let's have dinner." Eggers hung up.

Stone resisted a very strong urge to rip the phone from its connection and bang it repeatedly against the wall. Calming himself, he found the slip of paper on which he had written Billy Bob's phone numbers and dialed his home. A woman answered.

"Good morning, the Barnstormer residence."

"May I speak with Mr. Barnstormer, please; it's Stone Barrington calling."

"I'm sorry, but Mr. Barnstormer is traveling today."

Stone consulted the paper for the GIV's number and found it not present. "May I have the phone number for his airplane?"

"I'm sorry, I'm not allowed to give out that number. I should be speaking with Mr. Barnstormer later today; can I tell him you called?"

"Please. He has the number." Stone thanked her and hung up. He buzzed Joan.

"Yes?"

"Joan, have you already deposited Billy Bob's retainer check?"

"Sure, I told you that. We'd have had to sell stock without it."

"Thanks." He hung up and fumed for a

moment, then he dug out Warren Buffett's card and called his Omaha office.

"Good morning, Berkshire Hathaway," a woman said.

Stone was about to speak but he stopped himself. He was sure that the voice he was hearing from Omaha was the same voice he had heard at Billy Bob's home in Dallas. He hung up and looked at the area code on Buffett's card: 402. He got out a phone book and looked up the area code for Omaha: 402. He looked up the area code for Dallas; there were three, one of them 469, same as Billy Bob's. But the same woman was answering both phones. He called Omaha information and asked for a number for Berkshire Hathaway. He was given a number different from the one on Warren Buffett's card. He dialed the number, and a woman answered.

"Good morning, Berkshire Hathaway." Different voice, different accent.

"Good morning, can you tell me if this is the only number listed for Berkshire Hathaway?"

"It's the only one in Omaha," she said.

"Thank you." He hung up and looked at the Warren Buffett card. This Buffet was spelled with one *t*.

Stone reached for the phone to call Dino,

then stopped. He couldn't give the police unfavorable information about his client. Not that he had a hell of a lot of information about his client. He turned to his computer, went online and did a Google search for Billy Bob Barnstormer. He got a lot of aviation hits, and to his surprise, learned that quite a number of people were actually named Barnstormer. He got two hits on a Billy Bob, both of them on Web sites that reported society news in New York, both of them referring to Billy Bob's presence at the Woodman & Weld party, one of them featuring the photograph with the mayor. Nothing before that date. Apparently, Billy Bob Barnstormer had not existed before that, at least on the Internet.

He did another search, this time for addresses and phone numbers. That service had never heard of anybody named Barnstormer. He tried Barnstetter and got the same result.

Stone sat at the computer, thinking hard. Then a tiny lightbulb went on in his brain, accompanied by a sinking feeling. He went back to Google and typed in "Rodney Peeples." To his astonishment, he got three thousand, four hundred and twenty-two hits. For the next hour he scrolled laboriously through them and found two that mattered: a Web site for a used-car dealer in San Mateo, California, and another for a firm of certified public accountants in Enid, Oklahoma. The used-car Web site had photographs of the California Peeples standing in his car lot, a flashy girl on each arm. The man had a big mustache and sideburns, but he was, without doubt, Billy Bob Barnstormer. On the Web site of Peeples & Strange, accountants, he found photographs of the partners. This time he wore a conservative suit, button-down shirt and wire-rimmed spectacles, but he was, nevertheless, Billy Bob.

So Billy Bob, in addition to being a Texas entrepreneur, was also a flamboyant used-car dealer in San Mateo, California, and a nerdy CPA in Enid, Oklahoma. Stone wondered how many other identities the man had. The mind boggled. He buzzed Joan again.

"Yes?"

"Joan, call my broker and tell him to sell a hundred thousand dollars of stocks, and to minimize the tax consequences. Have him wire the funds to our checking account immediately, and draw a cashier's check for fifty thousand dollars, payable to Billy Bob. Then send the following letter to Billy Bob Barnstormer at the address we have for him:

'Dear Mr. Barnstormer, this firm is unable to continue to offer you legal representation. We enclose a cashier's check in the amount of $50,000, representing a return of your retainer.' Send it Express Mail, return receipt requested, and get it out today."

"As you wish."

"And ask the bank to let you know when the cashier's check is paid."

"Okeydokey."

Stone called Dino.

"Bacchetti."

"This is a confidential informant," Stone said. "Listen carefully: Call Warren Buffett's office again, but this time, get the number from Omaha information."

"Okay," Dino said. "You want to have dinner?"

"Why not?"

"Elaine's, nine o'clock?"

"Sure."

15

Stone was halfway through his first drink when Dino arrived and sat down. "So, what's this confidential informant crap?" he asked.

"If anybody ever asks where you got that information, I want you to be able to say, truthfully, that you got it from a confidential informant."

"Well, that's very lawyerly of you," Dino said, signaling a waiter for a drink.

"It's what I do. Did you call Berkshire Hathaway?"

"I did."

"And?"

"And we've both been had. Warren Buffett has never heard of Billy Bob."

"You could say that. Something else I can tell you, since I no longer represent Billy Bob, is that you should go on the Internet, do a Google search for one Rodney Peeples, and pay particular attention to the hits you will get on a used-car dealer in San Mateo, California, and a firm of accountants, Peeples and Strange, in Enid, Oklahoma."

"Why?"

"I think you will find the experience rewarding."

"Oh, for fuck's sake, Stone, stop talking like Alistair Cooke and tell me what's going on."

"You will find that the Rodney Peeples of San Mateo and the Rodney Peeples of Enid are both Billy Bob Barnstormer. Or vice versa. Or they're all somebody else."

"Oh? So Billy Bob made a complete fucking schmuck out of you, then?"

"Not quite. He paid me fifty thousand dollars for my trouble."

"So, you're only a schmuck, then."

"Except that I gave him back his fifty grand and told him to get lost."

"So, you are, after all, a complete fucking schmuck."

"One could say that."

"What's Billy Bob's game?" Dino asked. "Besides murder, I mean."

"I have no idea what his game is, but what do you mean, murder?"

"I mean the ME came back with a definite time of death of between eight A.M. and noon."

"When Billy Bob was still in the house?"

"Correct."

"Then I'm off the hook?"

"Not exactly. You haven't yet proved that

the two of you weren't in it together."

"You mean, you think that Tiffany may have been strangled by one of Billy Bob's hands and one of mine, working in concert?"

"Could be something like that."

"My God, the entire Nineteenth Precinct detective squad, along with its lieutenant, is going to have to repeat junior detective school."

"We are more in the business of implicating than exonerating."

"Is there a warrant for Billy Bob yet?"

"First thing in the morning; I only got the ME's verdict an hour ago. Do you know where he is?"

"No, but if you will telephone Mr. Barnstormer's former attorney's secretary tomorrow morning, she might give you his address and phone number in Dallas."

"Will he be there?"

"I have not been vouchsafed that information."

"There you go again — what is this, *Masterpiece Theatre*?"

"Or you could try him in Enid, Oklahoma, or San Mateo, California."

"Well, I have to say that Billy Bob, or whoever he is, is the most interesting comurderer I've run across for a long time."

"You want my theory?"

"I'm going to hear it, whether I want to or not."

"I think his murdering Tiffany, or Hilda, or whatever her name was, was more in the way of an accident."

"You mean you subscribe to that theory about strangling adding punch to the orgasm?"

"Either that, or they got rough, and he went too far. He doesn't strike me as a cold-blooded killer."

"Guys like Billy Bob strike you as whatever they want to. He's a con man, a pro, and guys like that will go to great lengths to protect whatever identity they've chosen for themselves, up to and including murder."

"You mean you think she got hold of his wallet or his passport or something and figured out he wasn't who he said he was?"

"Yeah, or maybe he confided in her, and she threatened to turn him in."

"A little blackmail?"

"Hookers have been know to indulge in that sport."

Stone glanced toward the front door in time to see Tiff enter. He waved her back to the table.

"Hi, there," he said, giving her a kiss on the cheek.

"Hi, back. Hey, Dino."

"Good evening."

"Good to see you," Stone said, trying and failing to remember if he'd invited her to Elaine's.

"I thought you might be here, and I didn't have anything else to do tonight."

"So the AG is done with you?"

"Not by a long shot, but he's on his way back to D.C., thank God." The waiter approached, and she ordered a drink.

"What was the panic about?"

"More enthusiasm than panic, but, of course, I can't tell you."

"I'll trade information with you," Stone said.

"What have you got to trade?"

"Info about your friend Rodney Peeples."

"I thought you didn't represent him."

"Technically, I didn't; however I've come into some information about your Mr. Peeples that connects him to someone I do, or rather, did represent. At one time."

"And who would that be?" The waiter returned with her drink, and she sipped it.

"You remember my client, now former client, the large Texan with the glittery tuxedo and the Tiffany, at the Woodman and Weld party?"

"How could I possibly forget?"

"Turns out he's not only my former client; he's also Rodney Peeples."

Tiff nearly choked on her drink. "What are you talking about?"

"I thought I was clear."

"Why didn't you tell this to the Secret Service guys who called on you? Don't you know it's a felony to lie to a federal investigator?"

"Because, when I spoke to them, I didn't know that Billy Bob and Peeples were one and the same."

"And how did you find out? Did he tell you?"

"I found out by doing a Google search for Peeples, an investigative technique available to any six-year-old with a computer, and one that I recommend to your Junior G-Men."

"And what did you find out about Peeples?"

"That he is a used-car dealer in San Mateo, California, and a CPA in Enid, Oklahoma."

"And you're sure that he's my Rodney Peeples?"

"No, just that he's *my* Rodney Peeples. Both Web sites sport his photograph."

"Well, we didn't know about either San Mateo or Enid. Did you get the two-dollar bill from Peeples/Billy Bob?"

"I can't say."

"I'll take that as a yes."

"Having received information, it is your turn to impart it."

"Let's just say that we have evidence of other activities of Mr. Peeples, but not the two you mention."

"Exchanging information with you is an unrewarding experience," Stone said.

"If I told you, I'd have to lock you up, so you couldn't tell anybody else."

"You'd do that?"

"Not if I could help it, but the AG would do it in the blink of an eye, if he thought you knew about it."

"You intrigue me."

"That's the nicest thing anybody has said to me all day," she said, batting her eyes furiously. "My office is buying dinner," she said, reaching for a menu, "in return for the information."

"Oh, no, you don't. I'm not becoming a confidential informant for the feds, and don't you dare write my name down anywhere."

"I'll have to tell some people where I got the information about Peeples."

"Tell them you got it from Google, which is the truth, sort of."

"Okay. If you insist on buying, let's split the porterhouse."

"Gold digger."

16

Stone was wakened from a sound sleep by the ringing of his bedside telephone. He answered it as quickly as possible, to avoid waking Tiff, who slumbered beside him, her hand on his belly.

"Hello?" he half whispered.

"Hey, Stone." The line was staticky and faint.

Stone felt a wave of irritation. "Billy Bob."

"You left me a message to call."

"Not at . . ." he looked at the bedside clock ". . . three-thirty in the morning."

"Sorry about that. It ain't three-thirty here."

"Where are you?"

"Maui."

"Hawaii?"

"Got a little deal going out here. What did you want to talk to me about?"

Stone checked the caller ID window on the phone. *Unavailable.* "It's hard to remember in the middle of the night."

"Well, I might not be able to get back to you for a few days. We're headed out for a little cruise on a big ol' yacht in the morning."

"Oh, yes, I remember. I've resigned from representing you as your attorney. I sent you a letter and a refund of your retainer to your Dallas address."

"Well, shoot, Stone. What'd you want to go and do that for? Ain't my money no good?"

"I don't represent clients who conceal their identities from me, or who employ more than one identity."

A silence.

"Or who murder women in my guest room."

"It wasn't murder, exactly," Billy Bob said, and he managed to sound sheepish.

"Exactly what was it?"

"She wanted me to choke her a little; said she got off better that way. I told her to tap me on the hand if she wanted me to stop, but she didn't. I don't know why."

"You're a big, strong guy, Billy Bob," Stone said. "Strong hands, I expect. By the way, the electric blanket was a clever idea. It threw the medical examiner for a loop, until he figured it out."

"I needed to buy me some time," Billy Bob said. "Are the cops looking for me?"

Stone wasn't going to become an accomplice to flight. "I can't comment on that."

"I'm looking for advice, here, Stone; that's what I'm paying you for."

"No, you're not. I've sent you a cashier's check for the full fifty thousand, so you haven't paid me a penny."

"So that's the way it is, then?"

"That's the way it is. I'd appreciate it if you wouldn't contact me again."

"Oh, you'll be hearing from me, Stone."

"And Billy Bob? The next time you print up some cards for Warren Buffett, try and remember that he spells his name with two *t*'s."

Silence, then Billy Bob hung up.

Stone tried to get back to sleep, but he spent the rest of the night staring at the ceiling.

Stone fell asleep about a minute before Tiff woke him, moving her hand down his belly. He groaned. "I got a phone call in the middle of the night and never got back to sleep. Forgive me if I'm not too responsive this morning."

"So Billy Bob is in Hawaii?"

"I thought you were asleep. You're a sneaky person."

"Where in Hawaii?"

"Let me think about this for a moment." He thought about it. "He told me where he was while he still thought I was his attorney, so I can't tell you."

"God, but you're a pain in the ass."

"I cherish my license to practice law," Stone replied.

She grabbed his balls. "I'll bet I could torture it out of you."

"We're not at Guantanamo, missy," he said. "Oh, Billy Bob did confess to murder, and that was after I told him I wasn't his lawyer anymore."

"Murder?"

"You haven't heard?" He told her about Tiffany's death. "Actually, he didn't confess to murder; he said it was an accident."

"Murder isn't a federal crime, unless the victim is a federal official."

"If it helps, I have no way of knowing if Billy Bob was actually in Hawaii; he just said he was. The time zone works, though; it's what, six hours earlier there?"

"Seven, I think."

"So it would have been midevening in Maui — oops, forget I said that."

"You're sweet," she said, tickling his balls. "And you're becoming more responsive, too."

She was right.

Stone was sitting in his office at midafternoon, trying to stay awake, when Dino called.

"Sorry I didn't get back to you sooner; it's been busy here. What's up?"

"Billy Bob called in the middle of the night; said he was in Maui."

"You believe him?"

"Who knows what to believe? He could be anywhere. Oh, he said he was going on a cruise on a yacht for a few days."

"Where do you cruise to in Hawaii?"

"Hawaii, I think. Anything else is a long way away."

"I could ask the Hawaii state police for an APB, I guess."

"Must be lots of yachts in Hawaii, so that's a lot of work, and if Billy Bob was lying about his whereabouts, the cops out there won't appreciate the wild-goose chase. Oh, something else: Billy Bob owned up to killing Tiffany, but your theory was right, or he says it was. He said she asked him to choke her, because it gave her a better orgasm. She was supposed to ask him to stop, but she didn't."

"Did you tell him we were looking for him?"

"I declined to address the subject."

"So he knows?"

"Probably. Another reason why he might not be aboard a yacht in Hawaii. He wouldn't be doing what he said he'd be doing, if he knew there was a warrant out for him."

"Okay, so I won't ask for a Hawaii APB."

"The phone call was kind of scratchy, like it was from a long way away."

"A cell phone, maybe?"

"Maybe."

"He could still be in the city, then?"

"Could be. He checked out of the Four Seasons, though; I called yesterday."

"Could have changed hotels."

"And names. Did you add Peeples to the warrant?"

"Yeah; that's on the record, now. Does he know we know about the Peeples identity?"

"I didn't tell him, but the feds are looking for him under that name, and they've got a head start. If they find him first, lots of luck on ever getting him back for a murder trial."

"Yeah, I'd like to get my hands on him first."

Joan came into the room, and she didn't look happy.

"Dino, hang on for a minute. What's up, Joan?"

"The bank called; the cashier's check cleared."

"Boy, that was fast."

"They wired the funds to a bank in the Cayman Islands."

"You hear that, Dino?" he said into the phone.

"Yeah, we'll never track him that way."

"There's something else," Joan said.

"What?"

"The check Billy Bob gave us bounced."

"What?"

Joan shrugged.

"I heard that," Dino said. "Stone, you are a complete, absolute, gold-plated, fucking schmuck!"

Stone could not find a reason to disagree.

17

Joan knocked on Stone's office door.

Stone looked up. "Yes?"

"Don't look so depressed."

"I have good reason to feel depressed," he said. "Somebody just stole fifty thousand dollars from me."

"Not to make it worse, but that leaves us overdrawn at the bank, and if I don't get some money in there pronto, *our* checks are going to start bouncing."

Stone sighed. "All right, tell my broker to sell another fifty thousand and wire it."

"Ah, that would only replace Billy Bob's fifty thousand, and we've already sent him that much, so we're going to need to raise a hundred and fifty thousand, if we're going to pay this week's bills."

"All right, a hundred and fifty thousand," Stone said. That meant that, in a single week, he had cashed in 20 percent of his portfolio.

Joan disappeared.

Stone grabbed his coat and walked down the hall to her office. "I've got to get out of the house, or I'll go crazy," he said.

"Go shopping," Joan suggested. "That usually makes you feel better."

"That makes *women* feel better," Stone said. He left by the street door and started walking west. A cold wind whipped around him, blowing down his neck. He had forgotten to wear a muffler or a hat. By the time he got to Park Avenue he was freezing, and he was certain he was being followed. Crosstown traffic was heavy, of course, not moving much faster than he was, but the same black Suburban with darkened windows kept pulling even with him, then dropping back, allowing other traffic to pass. New York drivers did not allow other traffic to pass; in fact, most of them would rather block traffic completely than let anyone else pass. It was unnatural.

He turned right on Park, walked to Fifty-seventh Street and turned west again. A few steps from Park, he went into Turnbull & Asser, his shirtmakers. He went up to the second floor and looked idly at ties, choosing a couple, then he found a cashmere scarf he liked. He looked at hats and chose a soft, foldable one, then he walked to the window and looked down: the black Suburban was parked across the street, next to a fire hydrant.

Stone went to the rear of the shop, to the

custom department, and started flipping through the book of Sea Island Cotton fabrics. He grabbed a pad and jotted down numbers of swatches, then a salesman approached.

"Good afternoon, Mr. Barrington," the man said. "May I help you?"

Stone tore the sheet off the pad and handed it to him. "I'd like to order these numbers, please."

The man got an order pad and made note of the numbers.

"How long?"

"Eight to ten weeks."

That wasn't exactly the instant gratification Stone was looking for. He charged the things he had selected and put on the scarf and the hat, then he walked back downstairs. The black Suburban was still there, its engine running.

Stone looked down the street and saw a meter maid, or whatever they called them these days, coming. He cracked the front door. "Excuse me, miss," he said.

She walked over to the door. "Can I help you?"

"Yes, that enormous black car over there has been parked next to that fireplug for at least an hour. I hate to see the law flouted like that."

"I'll take care of it," she said. She jaywalked across the street, to the rear of the car, took out her pad and began writing a ticket.

Stone stood and watched. The driver's door of the Suburban opened and a man got out, wearing only a business suit, in spite of the cold wind. The man pointed at the license plate and said something. The meter maid didn't even look up, just kept writing. The man reached into an inside pocket, produced a wallet, opened it and showed it to her. She ignored him, finished writing the ticket, walked to the other end of the truck and put it under the windshield wiper.

The man pursued her, waving his arms and yelling.

Stone pulled up the scarf to obscure part of his face, pulled his hat brim down, slipped out of the shop, walked to the corner and crossed the street. As he approached the Suburban, he checked the license plate: U.S. Government. Swell.

He walked down Fifty-seventh Street, then turned north on Madison Avenue, feeling better. A moment later, the Suburban passed him, then turned right on Fifty-ninth Street, apparently missing him. He went into Barney's, a department store in the low sixties, found the restaurant and ordered a double espresso. He got out his cell phone and called Tiff Baldwin. He got her secretary, who seemed to recognize his name and put him through.

"So," Tiff said, without preamble, "are you having an attack of bad conscience?"

"About what?"

"About not telling me how to find Billy Bob."

"You know everything I know, kiddo," he said.

"I doubt it."

"Is that why you're having me followed?"

"What are you talking about?"

"C'mon, Tiff, I left my house a while ago, and a black Suburban with government plates and men with badges has been following me ever since."

"They're not mine," she said.

"Then whose are they?"

"They could be anybody's," she replied. "Could be the Department of Agriculture or the Bureau of Weights and Standards — anybody."

"Well, that's helpful. Why would fed types be interested, if you didn't sic 'em on me?"

"Consult your conscience for the answer to that one, my dear. You want to talk dirty, or something? Because I've got people waiting, and if I'm going to stay on the phone with you I need a good reason."

"Let's do it tonight."

"Do what?"

"We'll figure out something."

"Okay. By the way, I need some letters of recommendation for my co-op board application. Will you write me one?"

"I'd love to, but I have to tell you, it's probably not a good thing to have a lawyer write a letter."

"Why not?"

"Because there might be somebody on the board who's been on the other side of some disagreement with one of his clients, and who remembers the situation unfavorably. Call Dino, and ask him. They'd love a letter from the head of detectives at the One Nine."

"I see your point, and that's a good suggestion. I'll pick you up at eight tonight, and I'll book the table."

"You're on, and ask around and see if any of your people are on my back, will you?"

"Maybe." She hung up.

As Stone was putting away his cell phone a man sat down at his table.

Stone blinked. "Hello, Lance," he said. Lance Cabot was a CIA officer he had had some dealings with a couple of years ago.

"Good morning, Stone," Lance said. "That wasn't very nice, what you did to my guy a few minutes ago." Lance was impeccably dressed, as always, in a camel-hair polo coat with a silk handkerchief in the breast pocket.

"I think everybody should obey the law, most of the time," Stone said. "So he was yours?"

"He was and is."

"And why are you interested in where I buy shirts?"

"Not so much that, as where you're going and who you're seeing these days."

"And why would you care?"

"Oh, we like to look in on our contract consultants from time to time, make sure they're not moving in bad company."

Stone had signed a contract with Lance a year ago to offer counsel when requested. "Oh, that's right, I'm a consultant for you people now. You know, I haven't seen a nickel out of that contract."

"We haven't needed your help until now," Lance said.

"What's up?"

"It's about a client of yours, one Whitney Stanford."

"Never heard of him," Stone said, then a light went on. "Unless . . ."

18

Lance's smooth brow furrowed, for once. "Who are Billy Bob Barnstormer and Rodney Peeples?"

"They are at least two of the names that a former client of mine has used." Stone told him about the Google search.

"And why do you think this fellow might also be Whitney Stanford?"

"Just a hunch; tell me about Whitney Stanford."

Lance ordered a cappuccino and looked at his watch. "I don't have a lot of time."

"You've got time to follow me around New York," Stone said. "Come on, who is he? Maybe I can help."

"Whitney Stanford is an old-money New Yorker who runs a private investment firm."

"And why are you interested in him?"

"Because his name has come up in connection with a possible sales transaction involving, shall we say, unusual goods to not very nice people."

"Lance, when you signed me on as a

consultant, did you run a background check on me?"

"Of course."

"And, as a result, do I have a security clearance?"

"Purely as a matter of form, yes. You have a top-secret security clearance."

"Then why are you being so cagey with me about this guy? I'm trying to help you."

"What do you want to know?"

"Have you ever seen him?"

Lance produced a cell phone and pressed a single button. "Bring me the file folder on the front seat," he said, then closed the phone. "No, I've never seen him, but I have a photograph."

"Now we're getting somewhere. Just what is Stanford supposed to be selling, and to whom?"

"A new kind of rifle-launched grenade, to an organization suspected of terrorist connections."

"This does not sound like my guy," Stone said.

"Why not?"

"Because I think my guy is a garden-variety con man. Oh, and a murderer."

"Whom did he murder?"

"A prostitute, and in my guest room."

"Stone, *really*," Lance said, wincing.

"Don't look at me like that; the guy came to me through Woodman and Weld, recommended by another of their clients."

"Which client?"

"I don't know."

"Find out."

"Oh, and did I mention that the guy has stolen fifty grand from me?"

"How?"

Stone told him.

Lance looked amused. "Let me get this straight: You took a bad check from this fellow, then refunded his money by cashier's check?"

"Don't rub it in; that's Dino's job."

"How is dear old Dino?"

"What's the matter, aren't you following him, too? Dino's just fine."

A man in a business suit appeared, handed Lance a file folder and left.

Lance opened the folder and handed Stone a photograph.

It was of a gray-haired man in a business suit taken in what looked like the lobby of an expensive hotel.

"That's Billy Bob Barnstormer," Stone said. "And Rodney Peeples. By the way, the Attorney General has an abiding interest in arresting Rodney Peeples."

"Why?"

"I don't know."

"Then how do you know the AG wants him?"

"Because the U.S. Attorney for New York hauled me in and asked me about him. I denied all knowledge, until I put one and one together, and now that adds up to three."

"This is all very queer."

"No queerer than your following one of your own people on a shopping trip. By the way, what are your people doing in an SUV with government plates? Aren't you supposed to be spies? And if so, doesn't that imply a certain stealth?"

"It was all the motor pool had," Lance said, looking annoyed. "Do you know how to find this Billy Bob character?"

"He called me in the middle of last night, said he was in Maui, about to go on a cruise aboard a yacht. But I wouldn't believe that any more than anything else he might tell me."

"Did he mention the name of the yacht?"

"He said it was big, and that was it."

"Did you check your caller ID?"

"Yes. It said, 'not available.' It could have been a cell phone; the connection sounded a little funny."

"This is all very annoying."

"What?"

"This triple-identity thing with Stanford."

"Yes, well, criminals can sometimes be irritatingly difficult to catch."

"I don't want to catch him; I want to track the sale of these grenades, then catch the buyers."

"Then it would annoy you, if the NYPD or the AG arrested him?"

"It most certainly would. I'm going to have to take steps to see that that doesn't happen."

"Good God, Lance, you're going to try to prevent the arrest of a murderer and illegal arms dealer?"

"Stone, it's not as though he is an imminent danger to anyone. You have to stack up the benefits of preventing very powerful grenades being used against American soldiers in Afghanistan or Iraq against the significantly smaller benefit of jailing Mr. Whoeverheis."

"Well, I guess I still have a policeman's mentality; I tend to want to get perpetrators off the street as quickly as possible. And, of course, I'd like my fifty grand back."

"Well, I'm sure Dino will take a different view, when I've explained things to him."

"And the AG? I'm told he has a very keen interest in capturing this guy."

"That may take a little longer," Lance replied. "Now, Stone, I'm going to have to insist that, if you hear from this fellow again, you contact me instead of the police or the feds."

"The police I can handle, but I'm not going to put myself in the position of lying to federal investigators. Oh, did I mention that Billy Bob has been distributing two-dollar bills stolen in a robbery at Fort Dix fifty years ago, during which two army officers were killed?"

"You did not. *Fifty years ago?*"

"I kid you not. The waiters at Elaine's are calling him 'Two-Dollar Bill.' "

"And how is dear Elaine?"

"As ever. Drop in and see her sometime."

"Why don't you and I have dinner there this evening?"

"I have a previous engagement with someone even more beautiful than you."

"Tomorrow, then? Nine o'clock? Perhaps I'll have more to tell you then."

"Okay, if you promise to pull your dogs off me."

"I'll make them disappear like *that*." Lance snapped his fingers.

"By the way, have you spoken to Holly Barker lately?" Holly was a friend of Stone's who was a police chief in a small Florida town.

"Oh, yes; she's coming to work for me as soon as she can disentangle herself from her current life in Florida."

"I rather thought she might," Stone said. "She seemed bored with the work."

"She won't be bored much longer," Lance said, standing up. He handed Stone a card with only a phone number on it. "See you tomorrow evening." He tucked the file folder under his arm and walked out of the restaurant.

Stone was feeling better, now. He thought he might look at some shoes.

19

Stone arrived home to find the two detectives, Morton and Weiss, walking up his front steps.

"Good afternoon, gentlemen," Stone said. "What can I do for you?"

Morton held up a document. "We have a warrant to search your house."

"Well, it's déjà vu all over again, isn't it?" He glanced through the document and saw particular mention of safes. "All right, come on in."

He hung his coat in the front hall closet.

"Let's start with that big safe in your dressing room," Weiss said. "Might save us some time."

Mystified, Stone led them up to his bedroom and into his dressing room. His safe was a big Fort Knox, with an electronic keypad. He entered the code, turned the spokes on the door and stood back to give them access. The light in the safe came on, revealing his electric watch winder, some files, cash and a gun rack. Suddenly, he had a bad feeling.

Morton pulled on a latex glove and reached into the safe. He came out with Billy Bob's six-shooter, then he looked closely at it and turned to Weiss. "It's a forty-four," he said, and the two exchanged a little smile.

"That doesn't belong to me," Stone said quickly.

"Oh?" Weiss asked. "It just made its way into your safe?"

"It belongs to a former client. I took it from him and stored it so that he wouldn't be in violation of New York City law."

"And who would the client be?" Morton asked.

"You've met him," Stone said. "That's all I can say."

"Thanks, Mr. Barrington, we're done," Morton said. He dropped the gun into a plastic bag, and the two detectives left.

"Shit!!!" Stone screamed at himself. Why hadn't he just shipped that gun to Billy Bob's Dallas address?

"Did you say something, Mr. Barrington?" Morton called from the stairs.

"No, nothing. Goodbye."

"Goodbye."

Stone called Dino.

"Bacchetti."

"Morton and Weiss were just here."

"I know."

"They took Billy Bob's six-shooter."

"Good."

"Why do you want it?"

"We had a murder in the precinct a couple of weeks ago, and the ME dug a forty-four slug out of the victim. Weiss finally remembered that you had an old-fashioned six-shooter."

"I told you, it's Billy Bob's. I took it from him outside Elaine's that night, when somebody took a shot at him."

"Well, that turns out not to have been very bright, doesn't it?"

"He had just become my client, and I couldn't allow him to be arrested for carrying a gun in a strange city."

"Commendable," Dino said.

"I meant to give it back to him when he left town, but I forgot."

"Not so commendable."

"So now you're going to try to tie me to another murder?"

"Stone, I'm not trying to tie you to anything. My guys are just doing their jobs. Now, after the appropriate fingerprint and ballistic tests, *then* they may try to tie you to something."

"Who was murdered?"

"An investment banker named Owen Pell.

In his Fifth Avenue apartment. It was in the papers."

"I think I saw something about it, but I didn't know the man."

"Well, that's a good start for your defense. You might start dreaming up an alibi."

"When did it happen?"

"Let's see, it was . . . two weeks ago today, in the evening."

"I'll check my calendar. What time?"

"The ME says between eight and midnight."

"Hang on." Stone went to his desk and flipped through his diary. "Here it is. I had dinner with you at Elaine's."

"Two weeks ago, today? I don't remember that."

"Oh, stop it, you know damned well we had dinner. Mary Ann threw you out of the house, or something."

"Oh, yeah, *that* night. I guess you're covered."

"There's something else, though."

"What?"

"I don't want word of my possession of the gun to reach the License Division of the department."

"Oh, yeah, that could cause them to yank your carry permit, couldn't it?"

"I think I could win the fight, but I'd rather not have to go through it."

"I'll see what I can do. You want to have dinner tonight?"

"I'm seeing Tiff."

"How about tomorrow?"

"I'm seeing Lance Cabot."

"Whatever happened to Lance?"

"Who knows? I ran into him this afternoon, when he was having me followed by a carful of spooks."

"Why were they following you?"

"You're going to love this. They're looking for somebody called Whitney Stanford, a venture capitalist."

"Who's he?"

"He's Billy Bob and Rodney Peeples."

"You're shitting me! Another alias?"

"You bet. Lance was shocked to learn that his guy was our guy. By the way, you can expect a phone call from Lance; he doesn't want you to arrest Billy Bob."

"Lance can go fuck himself."

"Tell him that, after he hoses you down with national security."

"Lance is protecting this guy?"

"Just until he can catch him himself and put him out of business."

"If he does that, we'll never get our hands on him."

"You're right about that. They'll either turn him to get at some other people, or send him to Leavenworth, and you'll get your crack at him in twenty years."

"Well, I hope Billy Bob's forty-four doesn't match our bullet; it'll make it easier to give Lance what he wants."

"And Lance always gets what he wants."

"We'll see."

"Thanks for your help; see you later."

" 'Bye."

Stone hung up. He was beginning to really hate Billy Bob Barnstormer, or whoever he was.

He called Tiff Baldwin.

"Hello?"

"It's Stone."

"I know, my secretary told me."

"You want some new information on Billy Bob, or you want to be a smart-ass?"

"Gee, that's a tough one; okay, what's your information?"

"He's turned up with another alias."

"What is it this time?"

"Whitney Stanford."

"Hey, I know that name; he's under investigation by this office for some kind of stock fraud."

"He may also have murdered an investment banker named Owen Pell. The

NYPD is running a ballistics test right now."

"No kidding? I would have thought he was too smart to leave the gun at the scene."

"He didn't exactly leave the gun at the scene."

"Then how did the cops get ahold of it?"

"He left it in my safe."

Tiff burst out laughing. "So Billy Bob has figured out yet another way to leave you holding the bag?"

"It's not funny."

"I'm sorry, it's just my sense of the ridiculous."

"You better get a grip on your sense of the ridiculous, if you ever expect me to cook you dinner again."

"I'm terribly sorry," she said, making an unsuccessful effort not to laugh.

"You'd better be."

"My co-op board meeting is tonight."

"Hey, that was fast."

"Lucky timing, that's all. I just barely got my financial statement and my letters together in time. They're passing those around among themselves now. I haven't felt this naked since the last time I was with you."

"Yeah, they're probably showing that stuff

to the guys at their clubs, too. Think you'll pass the investigation of your sex life?"

"What!!!?"

"You didn't know they do that?"

"They don't."

"There were two detectives on my doorstep when I came home this afternoon."

"And what did you tell them?"

"I had to tell them everything . . ."

"Everything?"

"I had to; it's a felony to lie to a detective in a sexual investigation. Haven't you read the whole text of the Patriot Act?"

Then she began laughing. "Good one; you almost had me. But I'm going to make you pay for that."

"I'll look forward to it."

20

Stone was waiting when Tiff's car pulled up out front. It had begun to snow, lightly at first, but now fat flakes were being deposited in large numbers, collecting on the sidewalks, while cars beat them to pulp in the streets.

"Good evening," she said as he got into the rear seat with her.

Stone kissed her. "Good evening. Where are we off to?"

"Rao's," she said. "Do you know it?"

"I've been there, but not nearly often enough. How did we get a table?" You didn't get a table at Rao's; you owned it, or you didn't: It was as simple as that.

"One of my colleagues willed it to me."

"He died?"

"He went back to Washington; it's the same thing. So I get his table, same night every week."

Rao's was in Spanish Harlem, way uptown, and they took the FDR drive up the East Side of Manhattan, while the Lincoln's wipers tried valiantly to deal with the increasing snow.

They arrived to find the usual collection of limos and expensive cars outside, some of them abandoned, with the keys left in them, in case somebody needed to move them. Prominent among them was a bright red Hummer, with a driver.

"Who the hell would drive a Hummer in New York?" Stone asked.

"It's your town; you tell me," Tiff said.

Inside, the place was packed, as it was every night. Their booth, along the south wall, was ready for them, and Stone took the seat facing the bar, where it was easier to see a waiter. It was also easier to see the motley crowd at the bar — people who had congregated there, hoping that somebody would have a coronary on the way to the restaurant and, thus, make a table available. The place seemed to draw its share of wiseguys, too. A few months back, one of them had shot another of his ilk, when he drunkenly complained too loudly about a dinner guest who had spontaneously begun to sing an aria. The events had been exhaustively covered in newspapers and magazines, and now a lot of people seemed to think that a shooting was a regular occurrence at the restaurant, though it was the only instance in the more than one hundred years of its existence.

A waiter brought them drinks, then Frank

Pellegrino, the owner and grandnephew of the founder, came over and pulled up a chair. Frankie looked familiar even to people who had never been to Rao's, because he was also an actor, most recently playing a recurring role on the FBI team assigned to bring Tony Soprano's mob to justice.

Kisses and handshakes were exchanged.

"So what's it going to be tonight?" Frankie asked. A detailed discussion of what was available ensued, and they ordered more dishes than they could possibly eat.

"It's okay," Tiff said, "I'll take the leftovers home to the Waldorf Towers."

Stone ordered a bottle of wine and looked around the room: His eyes came to rest on the nose of a man in a booth across the room. Most of the rest of him was blocked by the wing of his booth; the nose was terribly familiar, but Stone couldn't quite place it.

Dishes began to arrive, and they tried, but failed, to keep up. There was veal, shrimp, an eggplant dish, chicken and, of course, pasta.

"You know, this is the best plain tomato sauce I've ever tasted," Stone said. "I don't know how Frankie does it." Frankie also cooked.

"You're right. In Washington I used to buy it by the jar at my neighborhood grocery store."

They ate and ate, until they couldn't eat any more, then the remains were packed up for Tiff to take home. As they were waiting for the check, the man across the room rose from his booth and, with his female companion, began to move toward the door, picking his way through the expanding crowd at the bar. To Stone's annoyance, he managed this with his back turned to their table. Then, as the man disappeared out the front door, it struck him. "Billy Bob," he said.

"What?"

"I swear, that was Billy Bob who just left."

"I didn't see him."

"I could only see him from behind." Stone got up. "I'll be right back." He made his way through the crowd to the front door and stepped outside. The red Hummer was pulling away, driven by a chauffeur. The rear windows were darkened, and Stone couldn't see inside. He watched it disappear up the street, undeterred by the accumulating snow, which now amounted to about eight inches. He got out his cell phone and called Dino.

"Bacchetti."

"It's Stone; I'm at Rao's, and I'm sure Billy Bob just left."

"Sounds like you're not really sure."

"I never got a look at the guy's face, but I'm sure it was Billy Bob. He should be easy to pick up, he's in a bright red Hummer."

"Why are you telling me?"

"Oh, did you retire from the NYPD when I wasn't looking?"

"It's nothing to do with me; I handed this one off to Lance, remember? You were there. Call Lance." Dino hung up.

Stone called Lance's cell phone.

"Yes?" he drawled.

"It's Stone; I'm pretty sure I just spotted Billy Bob."

"Where?"

"Leaving Rao's. You know the restaurant uptown?"

"Of course; I'm a regular."

"*You've* got a table at Rao's?"

"Every week."

"How the hell did you do that?"

"Frankie and I go way back. Tell me about this person you think was Billy Bob."

"He was eating at a booth across the room from us, and I never got a clear look at his face, but I'm pretty sure it was him."

"Which way did he go?"

"Downtown, I imagine," Stone said dryly.

"Where else would he go but downtown? And in a bright red Hummer."

"Did you get the plate number?"

"It's a bright red Hummer, for Christ's sake! You don't need a plate number."

"Probably from a service; if I had a plate number, I could track it down and maybe back to Billy Bob."

"Well, I didn't get it; I'm up to my ass in snow, here, and the visibility isn't too good."

"It's snowing?"

"Where are you, in a cave?"

"I'm in my study."

"Well, take a look out a window sometime. I've done my duty; good night!" He hung up and went back into Rao's brushing snowflakes off his shoulders and hair. He was slightly damp all over, now. He sat down in the booth. "I called it in, but Dino wasn't interested."

"Wasn't interested? Isn't the guy wanted for murder in this city?"

"He's handed the case off to Lance."

"Who the hell is Lance?"

Stone realized he'd said too much. "Ah, I can't really talk about that."

"What do you mean? You're not making any sense at all."

"Are you going to call in this sighting to your people?"

"What can I tell them?"

"That a guy I'm pretty sure is Billy Bob is headed downtown from Rao's in a red Hummer."

"He was in the Hummer we saw?"

"Yes, and he's getting farther downtown every minute. Don't you think your feds would want to know that?"

Tiff got out her cell phone and dialed a number. "Tell your boss that someone strongly resembling Rodney Peeples has been seen leaving a restaurant in Spanish Harlem and is on his way downtown in a red Hummer." She listened for a moment, then covered the receiver. "Did you get a license number?" she asked Stone.

Stone shook his head. "Poor visibility; it's really snowing hard, now."

"No license number; poor visibility, but how many red Hummers can there be in New York City? Great, pass it on." She hung up. "Okay, I reported it; can we go home and make love, now?"

"You betcha," Stone said.

21

By the time they had had coffee and an after-dinner drink, the snow was a foot deep in the streets. They piled into the Lincoln.

"Home, James," Tiff said. "I've always wanted to say that," she said. "And his name really is James."

The car fishtailed slowly up the street and turned downtown. "I wish I had chains," the driver said.

"You're doing fine," Tiff replied.

The driver worked his way downtown and over to Park Avenue, passing cars in various levels of disarray along their route. They had just turned south again when Stone pointed ahead. "Look!"

Tiff peered through the windshield. "All I see is snow."

"It's the red Hummer," Stone said. "Stop right here, driver."

"I'm afraid that if I stop, I won't be able to get going again," James replied. They were passing the Hummer, now, which had apparently stopped to help another car out of a drift.

"Pull over right here, goddammit!" Stone orderd.

"Pull over, James," Tiff said.

James pulled over.

"Now what?" Tiff asked.

"James, are you an FBI agent?" Stone asked.

"No, sir, I'm just a hired hand."

"Are you armed?"

"Yes, sir."

"James is an employee of the Justice Department, and he's armed, but he's not a law-enforcement official," Tiff said. "He can't arrest anybody."

"James, will you loan me your gun, please?" Stone asked.

"I'm sorry, Mr. Barrington, but I can't do that," James replied.

Swearing under his breath, Stone got out his cell phone and called Lance again.

"Yes?"

"Lance, I'm in a black Lincoln, stopped at the corner of Ninety-fourth and Park, and the red Hummer is right behind me, pulling another car out of a drift."

"Hold, please," Lance said.

Stone could hear him ordering up people on a landline.

"I've scrambled some cars, but in the present circumstances, it's going to take them some time to get there. Are you armed?"

"No."

"In the future, I would prefer that you carry at all times. This fellow is dangerous."

"I'm aware of that, and we have an armed driver, but he can't arrest anybody, and he won't loan me his gun."

Stone looked out the window and saw the Hummer drive past. "The Hummer is on the move," he said, "driving down Park."

"Stay with him, and keep me posted; I'll stay on the line."

"Let's go, James," Stone said. "Stay with the Hummer."

"Right," James replied. He put the Lincon in gear and pressed the accelerator. The car did not move. "Oh, shit," James said.

"Try rocking it back and forth," Stone said.

James tried doing that, but it didn't help.

"Lance," Stone said, "We're stuck in the snow, and we're losing the Hummer. Are your people anywhere near?"

"Hang on." Lance went back to the landline, then returned. "They're making their way up Park from about Thirty-fourth Street," he said.

"Well, all you can do is to keep them on Park, looking for a red Hummer. If they spot him, then they can make a U-turn."

"That's what they're doing," Lance said. "I'm going to hang up, now; I'm missing Letterman's Top Ten." He clicked off.

"So much for the CIA," Stone muttered, putting away his cell phone.

"You've been on the phone with the CIA?" Tiff asked.

"Try and forget I said that."

"This Lance guy is CIA?"

"I told you, I can't talk about him."

"Stone, I'm a high federal official; you can talk to me about the CIA."

"No, I can't; I've signed a contract that . . ." He stopped himself. "I'm going to shut up now."

James was still trying to rock the Lincoln back and forth.

"I'm not going to leave you alone until you tell me about this," Tiff said, goosing him.

"Nope."

She grabbed his crotch and squeezed.

"Easy, there!" Stone cried. "That will get you a lot, but not the information you want."

Then the car started to move. "I got it going," James said.

"Stay on Park and find the red Hummer," Stone said.

"Ma'am?"

"Oh, all right, do it, James." Tiff sighed. "I'm never going to get you into bed, am I?" she whispered to Stone.

"Yes, you are," Stone said, "but let's take Billy Bob, first."

"I can't see ten feet in front of me," James said. "It's crazy to be driving in this stuff."

"James," Tiff said, "if you don't see the Hummer by the time we get to the Waldorf, we're stopping there."

"Yes, ma'am."

"I want Billy Bob," Stone said.

"You may have to settle for me," Tiff replied, snuggling up to him, leaving her hand, more gently, on his crotch.

Presently, James turned left, and the Waldorf swam at them out of the snow.

"Continue on to my house," Stone said.

"Oh, all right. Do it, James."

"Yes, ma'am."

By some miracle, they made it to Stone's, and they got out and made their way toward the front steps. Suddenly, Tiff pushed Stone, and he went facedown in a drift.

"I'm going to get you for that!" Stone

cried, struggling to his feet and throwing a handful of snow at her as she trudged up the front steps.

"Do it in bed!" she yelled back.

22

When Stone arrived at Elaine's the following night, Lance was already seated, and Dino was next to him. "Evening, all," Stone said. "And I thought it was just you and me, Lance, *tête à tête*."

"Oh, we have no secrets from Dino, Stone; you know that."

"I wish I had some secrets from him," Stone replied, as a waiter set a Knob Creek on the rocks before him.

"Never happen, pal," Dino said. "You'll always be an open book to me."

"Isn't it nice to have good friends?" Lance observed.

"It is, when they're not trying to hang a murder charge on you."

"Dino would never do that."

"He's done it twice in the last week."

Dino shrugged. "All I do is follow the evidence, wherever it leads. It's just more fun when it leads to Stone."

"This is just great," Stone said, raising his glass, "Lance is following me wherever I go, and my best friend is trying to send me to prison for the rest of my life. Who needs enemies?"

Elaine sat down. "Anything I can do to help?"

"Only if you're willing to defend me."

"Against what?"

"Whatever these two come up with."

"I'm staying out of this one," she replied.

"I'm hungry," Stone said. "Let's order."

"Well, that makes a nice change," Elaine said, then she got up and moved to another table.

The three of them ordered.

"So," Stone said, when the waiter had left, "did you two come to an understanding on . . . let's see, it's Whitney Stanford, this time, isn't it?"

"We did," Lance said.

"In spite of the ballistics test," Dino said. "The slug from your forty-four was a perfect match."

"I told you, it's not my forty-four."

"Well, if Lance is going to take Billy Bob off my hands, you're all I've got left."

"Lance," Stone said, ignoring Dino, "come on, give us the real poop on your Whitney Stanford guy."

"I told you, he's trying to sell some new hand grenades to bad people."

"What new hand grenades?"

"That's top secret, I'm afraid."

"Dino and I already have that clearance, and anyway, if Billy Bob knows about them, why can't we?"

"The army has developed a new, rifle-launched grenade that's about ten times as powerful as their current ordnance."

"Sounds dangerous," Stone said.

"That's why it's rifle launched. It can't be activated by hand; it's activated by the rifle, when it's fired, and it has a range of up to three hundred yards."

"Sounds more like a mortar," Dino said.

"In many ways it is. You can imagine what terrorists could do with it in a crowded city. From the top of a building they could lob the things in all directions at, say, a street demonstration or a parade."

"Or in Times Square," Dino observed.

"I shudder to think," Lance said.

"How did Billy Bob get ahold of them?"

"Stolen from an army proving ground in New Mexico; probably an inside job. An investigation is under way."

"How many did he get?"

"Thirty-six."

Stone rolled his eyes. "I can see why you want him so badly."

"And before he sells them," Lance said. "It exacerbates the situation that they're small and can be carried in a couple of brief-cases."

Their dinner arrived.

"He has an airplane, you know," Stone said.

"Who?"

"Billy Bob."

"What kind of an airplane?"

"A GIV. That has a range of, what, forty-five hundred miles?"

"How do you know this?" Lance asked.

"Actually, I don't know it. The first time Dino and I met him, he said he'd just arrived at Teterboro and an engine had eaten a bird and had to be replaced. For all I know, the airplane may just be another of Billy Bob's lies. God knows, everything else he's told me has been a lie."

"Not everything," Lance said. "He told you the truth about being in Hawaii."

"You found him?"

"We found out he'd been there, but he had checked out of a cottage at the Hana Ranch on Maui by the time we got there. We're checking on yachts now. I wish I'd known about the GIV earlier; he may already be gone, and he could go just about anywhere in that thing. I'll phone it in when I've finished this steak. I don't suppose you have a tail number?"

"Nope. You think he's already moved the grenades?"

"Maybe not; he's missing one thing."

"What?"

"The modification to the standard rifle launcher that arms the grenade when it's fired. All the ones in New Mexico are accounted for, and if he sold it to these people without the arming mechanism, he'd get a bullet in the brain, or worse."

"The grenades can't be fired any other way?"

"Nope. You could dribble one like a basketball, and it wouldn't explode. The mechanism does everything — launches it and arms it, with a single pull of the trigger."

"You know," Stone said, "every time we invent some new method of killing, the bad guys get it. That's been true from the slingshot to the atomic bomb, and now the administration wants to spend a lot of money developing tiny nuclear weapons. Don't they ever learn?"

"If they did, I'd be out of work," Lance said.

23

Stone was doing the *Times* crossword in bed the following morning, when the intercom buzzed. Stone picked it up. "Yes, Joan?"

"Good morning."

"Good morning."

"Did you listen to the phone messages when you came in last night?"

"No."

"There's one from Bill Eggers: He wants you at an important meeting at ten A.M., at Woodman and Weld."

Stone looked at his bedside clock; it was nine twenty-five. "Oh, God."

"Maybe it's something that will produce some income," she said. "You can't keep selling stock."

"I'm running," Stone said, heading for the shower.

He arrived at the meeting in Eggers's office ten minutes late.

"Good afternoon," Eggers said pointedly.

"I'm sorry. I got your message only a few minutes ago."

He turned and looked at the other person seated on Eggers's sofa. She appeared to be in her midthirties, dressed in a beautifully designed suit and expensive shoes, wearing a tasteful diamond choker and a heavy-looking engagement ring and wedding ring. "I'm Stone Barrington," he said, offering his hand.

She took it, smiled briefly, but said nothing.

"This is Barbara Stanford," Eggers said.

The name caused Stone to stop breathing for a brief moment. "I'm very pleased to meet you."

"Sit down, Stone," Eggers said.

Stone sat and regarded Barbara Stanford. He guessed that, when she stood up, she would be tall. She had chestnut-colored hair and tawny skin, and the silk blouse under her suit didn't bother to cover too much cleavage.

"Barbara has a rather unusual problem," Eggers said.

"Perhaps I'd better explain the situation to Mr. Barrington," she said in a beautifully modulated, accentless voice.

"Go right ahead, Barbara," Eggers said.

"A little over a year ago, I was married to a man I'd only known for a short time. During the time we've been married, we've spent a total of only a few months together, since he travels widely on business and prefers to do so alone."

Stone saw it coming, and he dreaded it. "May I ask his name?"

"Whitney Stanford," she replied.

Stone gulped. "Please go on."

"I began to think there might be another woman," she said, "and I began poking around among his things. I found a passport. I thought it odd, since he was in Paris at the time and would have needed his passport to travel there, but when I opened it, it was in another name: Forrest Billings. The photograph, however, was of my husband. I had barely gotten over the shock when a magazine called *Avenue* was delivered to my apartment."

Stone knew the magazine. It was a society journal that was delivered to every apartment building on the Upper East Side.

"The magazine features a lot of photographs of people taken at parties, and to my astonishment, I saw a picture of my husband with another woman and — you won't believe this — the mayor."

Eggers, who had seemed drowsy, was suddenly alert.

"The caption for the picture said he was somebody called Billy Bob Barnstormer."

Eggers got to his feet. "If you'll excuse me, I think it would be best if the two of you talked alone."

"No, it wouldn't," Stone said. "Sit down, Bill."

Eggers sat down, grabbed a tissue from a box on the coffee table and dabbed at his forehead.

Stone nodded. To Barbara Stanford he said, "Please continue."

"That's about it," she said. "It appears I'm married to a man with several identities, and I don't know which one is real. What should I do?"

"What do you want to do?" Stone asked. "I mean, what was your first instinct, when you learned about this?"

"Well, I thought about having him arrested for bigamy, but then it occurred to me that I don't know if he has another wife."

"Suppose you're his only wife: What would you wish to do then?"

"I think that depends on whether he is who he represented himself to be, or whether one of these other identities is real."

"Suppose none of his identities is real," Stone said, "including Stanford."

"Then I would want an immediate divorce," she replied.

"May I ask," Stone said, "have you given your husband any money?"

"No, he's insisted on paying all of my bills from the moment we were married — clothes, credit cards, the maintenance fees on my co-op — everything."

"You owned the apartment before you were married?"

"Yes, my first husband, who is deceased, left it to me."

"Well, I think that's good news," Stone said.

"Of course, there are the investments."

"He invested money for you?"

"Yes, that's his business, and he's very good at it."

"May I ask, on what basis do you assume he's good at it?"

"Well, his lifestyle, I suppose. And what he's said in conversation. He's had a number of telephone conversations with Warren Buffett about a start-up they're doing together. And he's never been short of money."

"How much did he invest for you?"

"Oh, not all that much; the bulk of my assets are overseen by a money manager who was the best friend of my late first husband. I let Whit invest only what was in my money market account at the time."

"And how much was that?"

"Something over eight million dollars."

Stone winced. "In what did he invest the money?"

"He put it into various companies that he had developed. The investments were quite well diversified."

"Have you seen monthly statements on the investments?"

She was looking worried now. "No. Do you think there might be something . . . funny about what he did with the money?"

Stone didn't answer her question immediately. "In recent days, has anyone called or visited your apartment looking for him?"

"Why, no. He hasn't had a single phone call or visitor since he left for Paris."

"And how long ago was that?"

"Not quite three weeks ago."

"Have you heard from him during that time?"

"Yes, he called daily until the day before yesterday. That was when I discovered the passport. The magazine arrived yesterday. He hasn't called since then."

"May I ask, what was your first husband's name?"

"Morris Stein," she said.

"Of Stein Industries?"

"That's right."

Well, Stone thought, she's never going to miss the eight million dollars. Stein had been well up among the top ten on the *Forbes* list of the world's richest people. "Mrs. Stanford," Stone said, "I don't think it will be necessary for you to obtain a divorce."

"Why not?"

"Because it would appear that your husband married you under an assumed name, and if we can demonstrate that he did so, then you would be legally entitled to an annulment."

"Oh, well, that's a relief."

"Did Mr. Stanford leave a lot of his things in your apartment?"

"Yes — most of his clothes and a lot of personal effects. Can you arrange the annulment?"

"Yes, but there are some steps we should take first."

"I'll do whatever you say, Mr. Barrington."

"To begin with, I'd like to bring some people to your apartment to go through his things and look for evidence of any other identities he might have used."

"All right; just let me know when you'd like them to come."

"Then, when they've been through everything, you should have Mr. Stanford's possessions packed up and put into storage. You should have the locks on your apartment changed and instruct the building superintendent that Mr. Stanford is not to be allowed in the building or in your apartment. You should also inform the management of your building that you will henceforth be known by your previous name, and you should inform anyone you do business with, and your friends, of that fact. In short, you will want to erase Mr. Stanford from your life as quickly as possible."

"I see."

"Do you have any joint bank or brokerage accounts?"

"Yes."

"Are you able to give instructions on those accounts without Mr. Stanford's permission or cosignature?"

"Yes."

"Then you should open new accounts in your own name immediately and transfer all assets in the joint accounts to the new accounts."

"This is going to be quite a lot of work, isn't it?"

"Yes, it is."

"Should I report Whitney to the police?"

"I'll take care of that."

"Should I hire a private investigator to look into Whitney's background?"

"I don't think that will be necessary."

"Why not?"

"Mrs. Stanford — perhaps I should say, Mrs. Stein — I think I should bring you up-to-date on what I already know about your husband."

"You know him?"

"In a manner of speaking." As gently as possible, Stone told her nearly everything. When he was done, Mrs. Stein sat silently, looking pale. Bill Eggers was no less pale.

Finally, she spoke. "And you still don't think I should hire someone to look into his background?"

"Mrs. Stein, there is a sufficient number of people already looking into everything about him," Stone said. "Does he have an office?"

"He works from an office in his old apartment, where he lived before we were married."

"Do you have a key to that apartment?"

"I believe there's one among his things."

"If I may, I'll accompany you home to get that key."

"All right."

Stone ushered her to the elevators. "Just a

moment," he said. He went back to Eggers's office and stuck his head through the door. "I want you to cut me a check for the fifty thousand dollars that your Billy Bob stole from me," he said. "Have it hand-delivered before the end of the day."

Eggers nodded, and Stone closed the door.

24

Stone walked Barbara Stein downstairs.

"Would you like to come and get the key now?" she asked. "You can ride with me."

"Yes, thank you." They got into her car, while the chauffeur held the door for her. Stone looked around the interior. It was the new Maybach, made by Mercedes-Benz, and he hadn't been in one before.

"Go ahead and play with the seat," she said, pointing to the controls. "Everyone wants to."

Stone tried the switches and discovered that it was much like a first-class airline seat. He could nearly recline.

"Fun, isn't it?" she asked, smiling.

Stone thought she looked very nice in a smile. "Yes, it is. I drive the small economy version of your car."

"I would never have bought the thing, but Morris ordered it before he died, and I thought, what the hell?"

"How long were you and your husband married?" Stone asked, as they made their way silently through traffic.

"Twenty-one years," she said. "I was twenty-two and working as a flight attendant on the transatlantic route. Morris flew with me twice, then asked me to dinner in London. I was swept off my feet. He had been widowed for less than a year."

Stone was doing the arithmetic. She was older than he had thought, but apparent youth was common among the well-tended women of the ultrarich class.

"Do the math, yet?" she asked. "You're blushing. It's so rare to meet a man with blond hair these days; you even have blond eyebrows. What are your national origins?"

"English on both sides, all the way back to the Bronze Age, but I suppose a Viking rapist must have insinuated himself, somewhere along the way."

"I expect it gets blonder in the summertime."

"I'm afraid so."

"I'm Polish, myself," she said. "My maiden name was Murawski."

"A handsome people, the Poles."

She laughed. "I like you, Mr. Barrington."

"Please call me Stone."

"And I'm Barbara. Where did the name come from?"

"My mother's name was Matilda Stone."

"The painter?"

"Yes."

"I've seen her things at the Metropolitan, in the American Wing."

The car drew to a smooth halt in front of 1111 Fifth Avenue, and they got out and went inside.

Barbara Stein lived in a three-story house, it turned out, but it was situated at the top of a fourteen-story apartment building. The elevator opened directly into the foyer, and a butler stood waiting to open the doors to the living room, which was on the top floor.

"There are two other floors downstairs," she said, "but we always enjoyed entertaining up here, because of the terrace." She led him through French doors to a beautifully planted terrace stretching the width of the building, with spectacular views west and south over Central Park and the Metropolitan Museum.

"Breathtaking," Stone said.

"Would you like something to drink? Iced tea, perhaps?"

"Thank you, perhaps another time. I'd really like to get that key and get some people over there as quickly as possible."

"Of course; please follow me." She led him down a floor to a gigantic bedroom and thence to a large, mahogany-paneled dressing room, filled with a man's clothing. She rummaged in the top drawer of a built-in stack and came up with a key. "Here it is." She gave him the address.

"Do you know if he has a safe there?"

"I expect so; there's one here, too, behind his suits."

"Then, if it's not too much of an imposition, I'd like to bring some people back here to go through his things and open the safe."

"Of course; whenever you like."

"In the meantime, you might ask your staff to pack all these things, and they needn't be careful about how they do it."

She laughed. "I'll see that they make a mess of it." She led Stone back upstairs and to the foyer. "Thank you so much for your advice. When can we start on the annulment?"

"First, let me see what we come up with in the search, then we can make a decision."

She rang for the elevator and held out her hand. "I'll look forward to hearing from you." She held onto his hand just a moment longer than necessary.

"I'll phone you later today," Stone said. "Are you in the book?"

"Under B. Stein."

He gave her his card. The elevator arrived,

and Stone rode down. On the sidewalk, he phoned Lance.

"Yes?" Lance drawled.

"Meet me at . . ." Stone looked at the address and read it to him. "Between Lex and Third."

"Why?"

"Because I have the key to Whitney Stanford's apartment at that address."

"Fifteen minutes?"

"Fine, and bring some help and a safecracker. Later, you'll need to go to an apartment on Fifth Avenue, too, where his wife lives."

"Wife?"

"Of some months. She was formerly married to Morris Stein."

"*The* Morris Stein?"

"The same."

"Good God!"

"Fifteen minutes."

They arrived at the building, in the East Sixties, simultaneously, Lance with two companions. It was a small apartment building, with no doorman. They took the elevator to the top floor and let themselves in. "We have Mrs. Stanford's permission, so a warrant won't be necessary," Stone said.

"A warrant is rarely necessary," Lance replied drolly. The place was a two-bedroom floor-through, professionally decorated in an impersonal style, with a roof terrace at the back.

"All right," Lance said, "take the place apart, but this is a covert search; everything must be left exactly as it was. Jim, find the safe and get started on that first." The two men went to work, and so did Stone and Lance.

"Watch me for a minute," Lance said. He donned a pair of latex gloves, went to a desk in the living room, pulled out a drawer, and set it on top of the desk, then he removed and replaced precisely the contents of the drawer. "Like that," he said. "I realize you haven't been trained to do this, so go slowly, and check the bottoms of the drawers, too." He handed Stone some gloves.

He left Stone to the desk and went to another room. Stone went through the drawers very carefully, and under the right-hand top drawer he found a small piece of paper taped in place.

"Lance," he called.

"Yes?"

"You're not going to need to crack the safe; I've found the combination."

Lance returned, looked at the piece of paper once, then went away again. A moment later, he called out, "Stone, come in here."

Stone found his way to the master bedroom and into a dressing room. Lance stood before an open safe.

"My God," he murmured. There were four passports stacked up in a corner of the safe, next to stacks of cash in dollars, pounds and Euros. Stone picked up a stack. "Two-dollar bills," he said, "unused and with consecutive serial numbers. The rest seem to be hundreds."

"Photograph everything," Lance said to his men, "then put it all back. I want an individual, readable shot of every page of every passport. Take down the serial numbers of every bank note."

Lance left them to it while he and Stone went quickly through the other rooms of the apartment. Except for the contents of the safe, not another scrap of paper yielded any useful information.

Two hours later they had finished and returned everything in the apartment to its original state. As they were about to open the door, there was a noise from the other side. Lance held a finger to his lips, and he and the other two men produced guns and stood away from the door.

There was a scraping noise that went on for, perhaps, thirty seconds, then the door opened and two men walked in, followed by a woman.

The woman was Tiffany Baldwin.

25

Tiff stared at Stone. "What the hell are *you* doing here, and who the hell are these guys?" She gestured at Lance and his two men.

Lance showed her his ID. "Allow me to introduce myself," he said, looking appreciatively up and down her. "My name is Lance Cabot."

"How do you do?" she said, then turned back to Stone. "You really are mixed up with the CIA?"

" 'Mixed up' is a good way to put it," Stone said.

"You haven't answered my question," Tiff replied. She turned back to Lance. "What are you doing here?"

Lance spoke up. "It would appear that we have a mutual interest in the gentleman who resides here. I should think we also have a mutual interest in not disturbing the contents of his apartment. If he knows either of us has been here, he'll bolt."

"I assume you've already turned over the place."

"You assume correctly. The only items of

any interest were four passports from as many English-speaking countries and some cash. They're all in a safe, and we left it undisturbed. May I suggest that, if we have anything further to discuss, we do it outside? The man could come home at any moment."

"All right," Tiff said. She led the way out of the apartment. The elevator had to make two trips to get them all downstairs.

On the sidewalk, Lance spoke to her again. "I assume you're after Mr. Stanford for financial crimes?"

"You could say that," Tiff replied.

"We are here on a matter of national security," he said, "and I'm afraid that trumps your investigation. I must ask you to stay away from the man. There's a great deal more at stake here than you realize."

"We'll see about that," Tiff said.

"Have your boss call my boss," Lance said. "So good to meet you." He herded Stone and his two men toward an anonymous-looking sedan.

Stone stopped and whispered in Tiff's ear. "Dinner tonight?"

"You're on," she said.

"Elaine's at nine o'clock. See you there."

Lance held the door of the sedan, and Stone climbed in.

He phoned Barbara Stein. "May I bring over my people now?"

"Of course," she said. "I have an appointment at my hairdresser's, but I'll instruct the butler to let you in and give you the run of the place. I won't be back before five this afternoon. I'm leaving a note with the doorman for Whitney."

"Thank you, Barbara; we'll leave the place as neat as possible." He hung up and turned to Lance. "We're on." The car drove away.

"I'm impressed with your resourcefulness, Stone, not to mention your acquaintanceship," Lance said. "I was optimistic about your eventual value to us, but you've surpassed my expectations."

"I'll bill you," Stone said.

"How ever did you learn about the wife and the apartment?"

"I have my methods."

"We must discuss those sometime. You know, I think it might be valuable for you to take a little trip down to rural Virginia for a few weeks sometime, to undergo some useful training."

"Useful to whom?"

"To us and to you. I think you might find the experience entertaining."

"Is this the famous 'Farm' you're talking about?"

"Camp Peary, to be precise."

"Lance, I would not find it entertaining to run around in the woods, being barked at by drill sergeants. I'm a little . . . mature for that sort of thing."

"Oh, it's not like that at all. You'd enjoy learning some of the dark arts."

"You make it sound like Hogwart's Academy."

"Well, I suppose it is, in its way."

They pulled to a halt in front of Barbara Stein's building and got out of the car.

"You know," Lance said reverentially, "someone once said that, if there is a God, he probably lives at Eleven Eleven Fifth Avenue."

Stone spoke to the doorman, and they were sent upstairs, where the butler greeted them.

"Gentlemen," the man said in a tony British accent, "my name is Smithson. Mrs. Stein has told me that you are to have access to the entire apartment, and that I am to assist you in any way I can."

"Thank you, Smithson," Stone said, "but I don't think we'll need anything."

"There are bells scattered around the three floors, for butler, maid and cook. Should you require my help, please press the 'butler' button."

"Thank you." Stone turned to Lance. "Let's start with our man's dressing room; there's a safe in there."

Stone led them downstairs to the master bedroom and thence to Stanford's dressing room.

"The man does live well, doesn't he?" Lance said, looking around at the racks and cubicles full of expensive clothing.

Stone pushed back some suits, revealing the safe.

"Get started on that," Lance said to one of the men. "The rest of us are going to go through the pockets of every jacket and pair of trousers in this room, collecting every stray piece of paper we find."

Stone took a suit off a rack, hung it on a hook, and started to go through it.

Downstairs the doorman watched as a red Hummer trundled to a stop at the end of the building's awning, and Mr. Whitney Stanford got out.

The doorman stepped directly into the man's path. "Good afternoon, Mr. Stanford," he said, removing an envelope from his pocket and handing it to him.

Stanford accepted the envelope. "I'll read it upstairs," he said, starting to move around the man.

"I'm sorry, sir," the doorman said. "But Mrs. Stein has asked me to tell you that you may not enter the building."

"What?"

"I believe the letter in the envelope will explain."

Stanford ripped open the envelope and read the letter, which was short. He tucked it into an inside pocket. "Please tell *Mrs. Stanford* that I'll be at my apartment, and ask her to phone me."

"I'll give *Mrs. Stein* the message, sir. Good day." He opened the rear door of the Hummer. Stanford got in, and the truck drove away.

"All right, what have we got?" Lance asked.

"The contents of the safe are much like those of the one in his own apartment," one of the men said. "Three passports — Irish, South African and British — and about a hundred and twenty thousand in dollars and Euros. And a stack of two-dollar bills."

Stone pointed to a paper on the dresser top. "We've got credit card receipts, one from a tailor and several phone numbers jotted on scrap paper," he said.

"Write everything down and put it all back," Lance said.

"Mrs. Stein is moving all this stuff into a storage facility tomorrow," Stone said.

"In that case, we'll take the paper with us — the passports and cash, too." He turned to Stone. "How do you suppose he's generating all this cash?"

"Various scams, I guess, but he's working with eight million dollars that he claims to be investing for his wife."

"That should keep him going for a while," Lance said. "Does Stanford have a study here?"

"His wife says not."

"Then we're done; let's get out of here."

The went back downstairs, and as they left the building, the doorman spoke.

"Excuse me, Mr. Barrington?"

"Yes?"

"You might like to know that Mr. Stanford was here less than an hour ago."

Lance took an immediate interest. "Do you know where he went?"

"He said that he was going to his apartment, and Mrs. Stein could phone him there."

"Let's go," Lance said, heading for the car.

"Oh, and he was riding in a red Hummer," the doorman called after them.

26

They piled back into the car and drove back to the Stanford apartment building. As they got out, Lance looked at Stone.

"Are you armed?"

"Ah, no."

"Do you recall my advising you that you should be armed at all times, until we catch this man?"

"Ah, yes."

"Then why aren't you armed?"

"I forgot."

"Wait here."

"I'll keep to the rear," Stone said.

"You're vulnerable, and that makes us vulnerable. Stay here." Lance turned and led his two men into the building.

Stone looked up at the top-floor windows. A moment later Billy Bob appeared on the roof, a cell phone clapped to an ear, a briefcase in the other hand. He looked down at the street for a second, saw Stone, then starting running along the rooftops toward Lexington Avenue.

Stone grabbed his cell phone and pressed

the speed dial button for Lance's number. Busy. He began jogging toward Lexington, watching the rooflines of the buildings he passed. Once he caught a glimpse of Billy Bob's head, then he didn't see him anymore. As he reached the corner, the light changed, and a flood of traffic started downtown, among the cars and trucks, a red Hummer.

"Shit," Stone said aloud. He tried Lance's number again.

"Yes, Stone?"

"He got out over the roof and made it down to Lex, where the red Hummer was waiting."

"Why didn't you stop him?"

"Stop him? He was five floors up. I don't know how the hell he got from the roof down to the street."

"And you couldn't shoot him, because you weren't armed."

"No, but I wouldn't have had a shot at him, even if I had been armed. I only got a glimpse of him. Anyway, I didn't know we were out to kill the guy."

"We'll be right down," Lance said.

Stone waited by the car, and a minute later, Lance and his two men came out of the building.

"Which way did he go?"

"Downtown on Lex, but that was three or

four minutes ago; he could be anywhere by now."

"Outstanding," Lance said sourly.

"I don't need the attitude, Lance; there was nothing I could do, except watch him drive away. Tell me, how did he get away from you?"

"The living-room television was on when we burst in," Lance said. "It was displaying the images from four video cameras that we never saw. He saw us enter the building and scampered, first cleaning out the safe."

"Well, at least you have photographs of the passports in the safe and the serial numbers on the currency."

"Yes, there is that. I'll flag the passports at all ports of entry and exit."

"What would you like me to do now?"

"Do you actually own a firearm?"

"Several."

"I want you to go home, select one, strap it to your body in some fashion and don't take it off until I tell you to, unless you're in the shower. Is that perfectly clear?"

"Stop giving me orders, Lance."

"While you're at home, read your contract with us; it allows me to give you orders and obligates you to follow them."

Stone thought about that.

"Trust me, it does. Until we find this man I want you to think of yourself as on active duty with us. Keep your cell phone handy at all times. If I need you, drop whatever you're doing and follow my instructions. Is that perfectly clear?"

"I'll read the contract," Stone said.

"Sorry we can't drop you," Lance said, getting into the car and driving away.

Stone got a cab home, went straight to his office and pressed the intercom button on his phone. "Joan, please get me that contract that I signed with Lance Cabot last year."

"Right." A moment later she came into his office and handed him the contract.

"Thanks."

"You'll be glad to hear that Woodman and Weld sent over a check for fifty thousand dollars."

"I am *very* glad to hear that."

Joan went back to her office, and Stone began to read the contract with increasing alarm. How the hell had he ever signed such a document? Lance could do with him as he wished and probably shoot him, if he objected. He went upstairs, opened the big safe in his dressing room, and chose a Colt Defender that he'd had custom-converted from a .45 to a 9mm. He shoved it into a holster and threaded that and a double magazine holder onto his belt.

"All right, Lance, goddammit," he said aloud, "I'm armed."

Tiff was late for their dinner date at Elaine's, and Stone was on his second Knob Creek when she arrived.

"I want one of those," she said, sitting down. "A double."

Stone gave her order to a waiter. "Rough day?"

"You don't know the half of it. Because of your CIA buddy, I had to sit still for an hour on a conference call with the AG, while he chewed me out in front of a dozen people."

"I take it Lance's claim to Billy Bob trumped yours?"

"The AG tried to take it to the president, but the White House chief of staff slapped him down. He is very, very pissed off."

"The experience will be good for him," Stone said.

Tiff sucked up a quarter of her drink, swallowed it and sighed. "Okay, how did you get involved with the Agency?"

"I can't tell you much," Stone said. "I read my contract this afternoon, more carefully than the first time, and well . . ."

"You mean, if you tell me, you'll have to shoot me?"

"No, but if I tell you too much, they'll probably shoot *me*. I met Lance a couple of years ago in London, and I became embroiled in an Agency operation that I didn't even understand. I thought the whole thing was completely screwed up, until Lance explained that that was what I was supposed to think. He asked me to sign on as a consultant — Dino, too, and another friend of mine named Holly Barker. I was flattered, the money was good, and it sounded intriguing."

"And none of that turned out to be the case?"

"All of it turned out to be the case, but I find myself in a position where I have to follow orders, something I have never enjoyed doing."

"Welcome to the club. Why does the Agency want Rodney Peeples?"

"Look, we've got to agree on what to call him; it's too confusing. Can we just call him Billy Bob?"

"Oh, all right. Why do they want Billy Bob?"

"I can't tell you that, on penalty of God knows what. Why do *you* want him, Tiff? Surely that can't be a secret, since you're out of the picture anyway."

"The guy has pulled off a series of scams. He used the car dealership in San Mateo to screw a dozen loan companies out of millions, financing nonexistent cars; he used the accounting firm in Oklahoma to set up phony tax shelters that nobody in his right mind, except a doctor or dentist, would invest in, soaking a group of them for more than thirty million dollars; and now there are half a dozen Dallas zillionaires — all of them heavy contributors to Republican causes — who got rooked out of millions and who are screaming bloody murder and wanting Peep . . . Billy Bob's balls nailed to the barn door, and people like that get listened to by this administration."

"Okay, I get the picture."

"And, as far as the AG is concerned, I dropped the ball. Shit, I went to that apartment to arrest him. I can't help it if the Agency one-upped us."

"No you can't," Stone said sympathetically.

"Try explaining that to the AG."

"What you need is a good dinner and lots of sex."

"You're right, and that's the only good idea I've heard all day." She picked up a menu. "Let's get started."

27

Stone gazed up at Tiff, who sat astride him, lit by shafts of moonlight through the window. Tiff was moving rhythmically up and down, a small smile on her face.

"I've got an idea," she said.

"Better than this one?" Stone asked, panting.

"Nothing to do with this."

"Then let's concentrate on this and talk about it later."

"What's the matter, can't you think about two things at once?"

"Not at the moment." He gave her a bigger thrust.

"Oooo," she said. "Being able to hold two opposing thoughts at once is a sign of high intelligence."

"I'm thinking about this and doing it at the same time. That's as smart as I get."

"Come now, Stone."

"I'm trying."

"Can you watch a TV movie and do a crossword at the same time?"

"If the movie's bad enough."

"So, the sex would have to be bad for you to be able to discuss my idea at the same time?"

"Bad sex is an oxymoron."

"Surely you've had bad sex at some time."

"Not that I can recall."

"You're getting smaller, I can feel it."

"You're distracting me."

She reached behind her and took his testicles in her hand. "Is this distracting?"

"Not in the least." He thrust again.

"I see I've got your undivided attention."

"You have."

"So, can we discuss my idea now?"

Stone thrust again.

"Now you're trying to distract me."

"Is it working?"

"Sort of."

"Then concentrate on the task at hand."

"You think of this as a *task?*" she said.

"I was speaking figuratively."

"You like my figure, then?"

"Oh, yeah."

She bent over him and swung her breasts across his lips. "Have some."

He caught a nipple and gently bit it.

"What were we talking about?" she asked.

Stone thrust again. "Coming."

She increased her tempo. "Now?"

"Yes, oh, yes!"

"Me, too!"

They both made noises for a little while, then she rolled over and lay beside him. "Now can we talk about my idea?"

"Talk?" Stone panted. "I can't even move my lips."

"You don't need to; I've seen to that."

He took a deep breath and expelled it. "Okay, what's your idea?"

"My idea is that you should tell me everything you know about the CIA's investigation of Peep . . . Billy Bob."

"Have you had much experience with the CIA?" he asked.

"Not really."

"Then you can't tell me what they'd do to me, if I told you about their investigation?"

"Not exactly."

"Well, I think before we discuss your idea further, I should know what the consequences might be. I mean, there's a full range of possibilities, considering the way my contract reads. They could shoot me; they could torture me; they could put me in an airplane and kick me out over the ocean."

"They wouldn't do that to you."

"You've just admitted that you've had

little experience with them. How do you know what they might do?"

She kissed him on a nipple. "Well, whatever they did to you, it would be worth it."

"Worth it to you, you mean?"

"Well, yes."

"So you'd sacrifice me to further your career?"

"Of course. I'm an ambitious woman."

"God save me from ambitious women."

"Come on, Stone, I want to know why they're interested in a con man and thief."

"Maybe they want to hire him."

"I wouldn't put it past them, but I think it's more than that."

"What reason do you have for thinking it's more than that?"

"Now you're trying to pump me for information," she said, slapping him on the belly.

"Isn't that what you're doing to me?"

"Well, yes, but I'm the girl; it's my job."

"How'd you ever get out of Harvard Law with reasoning like that?"

"How about if I tempt you sexually?"

"I think you've just removed sexual temptation from the equation, considering my current state."

"I'll bet I could get you going again."

"You're trying to kill me, aren't you? Are you working for the CIA?"

The phone rang. Stone looked at his bedside clock: a little past two A.M. "That's gotta be Lance," he muttered, picking up the phone. "Hello?"

"Hi, there, Stone."

"Billy Bob?"

"Sometimes."

"Your accent is slipping."

"Well, we don't need that anymore, do we?"

"Why do you always call in the middle of the night? You aren't in Hawaii this time." He looked at the caller ID screen on his phone: a 917 number, a New York cell phone.

"Because in the middle of the night, I know where to find you. I hope I'm not interrupting anything."

"My sleep."

"Oh, come on, Stone; you're not sleeping, not with the lovely U.S. Attorney in your bed."

Stone sat up and began looking for a pen. He found one and jotted down the calling number.

"What is he saying?" Tiff asked, trying to listen in on the call.

"Have you been following me, Billy Bob?"

"Well, someone has, obviously. How else

would I know Ms. Baldwin is in bed with you?"

Stone found the thought disturbing. "Listen, can we drop this Billy Bob stuff? What's your name?"

"What? You expect me to tell you my real name, so you can use it to track me down? Tell you what: You tell me what you're doing messing with the CIA, and I'll tell you my real name."

"I'm a consultant to them," Stone replied. "Now, what's your real name?"

"Well, I don't guess it can hurt. The name I was born with is Harlan Wilson."

"When did you stop using it?"

"Right after I got out of the army," he replied.

"How long ago was that?"

"Oh, the CIA can tell you that."

"They don't talk to me all that much."

"Sure, they do. You talk all the time. Why, you were at my wife's apartment with them this afternoon, weren't you?"

"How many wives do you have, Harlan?"

"Don't call me that; I prefer Billy Bob."

"The waiters at Elaine's call you Two-Dollar Bill."

Billy Bob laughed. "I like that."

"Where'd you get the two-dollar bills, Billy Bob?"

"I bought 'em at a nice discount from a fella I know."

"The same fella that stole them from Fort Dix and murdered two army officers?"

Silence. "I'm getting bored with this conversation," Billy Bob said.

"Oh, you didn't know about the robbery? Surely, you didn't think you could buy money at a discount, unless it was hot."

Silence. Then he hung up.

Stone replaced the receiver.

"I want to know everything he said," Tiff said, digging him in the ribs.

"He said you were in bed with me," Stone said.

28

Stone woke up to an empty bed. Tiff was gone, and it was nearly ten o'clock. There was something he had to do, but he couldn't remember what, until he rolled over and looked at his bedside table. The slip of paper he'd written Billy Bob's number on was gone. That woke him up.

He sat on the edge of bed and called up the list of caller ID numbers, people who had called him. Billy Bob's 917 number wasn't there. Shit.

He called Lance.

"Yes?"

"It's Stone."

"I can see that from my caller ID."

"Billy Bob called me last night."

"From where?"

"I don't know; he was on a cell phone, a New York number."

"What's the number?"

"I don't know."

"You have caller ID, don't you?"

"I tried that; it didn't register somehow. Technical glitch, I guess."

"Then how did you know it was a 917 number?"

Stone tried to get his mind in gear; it wasn't working.

"Stone?"

"I asked him his real name, and he said it was Harlan Wilson."

"Harold Wilson?"

"Harlan." Stone spelled it for him.

"Why would he tell you his real name?"

"Maybe he's lying, but I thought it wouldn't hurt to ask."

"Right. The bastard is so arrogant, he might actually tell you."

"Maybe he did."

"I'll check it out."

"Talk to you later."

"Stone?"

"Yes?"

"Why don't you have Billy Bob's number?"

"I can't explain it."

"Were you alone last night?"

"Funny, Billy Bob asked me the same thing. Or rather, he told me."

"He told you you were in bed with somebody?"

"Yes."

"And that would be Ms. Baldwin." It wasn't a question.

Stone said nothing.

"And did you write down the number?"
"Sort of."
"And was it still there when you woke up?"
"Not exactly."
"And had it been deleted from your caller ID log?"
"Possibly."
"You incredible schmuck."
It was out of character for Lance to employ Yiddish epithets, Stone thought. He must be really pissed off. "I can't argue with that."
"What else did you tell her?"
"Nothing. I told her that my contract with the Agency prohibited me from discussing it."
"Except you told her that you had a contract with the Agency."
"I think she figured that out when she found me with you in Billy Bob's apartment. She's not stupid."
"No, she's not, but she's a pain in the ass. Right now, she's running down that number and putting an electronic watch on it, which means that she and her people have a better shot at getting their hands on Billy Bob than we do. I do not like that."
"I understand."
"It's much easier to deal with the At-

torney General when he doesn't actually have custody of the man we're looking for."

"Look, Lance, I don't want to get involved in your interagency warfare."

"You already are involved, Stone. When you signed that contract, you joined our little army, and right now, you appear to have committed treason."

"I didn't commit anything," Stone said. "She stole the piece of paper and erased the number while I was asleep. That makes me a victim, not a perpetrator."

"And that's the only thing that is preventing me from hauling you before a . . ."

"A what?"

"Never mind; just know that you can be hauled before it, should something like this happen again."

"I'll try to remember that."

"See that you do. Now, you said that Billy Bob told you you were in bed with Ms. Baldwin?"

"Ah, yes."

"Don't leave the house; I'm sending a tech over there right now to sweep the place."

"Do you really think that's necessary?"

"Don't you?"

"All right, send him over. Goodbye." Stone hung up, got out of the bed and showered and shaved. His ears burned the whole time. He was in the middle of breakfast when the doorbell rang.

Stone picked up the phone. "Yes?"

"Our mutual friend sent me."

"I'm in the kitchen; ground floor, rear." Stone buzzed the door open.

A moment later a young man appeared. Jeans, T-shirt, leather jacket, longish ratty hair, stubble. A fashion plate, by current standards. "I'm Sandy," he said. "Where's the room you slept in last night?"

Stone pointed to the spiral back staircase. "Second floor, rear."

Sandy disappeared up the stairs.

Stone finished his breakfast and put his dishes into the dishwasher. He began reading the *Times* and was on the editorial page when Sandy came downstairs.

The young man walked over to the kitchen table and tossed four small devices onto it, each about the size of a walnut. "I hope you smiled; you were on *Candid Camera*."

"*Those* are cameras?" Stone asked disbelievingly, picking one up.

"The latest thing — color, sound, high resolution, wireless and almost invisible. When you came home last night, was there a van parked outside?"

"I've no idea."

"Had to be," Sandy said. "The range on these things isn't all that great. Whoever did this is well equipped."

"I guess so."

"I'm going to go over the rest of the house, now," Sandy said. "Where should I start?"

"My office," Stone said, pointing. "I'll tell my secretary you're coming." He picked up the phone and spoke to Joan.

Stone was finishing the crossword puzzle when the phone rang. "Hello?"

"Are you near a computer, Lance?"

"Yes." There was a laptop on the kitchen counter.

"Go to the Justice Department Web site." Lance gave him the address, then hung up.

Stone put down the crossword and went to the laptop, which had a wireless Internet connection. He typed in the address and waited a few seconds for the front page of the Justice Department Web site to appear. It did not appear. What came up was a fairly good, color photograph of the U.S. Attorney for the Southern District of New York, her back arched, her teeth bared, her hair down. Naked. Sitting on a body that Stone knew to be his own. What was more, it moved, and her voice could be heard, making an animal sound. It was on a loop, repeating about every ten seconds.

Though stunned, Stone managed to feel grateful that the face on the body underneath her was out of frame.

29

Stone took a few deep breaths and tried to think. Better she should hear it from him, he thought. He dialed Tiff's direct office line.

"Tiffany Baldwin."

"It's Stone."

"Now, don't start with me about the number, Stone."

"That's not why I called, but since you mention it, couldn't you have at least left it on the caller ID list?"

"Certainly not; that would give the CIA an advantage."

"They're *supposed* to have an advantage, because the call came to me, and I am their consultant."

"Irrelevant."

"Don't talk to me like a judge."

"If that's your attitude, I'm not going to talk to you at all. Good . . ."

"Hold it. There's something you need to know."

"What? And be quick about it; I've got a hellish morning ahead of me."

"You have no idea. Go to the Internet and

to the Justice Department Web site. Right now."

"Why?"

"Just do it."

"Hang on." She set the phone down, and he could hear the clicking of keys. There was a brief pause, then an angry, wounded-animal shriek, as if she might have taken an arrow in the chest.

"Tiff?" Stone said. All he heard was a long silence.

Finally, she picked up the phone, and her voice was cold and calm. "That is *not* me! Do you understand? Why would you do a thing like that to me?"

"I didn't do it, Billy Bob did. This morning a technician found four tiny video cameras in my bedroom."

"How do you know it was Billy Bob?"

"Because, last night, on the phone, he told me he knew that you and I were in bed together. He just didn't tell me *how* he knew. I thought he had guessed."

"I say again: That is *not* me. Do you understand?"

"If that's your story, okay."

"It's *your* story, too. Got that?"

"Okay."

"I will deny this to my dying day, and you'd better, too."

"Okay, I understand."

"Until *your* dying day, which will be sooner than you think, if you utter so much as a word implicating me."

"Tiff, there's no need to threaten me; I'm with you on this."

"If I hear a word; if I read a snippet; if a rumor starts, I will unleash the full force of federal law enforcement upon your person."

"Tiff, I told you not to threaten me. I understand, and I will support your denial."

"Threat? You think that's a threat? I haven't even begun."

"Goodbye, Tiff."

"Goodbye, indeed." She hung up.

Stone hung up and dabbed at the mist of sweat that had formed on his brow. Then he noticed that Sandy was standing there.

"They're hell, aren't they?" the tech said.

"What?"

"Women. They're from hell."

Stone sighed. "Sometimes."

"This guy really did a number on you."

"What do you mean?"

"I mean there are two devices in your office, and your phones were bugged. Kind of redundant."

Stone sagged. "Swell."

"Don't worry, I've removed everything, and I've installed some equipment that will let us know if anyone tries anything like that again. Say, how did this guy get access to your office and bedroom?"

"He was a house guest for a few days. He had all the time in the world."

"You better get pickier about who you invite to stay."

"No kidding. Thanks for the advice."

"Anything else I can do for you?"

"I don't believe so. Thank you very much for your help."

"Glad to do it." Sandy turned to go.

"Hang on a minute," Stone said.

Sandy stopped. "Yeah?"

"You any good with computers?"

"They are my *métier*."

Stone turned the laptop around so he could see the screen. "This video has been placed on the Justice Department's Web site. Can you do anything about getting it off?"

Sandy peered at the screen. "Wow," he said. "Who is *that*?"

"I have no idea; can you get it off?"

Sandy watched the screen, a little smile on his face.

"Stop watching it!" Stone said. "Can you get it off their Web site?"

Sandy pointed at the screen. "Looks like that's being taken care of."

Stone turned the computer around again. A message had appeared on the screen, replacing Tiff's image: "This Web site is temporarily down for repairs. Please try again later."

"Thanks again for your help," Stone said. "Goodbye."

Sandy turned and left.

The phone rang, and Stone picked it up. "Hello?"

Dino's voice. "Man, have you seen the Justice Department Web site this morning?"

"Sure. I start my every day by checking out the Justice Department Web site."

"Well, if you haven't, you should, because your current girlfriend, the gorgeous Tiffany, is all over it, and you're underneath her."

"That is *not* Tiffany, and I am *not* underneath whoever that is."

"So you did check it out?"

"No, and I have no intention of doing so."

"And you deny that that's Tiffany and you?"

"Most emphatically."

"Well, maybe you can tell me why your mother's painting of Washington Square is on the wall, just over her shoulder."

"Nonsense."

"Not that anybody would ever notice it while Tiffany is on the screen."

"You are mistaken."

"Who would ever have thought that the fucking U.S. Attorney would . . ."

"It is not she."

"Did you take the video and put it on that Web site?"

"Certainly not."

"Then who did?"

"If it didn't happen, nobody did it."

"Do you think Tiff has had a boob job?"

"I have no idea."

"Because, if those are original equipment, they are really something."

"Dino . . ."

"This is the funniest thing I've ever seen. The whole squad room is going nuts."

"Did you tell anybody about the picture on the wall?"

"Let's see, I'm not really sure."

"Because if you did, I'm going to come down there and kill you with my bare hands."

"Relax, nobody knows but me."

"And Tiffany will have you taken out and shot, right after she has me taken out and shot."

"So, I take it, your position is, you're denying everything."

"I'm denying everything. We're both denying everything. And I'd be grateful if you would plant the notion in the minds, if such exist, of the gentlemen in the squad room that the person appearing in the video is not, repeat, not who they think it is or who you thought it was."

There came a disappointed roar through the phone.

"What was that?" Stone asked.

"Hang on, I'll check," Dino said. A moment later, he came back. "Somebody at Justice caught on; they've shut down the Web site. My detectives are crushed."

"Excellent. Do not ever speak to me about this again. Goodbye." Stone hung up and buried his face in his hands.

After a moment, he went upstairs and moved his mother's picture to another spot in his bedroom.

30

Stone went down to his office and sat at his desk, wondering if there were anything he could do to short-circuit the mess he was in. Joan buzzed him.

"Yes?"

"There's somebody from Page Six at the *New York Post* on the phone for you. You want me to tell them to get lost?"

Worst thing he could do. "No, I'll take it." He picked up the phone, pressed the line one button and tried to sound bored. "Stone Barrington."

"Mr. Barrington, this is Henry Stead, Page Six at the *Post*."

"Good morning."

"Have you visited the Justice Department Web site this morning?"

"Are you kidding? Who visits the Justice Department Web site?"

"A number of our readers, as it happens. Our phone is ringing off the hook."

"What are you telling me? Have I been arrested and held without bail and deprived of legal counsel? I hadn't noticed."

"No, but there was a very interesting piece of video on the site this morning."

"I have a feeling you're going to tell me about it."

"Are you acquainted with a Tiffany Baldwin, who is the U.S. Attorney for the Southern District of New York?"

"What, is there more than one Tiffany Baldwin who is the U.S. Attorney for the Southern District of New York? Yes, I know Ms. Baldwin."

"Well, the video on the Web site features a woman who bears what some think is a striking resemblance to Ms. Baldwin."

"Mr. Stead, I have a busy morning ahead of me. Do you have a point?"

"Well the woman in the video is naked and is apparently having sex with a man underneath her whose face is not visible."

"Somehow, that doesn't sound like the U.S. Attorney I know."

"My question is, are you that man?"

"Mr. Stead, to the best of my knowledge, I have never been photographed having sex with *anybody*, let alone with the U.S. Attorney."

"To the best of your knowledge, maybe. Could you have been videotaped having sex with Ms. Baldwin without your knowledge?"

"Certainly not."

"So there has never been any video equipment present when you were having sex with Ms. Baldwin?"

"Mr. Stead, Ms. *Baldwin* has never been present when I was having sex. Are you beginning to get my drift?"

"Mr. Barrington, have you seen the video?"

"No, I have not. It doesn't sound like a lot of fun."

"So you think having sex with Tiffany Baldwin is not fun?"

"I would not be so ungallant as to characterize in that manner sex with a woman I have never had sex with."

"But you and Ms. Baldwin have been seen in public together, having dinner at Elaine's."

"Mr. Stead, it is a very large leap from dining at Elaine's to making sex videos for the Internet. Now you have my denial on record, and if you don't already have Ms. Baldwin's denial, I'm sure you soon will. Speaking as an attorney, I think you should consult with your newspaper's legal counsel before printing any preposterous nonsense."

"I will certainly do so, Mr. Barrington. Just one more question. Your mother was the painter, Matilda Stone, was she not?"

"Yes, all my life."

"Do you have a painting of hers hanging in your bedroom? Because one appears in the video."

"That's two questions, Mr. Stead, but I should tell you that a number of my mother's paintings have been reproduced and sold in the thousands in the shop at the Metropolitan Museum of Art, and I imagine that they adorn many bedrooms. I bid you good morning." He hung up, sweating again. He was getting tired of sweating.

Joan buzzed him again.

"Yes?"

"Lance Cabot has been holding on line two."

"Great." Stone pressed the button. "Lance, sorry to keep you waiting."

"Stone, have you done anything to deal with the Internet video problem?"

"I've just denied everything, except knowing Tiffany Baldwin, to the *New York Post*, and I will continue to deny it to anyone who brings up the subject. I've also spoken to Tiffany, who denies it."

"Good idea."

"What is it, Lance? Am I somehow compromising the CIA's reputation?"

"Not yet. Tell me, is there one of your

mother's paintings hanging on your bedroom wall?"

"I'll tell you what I told the *Post*: My mother's paintings have been reproduced and widely sold."

"I'm going to send Sandy back over there to check out your alarm system."

"Why?"

"Stone, there are, after all, publications that would stoop to sending photographers to surreptitiously enter your home and photograph your bedroom."

"Oh, all right, send him over."

"And, if I were you, I'd take that particular picture down, hide it, and hang a nice Keane portrait of a small child with big eyes in its place."

"Thank you for the advice."

"When you spoke to Ms. Baldwin, did you mention the matter of Billy Bob's cell phone number?"

"As it happened, she mentioned it and took full credit."

Joan buzzed and spoke on the intercom. "Stone, Tiffany Baldwin is on line one, and I think you'd better speak to her."

"I'll have to call you back, Lance."

"Don't bother." Lance hung up.

Stone pressed the line one button. "Tiff?"

"You miserable sonofabitch," she said. "Did you tell Page Six that I'm no fun in bed?"

"Absolutely not. Did they say that?"

"Yes, and a lot more."

"I simply denied everything, as you asked, and as I would have done even if you hadn't asked."

"What about that picture on your bedroom wall?"

"That's being dealt with."

"Burn it."

"My mother painted it."

"All right, I'll buy it from you."

"It's not for sale. Tiff, calm down. The video was taken off the Web site almost as soon as it appeared."

"Yes, I saw to that."

"Then there's nothing to worry about. This will go away by tomorrow, and then . . ."

"And then nothing," she said. "I never want to see you again." She hung up.

"And just when it was going so well," Stone said aloud to himself. He hung up the phone.

Joan buzzed again. "Stone?"

"Now what?"

"Someone to see you."

"Who?" But his question was answered

before she could speak. He looked up to find Arrington Carter Calder standing in the door to his office.

"Hello, Stone," she said.

She stood there in a tight, short, brown dress, her hair golden, a sable coat over her shoulders, looking better than he had ever seen her. Something inside him melted, as it always did when she entered a room. She had not entered a room of his for more than two years, and a dinner they had had together in London a year before had ended disastrously. Involuntarily, as happened every time he saw her, he wondered whether he or the late movie star Vance Calder was the father of her son, Peter. And he wondered why she was here.

"Well, aren't you going to invite me in?" she asked.

He got to his feet and walked around the desk to greet her. "Of course." He leaned over to kiss her on the cheek, but she turned so that their lips met. "Come in and sit down. Would you like some coffee?"

She sat down on the sofa. "I'd like some lunch, but would you answer a question, first?"

"Sure."

"This morning, on the Imus show, they were talking about something that seemed to involve you, something about your appearing in a sex video with the United States Attorney? Surely you aren't gay, Stone, not you."

31

They lucked into a table in the busy Grill Room of the Four Seasons, probably because Arrington was Vance Calder's widow. When a bottle of Chardonnay had been brought and their lunch had been ordered, Stone began to explain.

"First of all, the U.S. Attorney is female; second, she has denied that the video is of her; third, I am not the person in bed with whoever the woman is."

Arrington nodded. "All right, whatever you say."

"Do I detect a note of disbelief in your voice?"

"Yes, you do. This is just the sort of trouble you're always getting yourself into, Stone, and I know very well that there is one of your mother's pictures on your bedroom wall."

"I have done nothing whatever to get myself into trouble; it's been done for me. And there are thousands of reproductions of my mother's paintings on bedroom walls all over this city. They seem to have replaced

Utrillo prints as the thing to exhibit one's good taste in art."

"Whatever you say."

"While we're speaking of my troubles, I'd like to take this opportunity, not having previously had one, to explain what happened when we were having dinner in London."

"Are you referring to the occasion when you walked out of the Connaught Hotel's restaurant and vanished into the night without a word?"

"I was arrested, sort of."

"How do you get arrested, 'sort of'?"

"The London police turned up at the Connaught and demanded to see me. They took me up to my suite and grilled me for more than an hour and would not allow me to leave or make phone calls. When I finally came back downstairs, you, quite understandably, were gone. All my efforts to contact you and apologize were fruitless."

"Well, that's a very entertaining story, even if I didn't find it entertaining at the time. What were they grilling you about?"

"I can't tell you; it's a client confidentiality thing."

"How convenient."

"Oh, all right, I'll tell you. The London police found a car with two dead Israeli

Mossad agents in the trunk; one of them was wearing my raincoat."

Arrington burst out laughing. "Stone, you should be writing novels, really you should. You're able to come up with the most preposterous stories at the drop of a hat."

"Arrington, have I ever lied to you?" This was a dangerous question, he knew.

"Of course you have."

"On what occasion?" he demanded, trying to sound wounded.

"All right, all right, Stone," she said, patting his hand, "I believe your story, even if it is preposterous, but may I ask a question? Just to see how quick you are?"

"What?"

"How did the dead Israeli agent end up wearing your raincoat?"

"He owned a nearly identical raincoat, and apparently, we had inadvertently exchanged them at a pub or a restaurant. Fortunately, I was able to show the police his raincoat, which was hanging in my closet."

"You are a wonder, really you are." She took his hand. "I've missed you."

The melting inside him started again. "I've missed you, too," he said, without missing a beat, and meaning it, even if she didn't. "What brought you to New York?"

"You did, of course. I wanted to be near

my New York friends — and you — again, so I'm looking at apartments."

"If you really want to be near me, you needn't buy an apartment; I have a perfectly good house."

"I think it's best if we don't rush into things, don't you? Our . . . distance, for want of a better word . . . has been a strain, at least on me, and . . ."

"On me, too."

"Well, then, let's take it slowly and see where it leads us. Anyway, I can't be here all the time. Peter is starting school in the autumn, so I still have to be in Virginia much of the year."

"It may surprise you to learn that there are very good schools in New York City."

"I think the country life and the horses are better for him than adventure trips to Central Park. I'm not sure he's the sort of boy who would thrive in the big city."

"What sort of boy is he?"

"Sensitive, a bit shy. Happy to ride his pony, or spend the afternoon alone in the barn, grooming him."

"He sounds a lot like me."

"Now, let's don't start that again. As far as I'm concerned, Vance was his father."

"Don't you want to know for sure?"

"What would that solve?"

"It might supply him with a father. Don't you think he needs one?"

"I don't think he needs the confusion, and I would not look forward to explaining things to him. Now, let that be an end to it, please."

"Whatever you wish."

"Ah, just the words I long to hear from a man."

"You've been manless for too long."

"Oh? What makes you think so? There is an ample supply of men in Albemarle County."

"Chinless wonders in baggy tweeds; wastrel trust-fund boys with no character."

"Well, there is an element of that, but there are other types. Tell me, who have you been seeing?"

"Until this morning, the U.S. Attorney, but apparently, never again."

"Are those the words she used?"

"That was a direct quote."

"Well, you can hardly blame the woman, can you? What with all this unwanted notoriety."

"I can't be blamed, either, although she's blaming me, anyway. It's not my fault she has a doppelgänger disporting herself on the Internet."

"But how did this get on the Justice Department Web site?"

"I've no idea, but it seems to have been done to embarrass her before her peers, and I certainly had no reason to do that. It seems the only thing I can do now is to try to stay out of federal court, lest I encounter her."

"That would seem a good idea, in the circumstances."

A young man in a bad suit with spiky hair stepped up to their table. "Hello, Mr. Barrington," he said, "and Mrs. Calder."

Stone looked at him, baffled. "Could you excuse us, please?"

"Well, yes, but the U.S. Attorney probably won't. Do you have any comment for our viewing audience?"

"What viewing audience?" Stone asked, looking around.

The young man pointed to his lapel, to which was pinned a round object. "Right here," he said. "Twenty million Americans watch us every night, right after the news. Our viewers want to know your side of the Internet sex scandal."

The headwaiter suddenly appeared at their table, looking distastefully at the young man. "Is everything all right, Mr. Barrington?" he asked.

"This gentleman seems to be using a hidden camera to videotape your guests,"

Stone said. "I think he needs your assistance in leaving."

The headwaiter took the young man's elbow and marched him toward the stairs. "My apologies, Mr. Barrington," he called over his shoulder.

"I'm sorry about that," Stone said to Arrington.

Arrington shook her head. "Not the way I wanted to reenter New York life," she said, folding her napkin and laying it on the table. "I'd like to go now, and we'd better find another way out of the restaurant. I have a feeling there will be a knot of cameras at the front door."

Stone waved for a check.

32

When Stone got back to his house, after putting Arrington into a cab for the Carlyle Hotel, a thicket of seedy men with cameras surrounded his doorstep.

"What do you want?" Stone asked, playing the innocent.

A hail of questions swept over him. He held up his hands for silence. "Listen carefully; I'm going to give you a statement."

They became suddenly rapt.

"This morning somebody called me about a videotape on a government Web site. I haven't seen it; I had nothing to do with it; I'm sure it did not contain images of any government official. Sounds to me like you've all confused that image with some innocent person. Go away." He elbowed his way through the crowd and let himself into the house, leaning on the door to catch his breath.

"Hi."

Stone jumped about a foot. "Sandy, what are you doing here?"

"Lance sent me over to look at your alarm system, remember?"

"Oh, yeah, I forgot."

"It had been disabled."

"What?"

"Somebody had set it up so that it seemed to behave normally when you entered your code, either arriving or departing, but it was doing absolutely nothing. They could have kicked in the door, come upstairs and shot you in your bed, and the alarm would have been completely useless. I'm referring to video shooting, of course."

"Did you fix it?"

"Yes, but — I've already told your secretary this — I would be very careful from now on about who you let into the house. Be suspicious of plumbers and, especially, electricians."

"I will be suspicious of them. Thank you."

"Call Lance if you need me again."

"I certainly will. Maybe you'd better leave through the garden, unless you want to be on *Hard Gossip* tonight. I don't think Lance would like that."

"Right."

Stone let him out into the garden and instructed him on how to reach the street, then he went to his office.

Joan came in. "Did Sandy tell you about the alarm?"

"Yes, he did."

"What's going on?"

"I wish I knew."

She leaned against the doorjamb and grinned. "So, how's Arrington?"

"As you saw her."

"She going to be around for a while?"

"Maybe; she's looking at apartments."

"How nice."

"Get out of here, please."

Joan went back to her office, chuckling.

Stone called Lance.

"Yes?"

"Thanks for sending Sandy back. Turns out, the alarm system had been disabled, but he fixed it. Do you have any idea what's going on?"

"It seems that Billy Bob has decided to make your life hell."

"Why?"

"I would imagine, because you're making his life hell."

"No, you are."

"You're helping; he's seen you doing so. Because of you, his wife has kicked him out of her very nice apartment, and he can't go back to his own place. He's pissed off."

"I suppose he is. Of course, he left a corpse in my house and stole fifty thousand dollars from me."

"Billy Bob is a sociopath; he doesn't consider your feelings when he acts. His actions are taken only to gratify himself, and right now, he finds it gratifying to make you miserable."

"I know about sociopaths; I dealt with a lot of them as a cop."

"I doubt if you ever dealt with one as ingenious and as well financed as Billy Bob. The man has technical resources, too, so he's clearly not working alone. He's managed, in one fell swoop, to cause both you and Ms. Baldwin a great deal of difficulty. I imagine that a nude photograph of her is on half a dozen bulletin boards at the Justice Department by now. This could, conceivably, end her career, depending on how she handles it. You know how our Attorney General feels about exposed body parts."

"How are you going to catch Billy Bob?"

"It might help if we had the cell phone number he called you from."

"Don't start with that again, Lance. Tiff is now not speaking to me at all, so I can hardly get her to give it to me. Maybe her people can track him down with the number."

"That is *not* what we want, is it?"

"Does it really matter who puts the guy in prison, as long as he ends up there?"

"They want him for financial crimes; we

want to destroy an operation that is stealing military hardware and selling it to God-knows-who. Which do you think is more important?"

"I think they're equally important."

"We'll see if you still think that after Billy Bob lobs one of his newly stolen grenades through your bedroom window."

"You think he's *that* pissed off?"

"I don't know, and I don't want to find out the hard way."

"What's your next step in finding him?"

"I've got every available man on the streets with several photographs of him; we're trying to track down the red Hummer."

"How many red Hummers can there be in New York City?"

"We're going to find out, I assure you. By the way, I understand that Arrington Calder is back in your life."

"What the hell do you know about Arrington and me?"

"Oh, everything, I should imagine. Do you think I would have signed you on without the most thorough investigation of your habits? And Arrington certainly seems to qualify as a habit. I understand there's some question about the paternity of her son, too."

"You're unbelievable."

"Would you like me to find out whether you or Vance Calder is the father?"

"You can do that?"

"Certainly."

"How?"

"I don't think I should go into that."

"Well, don't, please; Arrington is very sensitive about it, and I don't want to run her off. What else do you know about my life?"

"Stone, if you've lived it, if it's happened to you, I know about it. I know everything about everybody who works for me."

"That's very scary."

"Why? Isn't your conscience clear, Stone?"

"Of course, it is."

"Maybe I should have allowed my people to put you through our polygraph program."

"Thank you, no."

"Are you refusing to take a polygraph, Stone? In the Agency, that's the first step on the road to perdition."

Stone didn't want to know what the CIA considered perdition. "I'm not refusing; I just would prefer not to do it."

"You're lucky you're dealing with me and not some case officer out of Langley, you know. I don't think you would enjoy the rigors of full-time employment with us."

"I cannot but agree."

"Watch your ass, Stone; Billy Bob is dangerous." Lance hung up.

Stone remembered that he had forgotten to go armed again. He went upstairs, opened the safe and strapped everything on. Then he took his mother's picture from the wall, wrapped it carefully in a bedsheet and tucked it away at the back of a closet.

33

Stone went to the kitchen and made himself a ham sandwich, his lunch having been interrupted. He was eating it when the phone rang. He let Joan pick it up. A moment later, she buzzed him.

"It's Arrington, on line one," she said.

"You're sure it isn't somebody from the *National Perpetrator*?"

"There's no such publication."

"Well, there should be." He punched line one. "Hello?"

"You're talking with your mouth full."

He gulped down the bite of sandwich. "There, is that better?"

"Much."

"I'm sorry our lunch was interrupted."

"So am I, but I know it wasn't your fault. At least, I'd like to believe that it wasn't your fault."

"Thank you for that resounding vote of confidence."

"You're welcome. Would you like to have dinner tonight?"

"I would. There's only one place we can

go where we'll be safe from photographers."

"Where's that?"

"Elaine's. The photographers are scared of her."

"All right. My driver is bringing my car up from Virginia this afternoon; I'll pick you up at eight-thirty."

"You're on."

"Until then." She hung up.

Stone hung up, too, hope renewed.

That night, Stone left the house and settled into the wonderfully comfortable rear seat of Vance Calder's dark green, long-wheelbase Bentley Arnage. Arrington kissed him lightly.

"Do you remember this car?"

"Yes, from L.A."

"It's a bit out of place in Albemarle County, but I couldn't part with it."

"It'll be perfect for New York," Stone replied. "The traffic moves at an average of nine miles per hour here, and it's better being stuck in this English drawing room on wheels than suffering the broken-down backseat of a New York City taxicab."

"I suppose it is."

"Have you started looking for an apartment, yet?"

"Not only have I started looking, I've found one."

"Wonderful! Where?"

"Fifth Avenue, overlooking the park. All I need is a designer, and I have some ideas about that."

Elaine's was only half full when they arrived, and they were shown to Stone's usual table. The waiters fawned over Arrington, welcoming her back, and she stopped to speak to a couple of people on the way to the table.

"I'd forgotten what a nice place this can be," she said, as they sat down. "One always knows somebody."

"True. What would you like to drink?"

"A cosmopolitan, I think."

Stone ordered that, and his usual Knob Creek came with it. They raised their glasses.

"Renewed friendships," Stone said.

"We are friends, aren't we?" she asked. "I mean, in addition to having been lovers, we've always been friends."

Well, not always, Stone thought. "Of course we have."

Elaine came through the door at the stroke of nine and spotted them immediately. She came over and gave Stone a hug and a kiss but offered only a hand to

Arrington. "Hi," she said, then went to another table.

"Well, that was rather frosty," Arrington said.

"Oh, you know how Elaine is with women," Stone said.

"I know she prefers the company of men, but I thought we always got along well."

"Once you're a regular again, all will be well. Elaine likes regulars. It doesn't matter to her that you haven't been coming because you live in L.A. and Virginia; all she cares about is that you haven't been coming."

"All right," Arrington said, sipping her cosmopolitan. Then her face lit up. Dino was coming through the front door. She waved, and he came over and gave her a big hug.

"It's great to see you back, Arrington," he said.

"And it's always good to see you, Dino. Please join us for dinner."

Stone aimed a kick at Dino under the table, which he deftly avoided. "I'd love to, and I know Stone would love it, too." He waved to a waiter for a Scotch.

"And how are Mary Ann and Benito?"

"My wife and son are both thriving."

"And when did you last see them?" Arrington asked, archly.

"As a matter of fact I just had dinner with them at home," Dino said. "Ben is now doing his homework, and his mother is doing whatever she does when I'm here."

"Which is, what, every night?"

"Only five or six nights a week. We have to go out to her father's for dinner one night."

"And how is the mysterious Eduardo?"

"Old, but hardy."

"Dare I ask about Dolce?"

"Mrs. Barrington is in a rubber room, or Stone would be dead now."

Stone made a face at Dino to ward him off the subject, but it didn't help. He had once been married to Dino's sister-in-law, Dolce, for a few minutes, before she turned out to be raving and murderously mad. "It was never legal in this country," Stone said.

"Thanks to Eduardo," Dino drawled.

"Stone still thinks of himself as a bachelor, not a divorcé," Dino said.

Arrington laughed. "Stone still thinks of himself as a virgin."

The two of them thought this uproariously funny, while Stone pretended to be amused.

"So, Stone," Dino said, "you had any offers from the porno industry, yet?"

"Dino . . ."

"Are you referring to the business of the

naked U.S. Attorney on the Justice Department Web site?" Arrington asked.

"What else?" Dino replied. "Hilarious, isn't it?"

"Priceless."

"I want you both to stop this," Stone said. "Both she and I are victims of mistaken identity, and that's the whole of it."

"Sure, Stone," Dino said. "Whatever you say."

"God, it was only on the Web site for a few minutes, and the whole world seems to have seen it."

"I heard that some kid in Jersey taped it and is already selling it on the Internet," Dino said.

Stone groaned. "Anybody hungry?" He waved frantically for a waiter to bring menus.

"Starved," Arrington said.

Stone looked up from his menu to see Tiffany Baldwin walk into the restaurant, accompanied by a well-dressed man.

"Stone, what's wrong?" Arrington said. "You look as if you've seen a ghost." Her gaze followed his toward the door.

"Not a ghost," Dino said. "A video porn star."

34

Stone nearly choked on his bourbon. Tiff glided by, flashing Stone a brilliantly threatening smile that seemed to say, "If you speak to me I will cut your heart out."

"Evening, Stone," she said, as she passed.

"Evening, Tiffany."

"Oh," Arrington said, "so that's the fabled United States Attorney for the Southern District of New York."

Dino laughed. "I'm surprised she'd show her face in here."

"Why not?" Arrington said. "I hear she's already shown everything else."

"Stop it, both of you," Stone said through clenched teeth. "She'll hear you."

"She's really quite lovely, Stone," Arrington said. "I hope your roll in the hay was worth the consequences."

"What consequences?" Dino asked.

"From what I hear, Stone is just about the most famous man in New York, and tomorrow's papers aren't even out, yet."

"God, is there no end to this?" Stone said aloud.

Arrington patted his hand. "Probably not, my dear, at least not until someone else does something even more outrageous, if that's possible. Dino, do you think you could get me a copy of that videotape from that fellow in New Jersey?"

"Just go to Google and type in 'U.S. Attorney,' " Dino said. "The tape will be right at the head of the list."

Stone glared at him. "You sound as if you've already been there."

Dino shrugged. "A couple of guys at the precinct stumbled onto it. Several of my detectives have already ordered their personal copies. You're their hero."

"I want both of you to listen to me very carefully," Stone said, keeping his voice low and calm. "Either we are going to have a moratorium on this subject from this moment on, or the two of you can dine together without my company." He was volcanically angry, but he was not going to allow himself to show it.

"Why, Stone," Arrington said, taking his hand, "you're angry. I've never seen you angry before."

"And I hope you never do again," Stone replied. "Now, shall we order?" He thanked God his back was to Tiff. His cell phone vibrated in his pocket. He ignored it.

* * *

They were finishing dinner when Stone's cell phone vibrated again, and still he ignored it. A moment later, it went off for a third time. He looked at the phone and read the number from caller ID — Lance. "Will you excuse me for a moment?" Stone said.

"Of course," Arrington replied.

Stone got up and walked toward the front door, while answering his phone. "Yes?"

"It's Lance."

Stone stepped outside into the cold. "What is it?"

"I need you right now."

Stone cursed under his breath. "I'm sorry, you're breaking up."

"Don't hand me that," Lance said. "I need you right this minute. A car will pick you up in front of Elaine's in about thirty seconds."

"I'm sorry, I still can't read you," Stone said. "Try again later." He turned off the cell phone and walked back inside, shivering.

"Who was it?" Arrington asked.

"A client. We had a bad connection, so I couldn't hear him."

"Do a lot of clients call you at eleven o'clock in the evening?" Arrington asked.

"More than I would like."

"It's gotta be a girl," Dino said.

Stone had to put a stop to this right now. "It was Lance."

"Lance who?" Arrington asked.

"Lance Cabot," Dino said. "He would be the New York station chief for the CIA, if they have a New York station."

"I used to know a Lance Cabot years ago," Arrington said.

"What did he look like?" Dino asked.

Arrington pointed toward the front door. "Very much like that," she said.

Lance strode through the restaurant to the table. "Why, Arrington," he said, his usual charming self, "how nice to see you after all these years."

"And you, Lance," Arrington said, offering her hand. "I hear you're with the CIA these days."

A flicker of annoyance ran across Lance's face, but he kept his composure. He turned to Stone. "I need to speak to you outside."

"I'm sorry, Lance, but we're about to have dessert," Stone replied. "Would you like something?"

"I'm afraid I haven't time right now, but I do need to speak to you."

Stone turned to Arrington. "Would you excuse me for a moment?"

"Of course."

Stone jerked his head in the direction of the mens' room and walked back there. It was a small facility, but he checked the booth to be sure they were alone.

Lance leaned against the door. *"Now,"* he said.

"Lance, I'm having dinner with friends. You'll have to get along without me tonight."

"Are you armed, Stone?" Lance asked.

"No," Stone replied.

"Another breach of my instructions."

"Lance, your instructions are becoming a pain in the ass."

Lance reached under his arm and produced a very small semiautomatic pistol. Simultaneously, he took a small tube from his pocket and began screwing it into the barrel. The whole assembly was no more than six inches long. "Please don't underestimate the power of this little weapon," he said. "It can put an end to your life instantly, or, more appropriate to this occasion, destroy a knee, which will require a mechanical replacement, if you don't bleed to death while waiting for the paramedics to arrive."

"No," Stone said.

Lance pointed the gun at Stone's right knee and fired a round, making a soft *pffft* noise.

Stone moved at the last second, and he felt something tug at his trouser leg. He looked down to see both an entry and an exit hole through the inside knee of his pants.

"Hold still," Lance said, taking aim again. "I wouldn't want to hit the femoral artery."

"All right," Stone said, holding his hands out before him. "That won't be necessary; I'll come with you."

"Thank you so much," Lance said. "Now say your goodbyes, and we'll be on our way."

Stone walked back into the restaurant and to his table. "Arrington," he said, "I must apologize, but something urgent has come up, and I have to accompany Lance somewhere. I hope you'll forgive me."

"If I must," she replied.

"Arrington," Lance said, "I hope we'll have an opportunity to renew our acquaintance at more length soon. Good night."

"Good night, Lance, Stone."

Stone got his coat and followed Lance from the restaurant. They got into a black car.

"Now," Lance said, "where did Arrington hear that I am connected with the Agency?"

"She didn't hear it from me," Stone said.

"Did Dino tell her?"

"She didn't hear it from me," Stone repeated.

"All right."

"So what's the emergency?" Stone asked.

"We've caught Billy Bob."

"What? Where?"

"He was sitting outside your house in the red Hummer; he was armed with a silenced nine-millimeter handgun and two of the rather special grenades I told you about."

"Outside my house?"

"That is correct. Stone, if you once again fail to follow an instruction of mine, I'll have you inducted into the armed services with the rank of private, so that if you should ever ignore another order, I can have you court-martialed and sent to Leavenworth for a few years. We have a rather special little detention unit there."

"All right, all right," Stone said.

"And if I find you unarmed again until this is over, I will, I promise, shoot you in a particularly painful place."

Stone slumped in his seat and wished he were at home in his bed.

35

Lance began idly unscrewing the silencer from his little pistol.

"What is that, some CIA secret weapon?" Stone asked.

"Hardly," Lance replied. "It's a Keltec three-eighty, weighs ten ounces, loaded. Of course, our gunsmiths have done a little work on it, but it's a wonderfully concealable weapon and very effective, if the range isn't too great. I'll send you one."

"I don't understand why you need me."

"I want you to interrogate Billy Bob."

"And why do you think he'll talk to me more readily than to you?"

"He seems heavily invested in you; no one else has so captured his attention, so, even if he's just angry with you, he'll communicate."

"I don't see how this is going to work."

"You're going to be the good cop," Lance explained. "After I've shouted at him or threatened him, you're going to interrupt. Surely, you've done this a thousand times."

"Very nearly," Stone said. He had always

played the good cop to Dino's bad, when questioning suspects. "Where is Billy Bob?"

"In your garage," Lance replied.

"What?"

"It was convenient to the scene of his capture."

"How did you get into my house?"

Lance looked at him, almost with pity. "*Really,* Stone."

Stone sat back and shut up.

"Now, here's the way it's going to go," Lance said. "Two of my men are with Billy Bob now, two very . . . ah, capable gentlemen. They may have slapped him around a bit by the time we get there, depending on his attitude. They're both rather short-tempered."

"Dino and I never got to soften them up," Stone said, half to himself. "Dino would have loved that."

"We do not operate under the same strictures placed upon the NYPD," Lance said, "or any other law-enforcement agency."

Stone wondered how far Lance would take that. "And just how far would you take that?" he asked.

"As far as necessary," Lance replied. "I hope it won't be necessary to spill Billy Bob's brains onto your garage floor. Incidentally, it's good of you to have a two-car garage and only one car. Otherwise, we'd have to do this in your office."

"Whatever I can do to help," Stone said, sarcastically.

"Now you're beginning to understand your position," Lance said. "I did not recruit you simply for legal advice or for the people you know, or for the table you have at Elaine's. I did so, because there are times I need someone like you, someone with a semipublic face, with gainful employment, who lives in full view of the world, or nearly so, and has some skills, no matter how rudimentary. It helps that you inadvertently made contact with and gained the attention of Billy Bob through other means.

"I recruited Dino, because there are times when I need the resources of a big-city police department without having to deal with its hierarchy."

"Why did you recruit Holly Barker?"

"I need Holly for other, more operational reasons. She is considering a more permanent offer from us as we speak, though I think it might take a few weeks or months for her to gather the resolve to leave her present, quite pleasant circumstances and join us."

They turned the corner onto Stone's block and stopped in front of his house.

"Let's go in through your office," Lance said, using a key of his own, to Stone's annoyance.

"I don't recall our contract saying anything about your using my house at will for surreptitious interrogations."

"There's a part of your contract that reads 'render all reasonable assistance,' " Lance suggested. He led the way through Stone's office, into his basement, then into the garage. Billy Bob sat in his shirtsleeves, tied to an armless kitchen chair with a wicker seat, which Stone had stored in the garage because he didn't need it, but it was too nice to throw away. Billy Bob's hands were tied behind him. He glared at Stone but said nothing.

"Now, Harlan," Lance said. "I know that may not be your name, but . . . oh what the hell, we'll just call you Billy Bob. Stone is used to that."

"Go fuck yourself," Billy Bob replied, not unpleasantly.

"I can see this is going to be more fun than I had hoped," Lance said. He turned toward his two men, who were leaning nonchalantly against the garage wall. "I would like for you two to cause Billy Bob, here, considerable pain, without marking him up too badly. I want him relatively bruise-free when we deliver him to Guantanamo, if possible. If not, then . . ."

"Sure thing," one of the men said, pushing himself off the wall and striding toward Billy Bob, whose expression did not change.

"Hold it a minute, Lance," Stone said. "Give me a few minutes alone with Billy Bob."

"Oh, all right," Lance said, as if it were against his better judgment. He beckoned to his two companions. "Come with me," he said. At the door he turned back to Stone out of Billy Bob's hearing. "Five minutes, Stone, and I want to know three things: One, who is his contact at the New Mexico weapons installation; two, where are the other thirty-four grenades he and Billy Bob stole; and three, the name, address and telephone number of the person to whom he intended to sell them." Lance left, and Stone returned to the garage.

He leaned against his car. "So, you were going to kill me?"

"I still am," Billy Bob said.

"Why? What did I ever do to you?"

"You inconvenienced me."

"That hardly stacks up against your murdering that girl in my house and trying to blame me for it, then stealing fifty thousand dollars from me."

"I was only getting started," Billy Bob said.

"You're in over your head, now, Billy Bob. Let me explain things to you: You're not under arrest; you're not going to be arraigned or allowed to see an attorney, except me; and when Lance's two thugs are done with you, if there's anything left, you're going to find yourself in a cage at Gitmo with a lot of companions who speak only Arabic or Urdu, and nobody will ever know you're there. You'll spend the next few years being interrogated a couple of times a day, until they've milked you dry, and then you'll disappear even from Cuba. Now, if you give me the information Lance wants, then maybe I can ameliorate those circumstances a bit, do some kind of a deal."

"What, no jail time?" Billy Bob asked, contempt in his voice.

"That's not impossible," Stone said, "but let's start with no torture, no death, and work from there, a bit of information at a time. If you'll tell Lance everything — and I mean *everything* he wants to know, then I'll see that you walk out of here by morning. Then you can take your stolen money and disappear, and Lance won't care. Only the police and the feds will be looking for you, and you don't seem to have had too much trouble evading them, up to this point."

"Oh, stop it," Billy Bob said. "I'm going to get whatever I'm going to get, and there's not a fucking thing you can do about it."

"So, you absolutely refuse to tell me anything?"

"Only to stick your slick personality and your legal skills up your ass."

"I'm really sorry to hear that, Billy Bob, and I wish they hadn't chosen to do this in my garage. Have you ever tried getting bloodstains out of a concrete floor?" Stone walked slowly to the door and opened it. "Lance?"

Lance came back into the room with his two henchmen.

"I'm afraid you're going to have to persuade him to talk to you," Stone said.

Lance turned to the two men. "Strip him, and cut the cane seat out of that chair so his genitals will be exposed. I'm going to get some tools; I'll be right back." He motioned for Stone to follow him, then closed the door behind him and started up the stairs.

"Let's see what being naked does to his self-confidence," Lance said, as they emerged into the first floor of the house. He went to the bar in Stone's study and poured them both a Knob Creek.

"You're not really going to torture the guy, are you?"

"No? Stick around."

"I don't want any part of this," Stone said.

Lance sipped his drink. "You're too squeamish, Stone," he said. "You wouldn't mind what we did to him, if you didn't know him, if he wasn't in your house, would you?"

"I would, wherever you had him," Stone replied. "I believe in the rule of law, even for Billy Bob. I'd be content to see him in prison for the rest of his life, and God knows, there's enough evidence to put him there — two murders, that we know about, just for a start."

"Oh, I'm not going to torture him, Stone, but a few minutes with that thought in Billy Bob's mind might do wonders to loosen his tongue."

There was a rattling noise from downstairs.

"What's that?" Lance asked.

"That is the sound of my garage door opening."

Lance set down his drink and started for the stairs. "What are those two fools doing? We don't want people passing by looking into your garage, do we?"

As Stone followed him down the stairs,

the rattling noise came again. "They're closing the garage door," he said.

Lance strode across the basement and flung open the inside door to the garage, which was in total darkness. "Where's the fucking light switch?" he demanded, groping along the wall.

Stone found the switch, and the garage was, once again, flooded with flourescent light. One of Lance's two men lay on his back, his throat gaping and blood pooling around him; the other sat on the floor, leaning against Stone's car, clutching his chest and coughing blood down the front of his shirt. One of them couldn't be helped, and Stone didn't know what to do for the other.

Lance calmly flipped open his cell phone and pressed a single button. "This is a Mayday," he said, slowly and clearly. "I need paramedics and a cleaning crew *now,* at the Barrington residence, garage entrance."

The man leaning against Stone's car coughed once more and keeled over sideways, coming to rest with his head on the concrete floor and his eyes open.

"Hang on," Lance said. "Scrub the paramedics; just send the cleaning crew."

36

Stone sat in his study with Lance. They were on their second Knob Creek.

"Don't worry," Lance said. "These fellows are very good; when they're through, not even luminol will pick up the bloodstains."

"That's a great comfort," Stone replied. He stared at Lance, who seemed perfectly calm, even a little bored. "I don't understand you," he said. "Two of your men are dead, and you're just sitting there, calmly drinking bourbon."

"What else is there for me to do?" Lance asked. "I've alerted my people to look for Billy Bob. I'm here now, only to see that the cleanup people do a good job, so you won't think I left a mess."

"The two dead guys are a mess."

"They've been cleaned up, too."

"What about their families? Shouldn't you be contacting them?"

"They don't have families," Lance said, "and they didn't seem to love anyone, except each other. It's one of the reasons I chose them, along with their special-operations backgrounds."

"So, they were trained killers?"

"Indeed."

"It seems that Billy Bob was even better trained."

"I've been pondering that," Lance said. "He must have had a knife they didn't find when we picked him up. When they untied him to undress him, well . . ."

"So, where did Billy Bob get good enough to kill two of your former special ops guys with a knife?"

"He had the advantage of surprise."

"There are only two ways somebody could do that — training or experience. Or both."

"There's always luck," Lance said.

"You don't believe that for a moment."

"No, I don't. We're doing a records check on Harlan Wilson; if that's his name, and if he was ever in some special unit, we'll find out. We're also questioning the driver of the Hummer and going over the car for fingerprints. One way or another, we'll find out who he is and where he sprang from."

"Let's get back to you," Stone said.

"Me?"

"Who the fuck are you, and how did you get to be this cold and hard?"

Lance shrugged. "I am who you know me to be. As you said, training, experience. Both, actually. And commitment. You lack commitment, Stone."

"Commitment to what?"

"To anything."

"I'm committed to the law and to . . ." Stone stopped.

"Yes? Finish that statement, please."

"No, you tell me what you're committed to."

"I," Lance said, "am committed to the preservation and success of my country and its way of life, and to the means my people have contrived to ensure that state of affairs."

"Well, that's succinct. Do you have no doubts about the means?"

"Not so far," Lance said. "Perhaps one day I'll run into a situation that might cause doubts. If so, I'll deal with them as best I can."

"Where do you draw the line? Murder? Mass murder?"

"The people who oppose us have no line," Lance said. "Otherwise, the World Trade Center would still be standing and three thousand dead people would still be alive. We cannot fight this enemy with reservations and qualms. If we do that, they will win."

"And how long must we do that? A year? A century?"

"For as long as it takes; forever, if necessary. Until we kill them or until they crawl back into their holes and pull the dirt in after them."

"There are hundreds of millions of potential recruits for them, standing in line, waiting their turn."

"They'll tire of their sport, when they don't win. Anyway, perhaps our leaders and diplomats will eventually find a solution someday. Until then, there is only me — and people like me — to stand between them and my country, between them and you."

"And what about Billy Bob? Is he worth the effort you're making, the price you've paid?"

"Billy Bob is one of an army of ants, and the only way to stop ants is to kill them all. He's a particularly harmful ant, since he's found a way to help that army use our own deadliest weapons against us. By the way, he took back the two grenades we found on him, so he has all thirty-six again. Do you want to see them used in Times Square on New Year's Eve? Isn't it worth whatever we have to do to Billy Bob to keep that from happening?"

"I wish I knew," Stone said.

"And what are you willing to do to him, Stone, to keep him from killing you? That seems to be his most immediate plan."

"Yes, he told me. I'm willing to kill him, if I have to, to keep him from killing me, but I'm not willing to torture him to death."

"Would you be willing to torture him to death to keep him from causing the deaths of those thousands in Times Square?"

"I don't know. I envy you your certitude, Lance; it relieves you of conscience or ethics. You're like those religious fundamentalists who believe that they know all the answers."

"Who knows?" Lance said. "Maybe they do."

"People who believe they have all the answers are *always* wrong," Stone said.

"I know my position may seem harsh, but I wouldn't trade places with someone who can't decide what his position is."

A man Stone hadn't seen before came up the stairs from the basement, carrying a wooden box, half the size of a briefcase. "They're about done down there," he said, "and they did a good job. You want to check?"

"Yes," Lance said, standing up.

"And you asked me to bring this." The man held out the box.

Lance took it and handed it to Stone. "This is for you."

Stone opened the box and found a Keltec .380 pistol, a silencer, three loaded magazines, one in the gun and two in a pouch, and a small holster.

"This is my personal advice to you, Stone, off the record," Lance said. "When you encounter Billy Bob again, shoot him twice in the head immediately. If you try to take him or reason with him or wound him, he'll kill you. My people don't want him dead, and that's supposed to be what I want, but I'm fond of you, in my way, and I wouldn't want to lose your life because you underestimated Billy Bob, as I have tonight."

Lance went down the stairs, leaving Stone alone with his conscience.

37

Stone slept, or rather, didn't sleep, with a .45 under his pillow, cocked and locked. As his mind raced through the night, considering alternatives, he considered Arrington. He had been out with her in public twice, and had perhaps been photographed or videotaped in her company, and that troubled him. He waited until after 7 A.M. to call her.

"Hello?" she said sleepily.

"Hi, it's Stone."

"Good morning," she said, her voice husky with sleep and, maybe, something else. "Did you conclude your business last night?"

"Not really," he said. "May we have breakfast together in your suite?"

"All right."

"Order me some bacon and eggs; I'll be there by the time room service delivers."

She gave him the room number. "See you then." She hung up.

Stone grabbed a shower and threw some things in a bag, then packed a Halliburton aluminum case with a couple of guns and ammunition. Then, with considerable reluctance, he went down to the garage. The place looked as it had before two men had been murdered there, but cleaner and neater. He got the car started and backed into the street, checking all around him, fore and aft, for any strange vehicle.

He pulled away and turned up Third Avenue, watching to see if a car, any car at all, followed him. None did. He drove up to the Carlyle on the Upper East Side, parked his car in the hotel's garage and walked next door to the lobby, again watching his back.

Arrington answered the door in a beautiful nightgown with a matching pegnoir, her blond hair brushed back but with no makeup. "Good morning."

"I'm sorry to get you up so early," he said, "but it's important."

The doorbell rang. Stone sent Arrington back to the suite's living room and looked through the peephole. A room-service waiter gazed blankly back at him. He let the man in and let him set up the rolling table; Arrington signed for their breakfast, and he left.

Arrington raised her orange-juice glass. "Remember the old Chinese curse? 'May you live in interesting times.' "

"It's appropriate," Stone said.

"What's going on?"

"I'm going to tell you this as concisely and as straight as I can," Stone said. "None of what I have to say is hyperbole."

"All right."

"A week or so ago, Bill Eggers introduced me to a new client, who he said had asked for me. His name was Billy Bob Barnstormer."

"And you believed that?"

"It doesn't matter. For reasons we needn't go into, Eggers talked me into putting him up at my house. He was there for several days, then he left, leaving a dead prostitute in my guest room."

Arrington's eyes widened slightly, but she said nothing.

"He arranged things so that I would be considered a suspect in her murder, then he vanished. Then I was introduced to Barbara Stein, a wealthy widow who had come to see Eggers, because she had seen a photograph of her husband, who was supposed to be out of the country, in *Avenue* magazine, with the mayor, and the same prostitute. It was Billy Bob, though she knew him as Whitney Stanford."

"I know that name," Arrington said. "Someone from Dallas recommended him to me as some sort of a financial whiz."

"You didn't meet him, I hope."

"No, but we talked on the phone. He was supposed to call me when I got to New York, but he hasn't."

"Good. He bilked a number of people in Dallas out of millions, and Barbara, as well, though you must keep that to yourself — client confidentiality, and all that. Did I mention that Billy Bob also murdered an investment banker in New York a couple of weeks ago?"

"No, you didn't."

"Well, he did. Now, about last night: As Dino mentioned, Lance is CIA."

"I knew him when I was a freshman at Mount Holyoke, and he was a senior at Harvard. I lost track of him after that."

"Some months ago, I signed on as a consultant to the Agency, and that is why Lance commandeered me. Last night."

"Did he also put a bullet hole in your trousers?" she asked. "I thought that looked odd."

"Yes, he did. When I declined to go with him, he became . . . persuasive."

"Where did you go?"

"Turns out, Lance's people had caught Billy Bob, waiting outside my house, apparently for me. He was armed with a silenced pistol and two explosive devices. Lance took him into my garage to interrogate him, and for some reason, he thought Billy Bob might talk to me more easily, since we had somehow formed this relationship where he wanted to kill me."

"That doesn't make any sense at all," Arrington said.

"A lot of what the CIA does doesn't make any sense to me," Stone replied. "I chatted with Billy Bob for two or three minutes, during which time he confirmed that he intended to kill me."

"But why?"

"I honestly don't know. He says I inconvenienced him by getting his wife to throw him out, but it's got to be more that that, I just don't know what."

"Well, you're safe from him, now that Lance has caught him."

"I'm afraid not. Lance and I left him alone with two of Lance's men, large men, who were supposed to, well, soften him up for interrogation. During the short time we were gone, Billy Bob managed to free himself and kill both men with a knife he had, apparently, concealed on his person."

"By kill, you mean, dead?"

"Very."

"In your garage?"

"Yes."

"With a knife?"

"Yes."

"I can't imagine what your garage must have looked like."

"Lance's people cleaned it very thoroughly, and did God knows what with the bodies."

"So Billy Bob is on the loose again?"

"He is."

"Which is very dangerous for you?"

"Well, yes."

She looked at him narrowly. "Are you here to tell me that *I* am in some sort of danger?"

"You are, possibly, in some sort of danger."

"And what do you recommend I do about that?"

"I have the house in Connecticut, and Billy Bob doesn't know about it. I think you should come up there with me, and . . ."

"When?"

"Right now, or as soon as we finish breakfast."

"Has Billy Bob seen the two of us together?"

"Possibly, I don't know. He had cameras in my house, but they had been removed by the time you arrived. He might have seen us at the Four Seasons, or at Elaine's."

"And if he did, he knows who I am?"

"Again, possibly. After all, he had your name, and you spoke to him on the phone."

"Stone, you must remember that, when Vance was murdered, my photograph was in every newspaper in this country."

"I do."

"So, if he saw us together, he might very well know who I am?"

"Perhaps. In any case, if he had been planning to con you out of money, he would have researched you thoroughly."

"And he would know that I have a child?"

"Yes."

Arrington got up and started for the phone. "I'm going home to Virginia," she said.

"I don't think you should go there, or to L.A., either."

"My little boy is there."

"Sit down and listen to me."

She sat, the frightened-deer look in her eyes.

"I think you should come to Connecticut with me. My car is downstairs; you should pack and send your luggage down. Do you still have access to the Centurion Studios airplane?"

"Yes, whenever I want it."

"I think you should ask them to send the

airplane to Virginia and have Peter brought to Connecticut. There's an airport twenty-five minutes' drive from my house. It will take the GIV. We'll meet Peter and take him to my house. No one will know we're there, so Billy Bob can't find us."

Arrington was quiet for a moment, but it was obvious that she was thinking fast. "What's the name of the airport?"

"Waterbury-Oxford. It has a five-thousand-foot runway and jet fuel."

"All right," she said. She got up and went to the phone again. She made two calls and returned. "We're in luck; the Centurion airplane is landing in Washington in an hour, after a flight from L.A. They'll refuel and go directly to Charlottesville, where Peter and his nanny will be waiting for them."

Stone shoveled down the last of his eggs. "Then let's get moving."

38

Stone checked out the bellman through the peephole, then let him enter and take the luggage. He called the garage and asked them to have his car ready, then instructed the bellman to precede them and load the luggage. They waited five minutes, then, with Stone going first, his hand under his jacket on his gun, made their way down the hall and into the elevator.

Stone asked Arrington to remain on the elevator while he checked out the lobby, then he escorted her quickly to the garage, where the car was waiting, its motor running. He tipped everybody, then got moving. He drove around the block twice to be sure he was not being followed, then crossed the park at Seventy-second Street, made his way to the West Side Highway, then north to the Saw Mill River Parkway.

"How long have you had this car?" Arrington asked. It was the first time she had spoken.

"Three years, I guess."

"It seems very powerful."

"It is; it's the E55 model, with the AMG-tuned engine, the fastest Mercedes made. And it has the advantage of being armored."

"*Armored?* Did you anticipate events?"

"No, it was serendipitous. I arrived at the dealership as they were wheeling it in. It had been ordered by an Italian-American gentleman, who felt he had enemies, but the car arrived exactly one day too late. His widow asked the dealer to resell it, and I couldn't resist."

"How armored?"

"It'll stop small-arms fire."

"That's comforting to know, in the circumstances." Then she went quiet again.

Stone took the Saw Mill all the way to I-684, then to I-84 and thence to exit 16. A left turn from the ramp took them to Oxford airport in two minutes. He checked his watch. They had been on the road for an hour and forty-five minutes. "We'll have a wait," he said.

They made themselves comfortable in the little terminal, and an hour and a half later, the GIV, with the trademark Roman centurion on its tail, touched down and taxied to the terminal. The engines died, and the door opened. The first person out was a small boy in a blue overcoat, carrying a small suitcase in one hand and a Gameboy in the other.

As Peter rushed into his mother's arms, Stone was struck by his appearance — dark hair, handsome face — and it suddenly occurred to him that Peter Calder, ostensibly the son of Vance Calder, bore an uncanny resemblance to Malon Barrington, Stone's father.

"Peter," Arrington said, "I want you to meet a very good friend of mine. This is Stone Barrington."

Peter extended his hand and said gravely, "How do you do, Mr. Barrington?"

"Hello, Peter," Stone said, taking the boy's tiny hand, "and please call me Stone."

"Thank you, sir," Peter replied.

Arrington then introduced Ilsa, the knockout Swedish nanny, and a moment later, they were headed north toward Washington, Connecticut.

Peter took in the bare trees and patchy snow. "It's colder here than Virginia," he said.

"I hope you packed warm clothes," Arrington said to Ilsa.

"Yes, ma'am," Ilsa replied.

They entered the village from the south, drove past the Mayflower Inn and turned left at the Congregational church.

"This is Washington Green," Stone explained, "and my house was once the gatehouse for the big place next door, called the Rocks."

"Then you should call your house the Pebbles," Peter said.

"The Pebbles it is, from this day forward," Stone replied, turning into the short driveway.

"Oh, this is charming, Stone," Arrington said. "Look at the little turret, Peter."

But Peter was already out of the car, peering through the windows.

Stone got the door open and turned up the thermostat. "Keep your coats on for a few minutes, until it warms up." He took Arrington aside. "There are only two bedrooms."

"Well," she said, "it won't be the first time we've shared, will it?"

Stone and the nanny got the bags upstairs and distributed, and by the time he got back downstairs, the furnace was producing heat. "Make yourselves at home," he said. "I have to make a couple of phone calls."

He called his office first.

"The Barrington Practice," Joan said.

"Hi, it's Stone. I'm at the Connecticut house, and I expect to be here for a few days."

"Okay, I have some things I can work on."

"No, I want you to take a few days off, too. Put an announcement on the answering machine saying that I'm away but that I'll pick up my messages. You can check it a couple of times a day and call me about anything important."

"Okay, boss."

"I'll call you when it's time to come back to work."

"Okay, I'll just do a few things this morning, then go home."

"Joan, I want you to lock up and go home right now, and I don't want you to come back, even for a minute, until I call you."

"Uh, oh," she said. "What's up?"

"A bad guy is looking for me, and I don't want him to find either of us."

"I'm out of here," she said. " 'Bye."

Stone called Dino.

"Bacchetti."

"Hi, it's Stone."

"What was that little dance you and Lance were doing last night, and why was there a bullet hole in your pants?"

"Lance picked up Billy Bob, but he managed to escape. It appears that killing me is high on his to-do list."

"Billy Bob's or Lance's?"

"Billy Bob's. Lance was just trying to get me to come with him."

"I guess it worked."

"I guess it did. But listen, Billy Bob might be mad at you, too."

"Why?"

"He doesn't seem to need a reason, but I want you to watch your back for a few days."

"I'll do that."

"Maybe even assign a man to watch it for you."

"You think Billy Bob's that dangerous?"

"Last night, he killed two of Lance's best people with a knife."

"In my precinct?"

"It's been dealt with; it won't come to your attention."

"Good."

"I'm at the Connecticut house, but don't tell anybody, not even Elaine. You can reach me here if anything happens."

"Okay, take care of yourself. Is Arrington pissed off at you again?"

"No, she and Peter are here with me."

"How cozy."

"Oh, shut up, and as I say, watch your back."

"And you watch your ass."

Stone hung up and went into the living room, which was warm now. Peter was expertly hooking up his game machine to the television.

"You can do that with the sound off," Arrington said.

"Don't worry, Mom, I brought my earphones."

Stone sat and watched, fascinated, while the little boy played his computer games.

Later that night, when Peter and Ilsa were asleep, Stone showered, then slipped into bed with Arrington. She was not wearing a nightgown. He touched her shoulder. "You're very warm."

"Come closer, and I'll warm you, too."

They came together as if they had never been apart.

39

For three days, they lived quietly, dining at the Mayflower Inn or cooking at home. They drove the country roads, gazing at the Connecticut winter. It snowed. Peter and Stone made a snowman in the front yard.

Late in the afternoon of the third day, while Arrington and Peter were napping and Ilsa was helping to get dinner started, Stone drove down the hill toward Washington Depot, the little business district, to get some wine for dinner. His cell phone vibrated, and he pulled into the empty parking lot of the Episcopal church, remembering that this was a place where cell-phone reception was possible.

"Hello?"

"It's Lance."

"Hello, Lance."

"Where are you?"

"Out of town."

"Where out of town?"

"I don't think I should say on the phone."

"I've been trying to call you."

"Cell-phone reception is dicey here."

"Don't you ever check your voice mail?"
"Not since I left the city. What's up?"
"We identified Billy Bob from a single thumbprint found in the Hummer."
"And?"
"It's not good news."
"Tell me."
"His real name is Jack Jeff Kight."
"You mean, Knight?"
"Without the *n*. Kight."
"So, who is Jack Jeff Kight?"
"Born in Plainview, Texas, thirty-nine years ago, son of a used-car dealer and a waitress mother. Attended the local schools, barely got out of high school. Juvenile delinquent, of a sort — joyriding in other people's cars, fights at the local roadhouses, that sort of thing. Got a local girl pregnant, stole some money to buy her an abortion in Juarez, got caught. He was given a choice — two years in jail or three years in the military. He picked the Marines."
"Sounds pretty ordinary."
"He wasn't. He tested very bright in the Corps. Very physical, breezed through basic at Parris Island, breezed through advanced infantry training. He qualified for the Navy Seals and was about to start training, when an Agency recruiter came across him."
"Uh-oh."

"Well, yes. He was lifted from the Corps fifteen years ago and sent to Camp Peary."

"The Farm."

"Yes. He did extraordinarily well there, learned many skills, seemed made for covert work, the wet kind. Then he killed another trainee. With his hands."

"So why isn't he at your little establishment in Leavenworth?"

"Claimed it was self-defense; a couple of witnesses backed him up. Another witness claimed he provoked the other guy, but he got through the investigation and was returned to training. Less than a month later, he got into a fight with an instructor and got his ass kicked, but when the instructor was walking away, Jack Jeff picked up a board and fractured the man's skull. This time, he got the boot. The Corps didn't want him back, so a general discharge was arranged, and Jack Jeff vanished into the hinterland. Five weeks later the instructor whose head he had broken had a seizure, collapsed and died. Apparently, too much time had elapsed between the original injury and the death to prove murder, and anyway, our boy was gone. The Agency never heard of him again, until now."

"What were some of those skills he picked up at the Farm?"

"Hand-to-hand combat, explosives, weapons, communications, document forgery, the opening of locks and safes, the bypassing of alarms of all sorts and how to create false identities and cover his tracks. Among others. He was there for nine months."

"Everything a boy needs to know to carve out a criminal career for himself."

"Everything but experience. He got that over the next decade and a half, doing the con jobs that we know about and, probably, a lot that we haven't discovered, yet. Apparently, he didn't kill anybody until the hooker at your house, but we can't be sure of that. Are you at your place in a nearby state? I'll send some people up to watch you."

"Don't bother; we're doing just fine."

"You took Arrington with you? What about her child?"

"Him, too. Look, Lance, we're okay. There's no way Billy Bob could know about this place."

"How about the little piece about your house in *Architectural Digest* two years ago?"

Stone felt ill. "How would he run across that?"

"How'd you find out about Billy Bob's past?"

"Google. That's a long shot."

"It's how I found you."

"Oh, shit."

"Exactly. You must learn that working for us entitles you to certain protections."

"I suppose you want to put us in the Agency's Protect Your Consultant's Ass program and ship us off to Omaha, or someplace?"

"Tell the truth, I'd rather send a team up there and hope Jack Jeff shows up."

"You want to turn us into bait?"

"Bait is alive. Corpses are dead."

"All right, but can you do it without Arrington noticing?"

"I can do it without *you* noticing."

"I'd rather notice."

"If you see a very Irish-looking fellow — thirtyish, red haired, red faced, chunky — he's mine. Name of McGonigle. There'll be others. McGonigle is all you need to notice."

"All right, when?"

"They're already on their way."

"Are you going to tell the local cops? You don't want to get them rousted."

"I've been in touch with them. I trust you are now armed?"

"To the teeth."

"Don't let Arrington or the boy go anywhere without you. The team won't be as effective, if they have to split up."

"Oh, there's a nanny, too, Swedish, name of Ilsa."

"Keep everybody close. If there are errands to be run, send Ilsa. I'll let McGonigle know about her. Oh, there was one other piece of information, goes to the motive of our boy."

"What's that?"

"You remember a little German man named Mitteldorfer?"

"Oh, Christ, yes." Stone and Dino had sent him to prison, and, once out, he'd made repeated attempts to kill them.

"There's a nexus: Jack Jeff has visited him a number of times in prison, using other names. We've no idea how they first made contact, but apparently, he's annoyed with you at having Mitteldorfer put away a second time."

"Yeah, he kept trying to kill us. Get some people on Dino, too, will you?" Stone said.

"I'll do that. Talk to you later."

"Lance?"

"Yes?"

"Thank you." But Lance had already hung up.

Stone drove on to the wine shop, but he hurried. He returned to find the house still quiet. Even Ilsa wasn't making any noise in the kitchen.

He went in there to put the wine in the kitchen rack, and Ilsa was still sitting at the kitchen table, where she had been shelling peas, but now, she had fallen asleep, her head on the table.

Stone put away the wine and went to wake her, then he stopped, confused. She had been shelling peas, not cutting tomatoes. There were no tomatoes for dinner. Still, there was a lot of tomato juice on the kitchen table, and some had spilled onto the floor. He walked slowly around the table and saw where the red came from.

Ilsa's throat had been cleanly, surgically cut.

40

Stone took his 9mm from the holster on his belt, looked into the hallway, saw no one, then slipped out of his shoes and ran silently up the stairs, two at a time, his heart pounding, steeling himself for more gore. His bedroom door was open. He put his back against one side of the door, listened for a moment, then went in, ready for anything. The bed was empty, its covers mussed. Arrington's shoes were still sitting neatly at one side.

He ran to Peter's room. The door was closed. He put his ear to it and listened, heard a murmur and the squeak of bed-springs. He looked through the keyhole and saw a hand hanging over the side of the bed, then he quietly opened the door and looked in. Peter was sleeping on his stomach, undisturbed. He closed the door quietly and checked Ilsa's room and the rest of the upstairs. Nothing, no one.

Stone started back down the stairs, then stopped. Through the glass pane of the upper door, behind the wrought-iron grillwork, lit from behind by a streetlamp, was the silhouette of a man. The man cupped his hands around his eyes and peered through the front door, then moved away.

Stone ran down the stairs, opened the door, and, his weapon at the ready, looked around. The man was now peering through the kitchen window.

"Freeze!" Stone said, not too loudly, as he didn't know if the man was alone. The man straightened up from the window. "Hands on top of your head," Stone said. The man complied. "Turn and face me."

The man turned, and the light from the kitchen window illuminated his face, which was red. So was his hair.

"I'm from Lance," he said. "My name's McGonigle."

"Come here," Stone said, still holding the gun on him.

McGonigle approached, his hands still on his red head.

"Show me some ID."

McGonigle produced a leather wallet with an ID card.

"Inside," Stone said. "You can relax."

McGonigle stepped inside the house, and Stone closed the door behind them.

"What's wrong with the woman in the kitchen?" McGonigle asked.

"Her throat has been cut," Stone said.

McGonigle's voice remained calm. "Anybody else hurt?"

"Arrington Calder has been lifted. Her son, Peter, is still upstairs, asleep. They apparently didn't know he was in the house."

McGonigle nodded. "Have you spoken to Lance?"

"Fifteen minutes ago. I was on my way into the village to pick up some wine when he called."

McGonigle produced a cell phone.

"It won't work here," Stone said. "With the exception of a few spots, Washington is pretty much a dead zone. There's a phone in the kitchen, on the wall, at the end of the counter."

"I think you can put the gun away," McGonigle said. "They're gone."

"Billy Bob won't be happy until he has me, too."

"That's why he took the woman when he didn't find you here. He can take you at his leisure, now. He knows you'll come to him, when he wants you." McGonigle went into the kitchen and used the phone to call Lance. They talked for a minute, then McGonigle called out, "Stone, he wants to talk to you."

Stone went into the kitchen, trying not to

look at Ilsa, and took the phone. "Yes, Lance?"

"I'm sorry we were too late," Lance said.

"Thanks for trying."

"Billy Bob didn't know about the boy; that's good."

"Yes."

"First things first. I'll have to notify the local authorities; a civilian is dead. I'll ask them to be discreet. I'll also call the Connecticut, Massachusetts and New York State Police and ask them to put out a bulletin on Arrington."

"Thanks."

"As soon as you're done with the police I want you and the boy to go with McGonigle and his people. We can't leave you there."

"All right."

"Pack some things for both of you."

"All right. You haven't said that we'll get Arrington back."

"I don't have to tell you why."

"No, I guess you don't."

"We'll get you through this," Lance said.

"Goodbye." Stone hung up.

"Why don't you go upstairs and pack," McGonigle said. "I'll call you when the local cops arrive."

"All right." Stone went upstairs and put some clean clothes into a bag, then went to

Peter's room and packed for him without waking him. When he came back downstairs, there was a uniformed Connecticut State Trooper sergeant standing in the hall.

"Mr. Barrington? My name's Coll." He offered his hand.

Stone took it. "Sergeant."

"I'm the local law. You want to give me your account of what happened?"

Stone did so, while Coll took notes.

"Thank you, I think that will do it. My people will take over here, now. You can go with Mr. McGonigle."

"Thank you."

"I've got a van out front," McGonigle said.

Stone went back upstairs and thought of waking Peter, but he remembered how he had slept when he was that age. He picked up the boy, wrapped him in a blanket and walked downstairs with him. "Will you get our bags and his coat from upstairs?" Stone asked McGonigle.

"Sure."

He went outside and got into the van. Another man and a woman were already inside.

"I'm Corey, he's Tucci," the woman said. Tucci backed the van into the street and drove away. "We'll be there in ten minutes,"

Corey said. "It's where we had planned to stay."

Stone held Peter against him, the sleeping boy's head on his shoulder. They drove through the village, in then out, then back, obviously checking for a tail. A few minutes later they turned into a driveway.

"I'm going to get out and open the door," Corey said. "When I've checked out the place, I'll call you, and you get Peter inside quickly." She got out of the van, and a moment later came back.

"All right."

Stone got out of the van and ran to the open door of the house. Inside, he was directed upstairs.

"You can put Peter in the first bedroom," Corey said. "Let's let him sleep."

Stone put the boy to bed and came back into the hallway.

"In here," Corey said.

He walked into a kitchen, and beyond that was a nicely furnished living room. The shades were all drawn. "Where are we?"

"We're in the carriage house of the Rocks, the house next door to you. The owner is away, but he's acquainted with Lance, so we're all right for as long as necessary. We have half a dozen people watching this place and your house, in case they come back for you. We can hope that happens, because it will make it easier for us to find them."

Stone nodded and sat down.

"Have you had anything to eat?" Corey asked.

"I'm not hungry. Peter will be when he wakes up, though."

"We've got some groceries; I'll make some soup." She busied herself in the kitchen.

A moment later, Peter walked into the room, rubbing his eyes. "Where are we?" he asked. "Where are Mom and Ilsa?"

"Come in and sit down," Stone said. "We had a call that someone in Ilsa's family is ill in Sweden, and she had to go home. Your mom has gone with her, to help her."

"That doesn't sound like Mom," Peter said.

"She'll be back next week sometime. In the meantime, you and I are going to stay here."

"Where are we?"

"In the house next door to mine. We had a pipe break over there, and there's water all over the place, so we moved over here, to a friend's house."

Peter looked around. "I don't like this as well as your house."

"Neither do I," Stone said, "but we'll be comfortable here until my house is fixed."

"Hi, Peter," Corey said. "I'm Annie; I'm a friend of Stone's."

"How do you do, Annie?" Peter said. He sat down and began to eat the soup she had put in front of him.

Stone tried to eat, too, and mostly failed. He had never felt so helpless.

41

There were four bedrooms in the place, and they put Stone in the one next to Peter's. It was windowless and not well ventilated, and Stone slept fitfully until nearly daylight, then he finally drifted off. He was aware of people coming and going in the flat; apparently there was another place downstairs, so there was plenty of room.

He finally came fully awake a little after 9 A.M. and lay there, thinking, going over every moment he had spent with Billy Bob, or Jack Jeff, or whoever the hell he was. Everything the man had told him was either a lie or invented to back up a lie, and the invented things — the phone numbers in Dallas and Omaha — would be gone and the people who answered them gone, too, and probably impossible to find. Billy Bob's apartments in New York had already been thoroughly searched; Lance would have run down whatever Billy Bob had told the rental company who supplied the Hummer and driver; and Lance would have people tracking the Jack Jeff Kight name, but that would take time, and he didn't have time. Sooner, rather than later, Billy Bob would reel him in with a threat to Arrington, and the best he could hope for in such a meeting is that he and not Arrington would be murdered. It didn't seem an attractive prospect.

He called Joan at home.

"Where are you?" Joan asked. "I've been trying you at the Connecticut house and on your cell phone, but I couldn't get an answer on either."

"We had to leave the Connecticut house, but I can't come back to New York, yet, and I still don't want you to go to the house."

"There's a strange phone message on the answering machine," she said. "I erased a couple of others that don't matter, but you should listen to this one yourself. I didn't understand it."

"I'll call now."

"Where can I reach you?"

"I'll call you every day. Bye-bye." He hung up and dialed his New York number, then entered the code for the answering machine.

"Hey, Stone," Billy Bob's voice said. "I figured you'd check in for your messages sooner or later. We ought to get together real soon, because Arrington isn't eating, and I don't know how long she can last. Here she is." There was a scuffling sound, and

Arrington came on. "Don't look for me," she said quickly, "just get out." This was followed by the sound of flesh striking flesh, and a cry, then Billy Bob came on. "Well, she doesn't really seem herself today. The girl's a good lay, though, if you tie her down. I'm going to let you think about that for a little while, then I'll call this number again and leave you some instructions. If you don't follow them explicitly, I'll send you Arrington's head in the mail. See ya!" He hung up.

Stone took deep breaths, trying not to feel what Billy Bob wanted him to feel. That had been the point of the message, and Stone had to fight it.

He had one other, very tenuous idea. He went to the living-room phone, where Corey couldn't hear him, and called Dino.

"Bacchetti."

"It's Stone."

"Lance told me; you okay?"

"Yes, considering."

"I've sent Mary Ann and Ben out to Eduardo's house; they'll be safe. Is Arrington's boy all right?"

"Yes. I told him his mother went to Sweden with the nanny. I'm not sure he bought it, but he's not asking too many questions yet."

"You heard anything?"

"I had a message on my answering machine, designed to shake me up and make me pliable."

"Let's get the fucker together; why should Lance have all the fun?"

"I had a thought; it's a long shot, but . . ."

"Tell me."

"A few months ago, the burglar alarm was acting up, and Bob Cantor came by to fix it. He did the original installation." Bob Cantor was an ex-cop who supplied technical services to Stone when he needed them.

"Yeah, Bob's good."

"I was standing there, and when he finished and buttoned up the system, he wiped it down very carefully, and I asked him why. He said he wanted it clean, so that if anybody ever tampered with it, he could lift his prints."

"Yeah, Bob's careful."

"Billy Bob, or someone who works for him, tampered with it last week, and one of Lance's people came to fix it. That means that the prints of two people could be somewhere either on the alarm system box or on the main telephone box. Can you get somebody over there and see what you can lift from those two pieces of equipment?"

"Right away."

"If you find prints and run them, there'll probably be a government block on Lance's man, but the other guy's might get us a name, and that's a start."

"I'll get on it. Where can I call you?"

"I'll call you. And you can always reach me by leaving a message on the machine in Turtle Bay."

"Your cell's not working?"

"Off and on where I am. It won't be reliable."

"I've still got a key to your place. I'm on it."

"Later." Stone hung up. Immediately, the phone rang, and he let Corey answer it.

"It's Lance, for you," she said, handing him the phone.

"Yes, Lance?"

"I heard Billy Bob's message on your answering machine. Don't let him get to you; that was the purpose of the message."

"I know that; I'm trying not to think about it."

"Arrington was smart enough not to mention Peter. I don't think Billy Bob has any idea he was with the two of you. He may check out the Virginia house and find out he's not there and begin to suspect."

"Let him suspect; it won't do him any good. Peter's well protected by your people."

"He certainly is. They don't come any better than McGonigle, and he has a first-rate team, Corey, especially."

"I figured."

"I've pulled out all the stops on this, Stone; we're running down every piece of information on Billy Bob and each of the aliases we know about. Something will turn up."

"I hope you're right."

"I could get the Bureau in on this, but it would get leaked. You want that?"

Stone thought about it for a moment. "No, I don't think so. I think it's better if we keep it tight."

"Good. If I get to a point where I think it would really help, I'll call them in."

"All right."

"Try to get some rest, and keep Peter entertained. I don't want you to leave the house, though."

"Where's my car?"

"Still in your driveway; you won't need it until this is over."

"Right. Thanks, Lance." He hung up. Peter had come into the kitchen. "Good morning, Peter."

"Good morning, Stone."

Corey gave the boy a brilliant smile. "Would you like some breakfast?"

"Yes, please," Peter replied.

Corey began making bacon and eggs. "How old are you, Peter?"

"Five and a half," he replied, pulling up a chair.

"Big for your age, aren't you?"

"No, I don't think so. Everybody in my kindergarten class is about my size." He turned toward Stone. "What are we going to do today?"

"Well, I saw some games over there on a shelf," Stone replied. "There's Monopoly and Scrabble and a couple of others, and you have your Gameboy."

"Can't we go outside?"

"Well, it's real cold today, and it could rain or snow. Maybe we'd better stay inside, where it's snug and warm."

"Okay."

Stone ate his eggs, counting the minutes until he could call Dino again.

42

Stone called his home number every hour to check for messages. Nothing for the whole morning. Then, at one o'clock: "It's Dino. I haven't been able to reach you for a couple of days. Call me when you get this."

Dino was playing it smart; he knew Lance might be listening in.

Stone started to call him on the landline, then stopped. If Lance were listening on his home number, he might be listening on this line, too. All the agents, except Corey, were out of the house at the moment, and she was playing Parcheesi with Peter. Stone got out his cell phone and began walking around the large apartment, checking for a signal at every window.

Finally, in the back bedroom, he got a one-bar signal. He called Dino.

"Bacchetti."

"It's Stone."

"You're weak, can you speak up?"

"No, I'm on my cell phone. What's happening?"

"Sometimes you're brilliant, Stone. Not

all that often, but . . ."

"What is happening, Dino?"

"We got three sets of prints. One of them, as you said, was government blocked. I ran the other two and came up with two names. One is a Martin Block, no record; he was printed in the army twenty years ago. The other is a Rocco Bocca, who got out of Sing-Sing just over a month ago."

"Did they send Mitteldorfer back to Sing-Sing?"

"Yeah, I checked. I almost had them put him in solitary, but decided against it. He might be able to tip off Billy Bob."

"Have you found out anything about Bocca?"

"You bet. He was doing five to seven on multiple burglary charges, served five and a half. And get this, he was working as a burglar alarm installer and hitting his clients."

"He's our guy. You get an address?"

"I got his parole officer's name, but the guy is out of the office all day, and I couldn't get a cell number. I left a message, so if he calls his office, I'll hear from him."

"Good news."

"You want me to pick him up when I find out where he is?"

"No, but if you can put a tail on him, do

that. If he meets Billy Bob it might be wherever he's holding Arrington."

"Will do."

"I'll keep calling my home phone every hour. Leave a message, if you learn anything more."

"Okay."

Stone hung up and looked out the window. There was a narrow porch at the rear of the carriage house, with a door leading to it, locked from the inside. That was a way out, but not in daylight, because men were stationed outside. Maybe not at night, either, because two agents slept in this room. He walked around the apartment again, checking windows. The back porch was definitely his best bet.

Stone spent the afternoon playing games with Peter and checking his answering machine for messages. Nothing more came in, until close to dark, when Dino called again: "I don't understand why you're not returning my calls," he said. "You out of the country, or something?"

It was completely dark by six o'clock, and agents were coming in for dinner. They were taking turns cooking or bringing in pizzas from the local parlor in Washington Depot. Peter preferred the pizzas.

Stone ate one slice, then clutched his gut. "Jesus," he said. "Please excuse me for a few minutes."

He left them sitting around the table and went to a bathroom in the hallway, closing the door, then he got his overcoat from his room, put it on and crept down the hall toward the rear bedroom. There was a roar of laughter from the people at the dining table.

Stone walked quickly across the bedroom, opened the door and stepped out onto the rear porch, closing it quickly behind him. He didn't want anyone feeling a cold draft in the house. There was a fire ladder at one end of the porch, and he climbed down it, then stood at the bottom, his back to the wall, and listened. Somebody coughed.

He peeked around the corner of the house and saw a cigarette glow in the darkness. One of McGonigle's team. His house was only fifty or sixty feet away, separated from the mother property by a high hedge. Stone ran along the hedge and around a corner. He was in full view of the Rocks's driveway, and if anybody drove in, he would be caught in the headlights.

He ran toward the road, looking for a gap in the hedge that had once been a passage between the main house and the gatehouse. It was mostly grown over, but it allowed him to push through the hedge without going to the main road, which might be watched.

He crept across the lawn to the kitchen door of his house and let himself in with his key. From there he ran upstairs in the dark to his bedroom and went to his dressing room. He had to feel for the keypad on the safe, but after a couple of tries, he got it open.

He stuck his small .45 in his pocket and a couple of extra magazines, then he took the box containing the little Keltec .380 that Lance had given him and went back downstairs. He let himself out the kitchen door and walked as quietly around the house as he could, looking for guards. He saw none.

His car was standing where he had left it, and there was no way to keep the interior light from coming on when he opened the door, so he did it and got in as quickly as he could. He put his key into the ignition and turned it to the first position, to disable the ignition lock, then he reached up and turned off the interior light, so it wouldn't come on when he opened the door.

He got out of the car and, with the door open and his hand near the steering wheel, put his shoulder against the central pillar and began pushing the car backward. There was a slight incline to the street, and he picked up speed, turning the wheel when he had to. Once in the street, he continued pushing the car backward until he was nearly to the church. Then he got into the car, started it and, with the lights off, turned past the church and drove down to the main road. He drove past a number of the Gunnery school buildings and took his first right, before he switched on the headlights. He felt exhilarated, as if he had broken out of prison, but he had only a few minutes before they began knocking on the bathroom door, looking for him.

He couldn't call Dino yet, because he wouldn't get cell-phone reception until Bridgewater, if then. He concentrated on driving fast on the curvy country road, much faster than usual. He wanted to get as far away from Washington as he could, as quickly as he could.

Fifteen minutes later he was in Bridgewater, and he switched on his cell phone. The signal was weak, but he finally found a part of the road where it was stronger, where he pulled over and called Dino's cell phone.

"Bacchetti."

"It's Stone."

"Okay, I finally got hold of the parole officer, at home. Rocco Bocca is living at his sister's house in Queens, and I've got two guys watching it. There are two cars in the driveway, so he might be home."

"Do this," Stone said. "Have the detectives knock on the door and ask to see him. Tell him, or whoever's there, that they're checking his alibi for a burglary that fits his MO. At least we'll know whether he's home."

"Okay. You on your cell?"

"Yes, I got away from the group."

"What about Peter?"

"He'll be fine with them; he likes the female agent."

"Are you coming back to the city?"

"Yes, but I don't want to go home; somebody might be watching."

"My place?"

"No. Are you at home?"

"On the way."

"Don't go there. Go to the Carlyle and get a room, under the name of Bocca. I'll come there."

"Okay; I'll go there now."

Stone hung up the phone, which rang immediately. That would be Lance. They would have missed him by now. He didn't answer.

He headed toward the city, staying off the interstate. It would take him longer, but he would be harder to spot. He felt better now, though there was not much reason to. At least he was *doing* something.

43

Stone's cell phone continued to ring, and finally, he switched it off. He entered the city from the East Side and drove to the Carlyle, parking in their garage. From the lobby, he asked for Mr. Bocca's room, and called Dino for the room number.

Dino let him into a very nice suite. "The manager is doing me a favor," he said. "You had dinner?"

"Half a slice of pizza, two hours ago. What's happening?"

"Bocca is at his sister's house, and the two detectives are sitting on him. They did the number about his alibi, told him he was clear and left. He's none the wiser. You may as well order some dinner."

Stone got the room service menu and ordered a steak and half a bottle of wine, while Dino poured him a bourbon from the wet bar. Then Stone called his home number and checked for messages.

"Hey, Stone," Billy Bob's voice said. "I'm ready to meet you now. What we're going to do is set up an exchange of

Arrington for you. She's a pain in the ass, you know? Yeah, you know. I want to get rid of her, so I'm going to set up something for tomorrow afternoon around three. I'll call your cell phone number, and you'd better answer it, if you want to see her again. I'll give you instructions then. You get one shot at getting her back, and one shot only, so you'd better make it work. If you get the cops involved, or your CIA buddies, then people will die, among them Arrington and you. You dream about that tonight, and I'll call you midafternoon tomorrow." He erased the message and hung up.

"That was Billy Bob," he said, and he repeated the message to Dino.

"When we get the instructions, we'll set something up," Dino said.

"It's going to be tough. Lance has probably heard the message, too, and he'll be all over us, if he finds out where we are."

"Some of his people were following me; I told him to hold them off, that my guys could take care of it, and I think he did. I made sure I wasn't followed here."

Stone's steak came, and he ate it hungrily, not having had much food for twenty-four hours. Then he stretched out on one of the beds and took a nap.

* * *

Dino shook him awake. "Bocca's on the move," he said.

"What time is it?"

"A little after one A.M. I'm on the cell phone with my guys. He's headed toward the Fifty-ninth Street Bridge."

"So Billy Bob is in Manhattan?"

"He may be on his way to New Jersey, for all we know," Dino said. "Let's just sit tight until we know more."

"Let's sit tight in your car," Stone said. "We might have to move fast when we learn more."

Dino spoke into his cell phone. "I'm going to my car. Call me in five minutes and let me know where you are."

Stone and Dino went downstairs to where Dino's car was waiting at the Seventy-sixth Street entrance to the hotel. They got into the backseat, and Dino told his driver to start the car. A moment later, Dino's cell phone rang.

"Yeah?" Dino listened.

"We'll pick you up at Seventy-sixth and Third," Dino said, "then we'll play switch with the two cars." He hung up and spoke to his driver. "Get us over to Third fast; use the lights to get across Park and Lex, but no siren, and turn off the lights after Lex."

The driver switched on the lights and moved down Seventy-sixth Street, made his way across Park against the lights, crossed Lex and switched off his flashing light.

Dino got back on his cell phone and pressed the speaker button. "Where are you?"

"We caught a light at Seventy-first, but we're moving again, crossing Seventy-second," the detective said.

"What's our guy driving?"

"A beat-up Ford van, tan in color, New York plates." They gave him the number. "We're in a gray Toyota."

"I'll pick him up at Seventy-sixth, and you drop back, but keep me in sight. I'm in a black Crown Vic."

"Gotcha."

"When the light turns green, turn left on Third and double-park on the right," Dino said.

The driver followed instructions, and a moment later, the van passed them.

"Now, you're the tail," Dino said. "Stay well back, but don't lose him." He spoke into the cell phone. "If you see our turn indicator go on, he's turning in the opposite direction at the next corner, and you pick up the tail."

"Gotcha."

They followed the tan van up Third Avenue to Eighty-sixth, where it turned right.

"Give a left-turn signal and make a left," Dino said, "then make a U-turn in the middle of the block. Don't use your turn indicator."

Stone looked back as the gray Toyota turned down Eighty-sixth after the van. A moment later, they made a U-turn and were back on the chase.

"Okay our guys are making a left-turn signal," Dino said. "The van is turning right on Second; follow him."

"Right," the driver replied.

Now the van drove down Second Avenue. There was little traffic, so Dino's driver stayed well back, and he and the Toyota changed positions frequently.

"What's he doing?" Stone asked.

"He's looking for a tail," Dino's driver replied, pulling over and double-parking in front of a news shop, to let the Toyota pass.

"Don't worry, he's not going to make us," Dino said. "This guy's a burglar; he don't know from tails."

The van went down to Twenty-third Street, made a right, went to Madison and made another right.

"This could go on all night," Stone said.

"We got all night," Dino replied.

"We'd better think about what we're going to do when he stops," Stone said.

"Call in the cavalry?"

"There are five of us; let's keep it to that. We're not storming a military installation. And we're not going in anywhere, unless we have reason to believe Arrington is there."

"Your call," Dino said. "Hang on, the guy's turning right on Thirty-second Street," Dino said into his cell phone.

They did their trick and switched cars again. Dino's driver made a U-turn and followed.

"He's stopping in the middle of the block," a voice said from the cell phone. "It's a bar. I'm driving past him. He found a parking place, and he's going in."

Dino watched Bocca go into the bar as they passed. They turned a corner and Dino told his driver to stop.

"Okay, on foot, now," Dino said into the cell phone. "You two guys walk past the place, one on each side of the street. Position yourselves where you can see the entrance, but where you can't be seen. If he gets back into the van, call me. Look for more than just him leaving; look for a woman."

"You think we ought to go in?" Stone asked.

"The guy could just be having a drink, you know. We go in, we're blown."

"What do you suggest?"

"Wait him out. If he leaves, we follow. If he leaves with a woman, we pounce. If the woman isn't Arrington, we sweat him."

"Makes sense to me," Stone said.

"I'll take the first nap," Dino replied. He turned up the collar of his overcoat, rested his head against the back of the seat and immediately seemed to fall asleep.

Stone just sat and waited.

44

Stone was dreaming that he was in bed with Arrington, when he suddenly woke to find himself in the backseat of a cop car. Dino and his driver were nowhere to be seen. He shook his head to clear it, then got out of the car and looked around. Nobody in sight. He walked to the corner and peered around the building into the block where the bar was. He could see nobody — not Dino's two cops, not the driver, not Dino. What the hell was going on?

As he watched, Dino and his driver came out of the bar and began walking back toward their car. Stone was waiting for them when they rounded the corner.

"What the hell are you doing?" he asked.

"Relax, we just went in and had a drink, chatted with the bartender."

"Two to one he made you as cops."

"You think I don't know how not to act like a cop? Jesus, Stone."

"What did you find out?"

"There's an all-night poker game going on in the back room of the bar."

"That's what the bartender told you?"

"After I bought him a couple of twelve-year-old Scotches. I'm invited to come back and play tomorrow night; their rule is no new players when a guy first finds out about the game."

"Why do you think he was telling the truth?"

"Two other guys went back there while we were drinking. It looks like a game; it smells like a game. When the door opened, it sounded like a game."

They got back into the car. "Are we going to sit in on a poker game all night?"

"You got a better idea?"

"What was the other guy's name? The one who owns the other set of prints found in my house?"

"Martin Block. No criminal record in any database."

"Get somebody to find out more about him. Just because he doesn't have a record doesn't mean he's not a criminal. After all, he was in my house, and I didn't invite him."

Dino made a call to the squad room, then hung up. "They'll get back to me. Why are you so interested in this Martin Block?"

"I told you, he was in my house. He cannot be a good guy."

"Maybe he works for the phone company — you think of that?" Dino's phone rang, and he answered it. "Yeah? What a big surprise." Then he looked more interested. "Now, *that* is a surprise." He hung up.

"What?" Stone demanded.

"There's a whole bunch of Martin Blocks in the various New York City phone listings, but one of them lives in the same house that Rocco Bocca does."

"His sister's house in Queens?"

"I make him as Bocca's brother-in-law."

"Didn't you say there were two cars in the driveway?"

"Yeah."

"Run the plate on the other one."

"My two guys down the street will have the make and plate number." He made the call and got the information, then phoned the squad room again. He held on for the answer, then hung up. "A 2004 Lexus four hundred fifty, registered to Martin Block of Queens."

"We followed the wrong guy," Stone said. "Bocca is just a burglar; the other guy, the brother-in-law, is the smart one; he's the one who'll be dealing with Billy Bob."

Dino called his two detectives. "Get back out to the Queens house and sit on it until a man leaves in the Lexus, then follow it wherever it goes and report to me." He hung up. "We were pretty dumb, weren't we?"

"You said it, I didn't," Stone replied. "Let's go back to the Carlyle and wait to hear from your people. I doubt if Block is going to go to work in the middle of the night. In the meantime, get your people to find out everything they can on Martin Block — occupation, education, military service, high school, the works."

Dino made the call, and they headed back uptown.

Stone and Dino were having breakfast the following morning, when Dino's cell phone rang.

"Bacchetti. Go ahead." He punched the speakerphone button and held it up so Stone could hear.

"Block is a Queens boy, born and bred. After high school, he went into the navy, served a four-year hitch, then reupped, but was discharged after another year. He came back to Queens a year after that and opened a car stereo and alarm business, which grew into something bigger. Now he deals in all sorts of electronic stuff and parts, too."

"Two questions," Stone said. "One: Why was he discharged from the navy one year after his second hitch began? Two: What did he do during the year after he left the navy, before he came home to Queens?"

"I'll look into it," the man said.

"Get back to me fast," Dino said, then hung up and turned to Stone. "What are you thinking?"

"I'm not thinking anything; I just find it odd that the guy left the navy a year into a four-year hitch."

"Bad conduct discharge?"

"Maybe, but he couldn't have reupped if he hadn't had a clean record the first four years. Did he suddenly go bad? Did he do some time? If he did, would it show up in your criminal-records search?"

"We searched the Pentagon database, too; if he'd done time in a military prison, it would have turned up."

"Maybe a hardship discharge? Sick mother, something like that?"

Dino got back on the phone again and asked for the reason for Block's discharge from the navy.

Shortly, the detective called back. "Okay, here's all I can get. The record of Block's discharge from the navy is unavailable, and we've been unable to find any trace of him for the year following — no phone listing, address, employment, nothing. There's no history for a year; it's a blank."

"Thanks," Dino said, and hung up. "What do you think?" he asked Stone.

"I think we're going to need Lance," Stone replied.

45

With great reluctance, Stone called Lance.

"Yes?"

"It's Stone."

"Where are you?"

"That's not important; I need your help."

"You bail out of a secure location that I went to great trouble to provide, go out into the world unprotected, endanger this operation and you want my help?"

"I just need some information," Stone replied.

"You want information from me? After . . ."

"I knew you'd be like this," Stone said.

"I ought to have you shot on sight."

"Lance, we both know you're not going to do that, so just calm down and . . ."

"I ought to bring charges against you. If there weren't a civilian in jeopardy, I'd . . ."

"Lance, *I'm* a civilian."

"No, you are a contract consultant, and as such . . ."

"I'm still a civilian, so will you just shut up and listen to me?"

Lance sighed deeply. "I'm listening."

"It occurred to me that there might be fingerprints on the alarm system in my house, and . . ."

"There could be dozens of prints on it."

"No, my own tech wiped it down the last time he worked on it. There were just three sets — your tech and two others."

"And I suppose you got Dino to run the two others?"

"I did. They belong to a guy named Bocca who has done time for burglarizing homes after installing their alarm systems . . ."

"That's interesting."

"Not very. The other set of prints belongs to a Martin Block, who owns an electronics business in Queens. He is more interesting."

"Why?"

"Because there are questions about his background." Stone explained about Block's unusual discharge from the navy and the blank year in his history.

Lance was quiet for a moment. "How do you spell his last name?"

Stone spelled it.

"I'll get back to you."

"Lance, there's something else."

"What?"

"I've heard from Billy Bob again."

"The message about a meeting this afternoon? I heard it."

"Oh. Well, get back to me. I don't want to have to take that meeting, if I can possibly help it."

"Goodbye." Lance hung up.

"So?" Dino asked. "He's going to help?"

"If he can find a way to help himself without helping me, he'll do it."

"He's pissed at you, huh?"

"He's pissed."

Dino's phone rang. "Yeah? Well, keep him in sight." He hung up. "Block's on the move in the Lexus."

Stone looked at his watch. "Eight-thirty; he's going to work."

"Probably. They'll let us know."

Ten minutes later, Stone's cell phone rang. "Yes?"

"It's Lance. Block was recruited from the navy by the Agency and sent to the Farm for further technical training. After a year, he got drunk and told a girl who he worked for and how he was being trained; he told her about several devices that we used at the time."

"And you caught him?"

"The girl worked for us, too; it was a test, and he failed it. He was bounced within days."

"Anything else?"

"Yes. His roommate at the Farm was Jack Jeff Kight."

"Bingo."

"I'm going to put people on Block immediately," Lance said.

"No need to; Dino's got people on him now. He left home a few minutes ago in his car, and we think he's going to work."

"He has offices and a warehouse on Queens Boulevard," Lance said.

"Then that's where Billy Bob is holding Arrington," Stone said.

"That's a big leap, and if you're wrong and we go in there, we could get her killed."

"You have a point. We'll have to confirm that she's there, before we can go in."

"My man, Sandy, who did the work at your house, has bought equipment there in the past. I'll send him back and see if he can learn anything. You sit tight, wherever you are. I'll get back to you."

"Lance, if Billy Bob calls and gives me instructions, I'll have no choice but to follow them."

"Before you do, you'd better call me; you'll have a better chance of survival with my help. Whatever you do, don't let Dino's people handle your cover. They'll stand out like sore thumbs."

"Call me when you know something." Stone hung up and turned to Dino. "Lance has no faith in the ability of the NYPD to operate undercover."

"Fuck him."

"He has a point, Dino; his people have a lot more experience at blending into the woodwork, and they don't look like cops."

"Cops don't look like cops, sometimes."

"Everybody in your squad room wears black shoes and white socks."

"I put a stop to that," Dino said.

"Maybe, but I'll bet they still wear the same black shoes."

"Some of them," Dino admitted. "They got used to them when they were in uniform."

"And every umarked police car might as well have an NYPD paint job; you can spot them a block away."

"And Lance's people drive black Surburbans with the windows blacked," Dino pointed out.

"There is some truth to that," Stone admitted, "but they have other transportation resources. Lance is sending a man into Block's business, which is on Queens Boulevard."

Dino's phone rang, and he pressed the speaker button. "Yeah?"

"Block drove to his business on Queens Boulevard," a detective said.

"Well, I'm glad he got there ahead of Lance's man," Stone said.

"He used a garage-door opener and drove inside," the detective said. "The place covers a third of a city block."

"Okay," Dino said, "sit on him. One of you take a walk around the block and see if there are exits other than on Queens Boulevard."

"Right," the man said, and hung up.

"Life would be sweet, if Arrington is there," Dino said.

"It would be sweet, if we could prove she's there before raiding the joint. Lance pointed out that, if she's not, we could get her killed. He's got this tech named Sandy, who's done business there; he's sending him in now to case the place."

"I could have done that," Dino said.

"Dino, the guy has done business there before; you have anybody like that?"

"Maybe."

"Let's just sit back and let Lance do his thing for the moment, all right? I mean, you were happy to give him the Billy Bob problem only a short time ago, as I recall."

"That was before I found out Billy Bob wanted to kill me," Dino said.

46

Sandy Peterson arrived at MB Electronics half an hour after Lance had dispatched him. He had been buying electronic components there for nearly a year, and the staff knew him, at least by sight. He always paid cash, and they liked that.

He parked across the street and looked at the building for a moment; it was a single-story building that covered a third of the block. On the corner was a retail electronics shop, which took up about a quarter of the building, and next to that was a corrugated steel door that could be operated with a remote control. He walked to the end of the block and a few steps farther. There was a wide alley behind the building, which had a loading dock. Across the street, he saw two men sitting in a car.

He walked back around the building, checking for windows — there were none on the side — and into the retail shop through the front door. He bought a hundred-foot reel of cat five wire and paid for it in cash, glancing at himself in the mirror behind the counter. "Is Marty in?" he asked the girl who was helping him. "I'd like to ask him about something."

"I'll check," she said. She went to a door, knocked and went inside, behind the mirror. A moment later she came out, followed by a stocky man in his midforties, balding, dressed in suit pants, shirtsleeves and a loosened tie.

"I'm Marty Block," he said and pointed a finger at Sandy. "And you are . . . ?"

"Sandy Peterson; I've been doing business here for a while."

"Yeah, I've seen you in the shop, didn't know your name. You don't have an account, do you?"

Sandy shook his head. "I prefer dealing in cash."

Marty grinned. "That's okay; we take American dollars."

"Can I talk to you for a minute?" Sandy asked.

"Sure, what's up?"

"It's kind of confidential."

"Come into my office," Marty said. He lifted the counter barrier, let Sandy through, then led him through the door into a large, comfortably furnished office with a six-foot-tall safe against one wall. "Take a seat."

Sandy sat down. "I've got a particular job to do for a client, and I need something custom."

"Tell me about your business," Marty said.

"I got started putting in alarms for people, and I did good work, so my business grew, and once in a while, a client would ask me to do some special work — personal stuff, usually — guy suspected his wife of screwing around, suspected his business partner of stealing, stuff like that."

"I know the kind of thing," Marty said. He held up his hands. "Not that I'd ever do anything illegal."

"Yeah, of course. It's like this . . ."

Marty held up a hand and came around the desk. "Before we have this conversation, I'm going to have to frisk you."

"Yeah, sure," Sandy said, standing up and holding his arms away from his body.

Marty proceeded to not just frisk him, but to do a body search more thorough than any Sandy had seen since he had finished his training at the Farm. He started with a normal search, looking for a recorder, then he went over Sandy's clothing in a minute way that would have detected a hidden microphone. He took Sandy's cell phone and set it on his desk, then he unbuckled

Sandy's belt, inspected it and handed it back to him.

"Let me see your shoes," Marty said.

Sandy shucked them off and handed them over.

Marty inspected the soles, the insoles and the laces. He handed them back, then ran his fingers through Sandy's hair and checked his wristwatch. After several minutes of this, he waved him back to his chair.

Marty picked up the cell phone, removed the back and the battery, then took a small screwdriver from his desk drawer and partially disassembled the phone. Satisfied, he reassembled it and handed it to Sandy.

"Sorry about that," Marty said. "I can't be too careful."

"It's perfectly okay," Sandy said. "Believe me, I understand. Can I speak freely now?"

"Go ahead; what do you need?"

"I've got a client who's in the middle of a big divorce. He wants me to bug his own house — he's moved out. He wants a mike in every room — just audio, no cameras. My problem is, his wife rarely goes out for more than a few minutes. The most time I'm going to get inside without being disturbed is, maybe, thirty minutes. You think you could put something together that would work for me?"

"Sure, but it ain't going to be cheap."

"How long would it take you to get it together?"

"How about ten minutes?" Marty said.

Sandy grinned. "Ten minutes would be good."

Marty went to a large safe in the corner, worked the combination with his body between Sandy and the safe, and opened it. He removed a plastic box, and as he turned to close the door of the safe Sandy was able to get a glimpse of the inside. It was filled with electronic components, what appeared to be a considerable amount of cash and two handguns on the top shelf. Marty locked the safe and returned to his desk.

"You recognize this?" he asked, opening the plastic box and handing Sandy a black, plastic object.

"Looks like a standard domestic circuit breaker," Sandy replied, turning it over in his hand.

"How about this?" Marty asked, handing him a plastic object about two inches long and half an inch wide. It was hinged lengthwise, and short spikes protruded from the back.

"You got me," Sandy said. "Never seen anything like it." In fact, he had seen something exactly like it. Marty was copying things that the Technical Services Department at the Agency had been making for years.

"Well," Marty said, sounding very pleased with himself, "here's what you do with your client's house. You go to the main breaker box and replace one of the breakers with mine. Then you go into each room of the house you want to bug, unscrew a power receptacle and crimp the other little thing so that the spikes penetrate both the positive and negative wires. Then you go outside and find an outdoor power receptacle and plug this into it." He handed Sandy a small, black box with a short antenna attached. "What you've done is turned the whole house's wiring grid into a receiver system that's picked up and retransmitted by the box with the antenna. I'll sell you a receiver with a dedicated, off-the-books frequency, and you'll be able to hear and, if you want to, record everything that's said in the house. You can even make it voice activated."

"Wow," Sandy said, pretending to be impressed. "How much?"

"The circuit breaker is eight grand, the crimpers are two hundred each and the retransmitter is two grand. Your receiver is a grand."

"Well, it's not like *I'm* the one paying for

it," Sandy said. "The client will pick up the tab."

"How many crimpers you want?"

Sandy counted on his fingers. "Eighteen."

Marty turned to a calculator on his desk and began tapping in numbers. "That comes to fourteen thousand six hundred bucks," he said. "Call it fourteen thousand even, and with cash, no tax."

"Done," Sandy said. "I'll need to make a run to get the cash; that's more than I walk around with."

"Sure; I'll have everything packed up and ready for you in half an hour; you can pick it up anytime today."

Sandy stood up to go. "You must have a great workshop here," he said.

"I do. You want a gander?"

"God, yes, please!"

Marty walked him through another door and into a large, beautifully equipped workshop where four men were hunched over worktables, wiring and soldering. "There you go. I can build you just about anything you want in here."

"This is really something," Sandy said. "I mean, I'm working out of my basement, you know?"

"Listen, I used to work out of my basement," Marty said.

"You've got a lot of building here," Sandy said. "What do you do with the rest of it?"

Marty walked him through another door into a storeroom filled with components and wiring, then into a large garage. Sandy counted four unmarked vans and half a dozen cars. "I keep larger equipment and my vans in here, and my employees park here, too. That's about as big a draw as health insurance. You got any idea what it costs to park in this city these days?"

"Tell me about it," Sandy said. He turned and saw a staircase going up to a windowed office in the high-ceilinged garage. "More work space?" He noted that blinds were pulled down over the windows.

"Nah, just storage," Marty said, steering him back toward the retail shop.

"I'll be back in a little later with your fourteen grand," Sandy said.

"You do that," Marty said, turning back toward his office. "Bye-bye. Nice doing business with you."

Sandy picked up his wire in the shop, then walked back to his car. He got out his cell phone and called Lance.

"Yes?"

"It's Sandy. Martin Block gave me the ten-cent tour. He's got four vans that the lady could be moved in, and there's a room I didn't get to see, up a flight of stairs in the garage. If Block has her, that's where she'll be. By the way, there are two cops in a Crown Vic sitting near the building, drinking coffee and eating doughnuts."

"Good work, Sandy."

"Oh, one more thing, Lance."

"What?"

"I'm going to need fourteen thousand dollars."

"*What?*"

47

Stone's cell phone rang, and he picked it up. "Yes?"

"It's Lance. My man is back; he's cased the building, and there's one room where Arrington is probably being held. Part of the building is a garage, and the room is up a flight of stairs. It's the only logical place they would keep her."

"Then let's get in there."

"No, I don't think so. Billy Bob is supposed to call you midafternoon, right?"

"Right."

"Billy Bob will give you some complicated routing to meet him at some place or other. They'll track your movement, then, at some stage, either exchange you for Arrington or keep you both."

"That had occurred to me."

"They'll move her in one of Block's vans — he's got four. We'll raid the place as they're leaving — they won't be ready for us then."

"And what if Arrington isn't there?"

"Then we'll sequester everybody on the

premises, so they can't call Billy Bob, and you'll have to go through with the meet. If Arrington isn't at Block's business now, it seems likely that they'll take you or both of you back there, and we'll be ready for them."

"And if Billy Bob doesn't have Arrington there now, and if he doesn't take her back there, what?"

"We'll be on your tail. We'll plant a transmitter on you, and we'll have a chopper on the job. When he gets wherever he's going, we'll be right on top of him."

"It sounds good, except for one thing."

"What's that?"

"Suppose he just shoots us both and dumps our bodies."

"Well," Lance drawled, "there is that. We can't cover *every* contingency, can we? The upside is, we'll at least take Billy Bob, and we'll roll up Block's operation."

"I'm sure that will be very comforting to me when I'm dead. How is Peter?"

"He's a sensible lad; he's curious about your and his mother's whereabouts, but Corey is handling him well, and he seems happy enough."

"Bring him back to the city, will you? When we've got Arrington back, I want to reunite them immediately."

Lance was silent for a moment.

"Take him to my house; I'm going there myself."

"Is there another way in besides the front door and your office door?"

Stone explained how to get into the common garden behind the houses and to his back door.

"All right, I'll have him there in two hours. Where's Dino?"

"He's right here."

"Tell him Sandy spotted two of his men, sitting outside Block's in a Crown Victoria, eating doughnuts. Tell him to pull them off before Block spots them. I've already got a team in the neighborhood."

"Right." Stone hung up. "Lance's man made your two guys outside Block's. You see what I mean?"

"How does he know they're mine?" Dino asked.

"They're in a Crown Vic, eating doughnuts, how else?"

"Shit," Dino said. He got on the phone and ordered the two men back to the precinct. "And when you get there," he said to them, "you'd better not be wearing black shoes and white socks."

"I'm going back to my place," Stone said, standing up.

"You think that's safe?"

"Billy Bob won't expect me to be there, and anyway, he thinks he's going to grab me later this afternoon."

"I'll come with you," Dino said.

Stone and Dino drove back to his house and parked in the garage, while Dino's car and driver followed.

"Call your driver and tell him not to park in my block," Stone said. "I don't want anybody to make the car, if we're being watched."

"Oh, all right," Dino said and made the call.

As they approached the house, Stone took Dino's shoulder. "Get down in the footwell. If they're watching, I want them to think I'm alone."

Dino grumbled but followed instructions.

When they were inside the garage and the door was closed, Stone said, "All right, we're in. You can get up."

Stone looked at his watch. "One o'clock," he said. He led Dino upstairs to his bedroom and began unpacking the guns and ammo he had taken with him. He handed Dino the box containing Lance's Keltec. "Take a look at that."

Dino opened the box. "Jesus, it looks like a toy."

"It's a three-eighty-caliber, and it weighs ten ounces, loaded."

Dino handled the little gun. "Billy Bob is going to tell you to come unarmed," he said.

"I suppose so."

"Then go armed. Wear something on your belt. You got an ankle holster?"

"No."

Dino pulled up his right trouser leg and undid the Velcro fastening of his own, which held a snub-nosed Smith & Wesson .38 special. "You can take mine."

"What's the point?" Stone said. "He's going to search me thoroughly."

"You still got that Thunderwear I gave you?"

"I don't know what you're talking about."

"For Christmas, dummy, the Thunderwear."

"Christ, I'd forgotten about that." Stone went into his dressing room and rooted around in the bottom drawer of his dresser. "Here it is."

"Put it on."

"Dino . . ."

"Just do it."

Stone took off his trousers and boxer shorts and put on the Thunderwear. Dino screwed the silencer into the Keltec, shoved a magazine into the butt, racked the slide and handed it to Stone. "See if it will fit with the silencer."

Stone took the gun and slipped it into the pouch in the undershorts. "Too long."

"Take the silencer off and try again."

Stone unscrewed the silencer and stuck the gun into the Thunderwear, then inserted the silencer next to it. "Fits nicely."

"Put your pants back on, you're embarrassing me," Dino said.

Stone put his pants back on.

"You've got a three-eighty or two, haven't you?"

"In the gun safe."

"Put on a three-eighty holster and a double-magazine pouch."

Stone did so and stuck his Walther PPKS into the holster.

"Now put the two spare Keltec magazines into the pouch. When they search you, they'll take the Walther, but probably not the ammo."

Stone did so.

Dino handed him the ankle holster with the S&W. "Now put this on."

Stone wrapped the Velcro around his ankle and secured it.

"Now, when they search you, they'll find

the Walther and the snub-nose — your piece and backup piece — but guys don't like to feel around other guys' crotches, so they'll probably miss the Keltec."

"It's worth a try," Stone said.

"You bet your ass it is," Dino replied.

48

At two-thirty, Stone and Dino were having a sandwich in the kitchen, when there was a soft knock at the back door. Stone opened it to find McGonigle, Corey and Peter standing there. "Come in," he said, scooping up Peter.

"Stone," Peter said, "where did you go?"

"I'm sorry, Peter, I had to sneak out for a while to run an errand. Did you and Corey have a good time?"

"We played all sorts of games, but we couldn't go outside."

"Tomorrow, I'll take you to Central Park," Stone said, setting the boy on the kitchen table.

"What's Central Park?" Peter asked.

"It's a great big, beautiful park, right here in the middle of New York, and you'll love it. Have you had lunch?"

"We went to Burger King," Peter said. "I had the double bacon cheeseburger."

"I'll bet your mother doesn't let you have that."

"No, she's nutrition conscious. Don't tell her."

"Don't worry, that's just between you and me."

"Oh, Dino, this is McGonigle and Corey; they're Lance's people."

"I've heard about you, Dino," McGonigle said.

"I haven't," Corey said, shaking his hand.

"Corey," Dino said, "will you do me a small favor?"

"Maybe," Corey said.

"Will you frisk Stone for weapons?"

"Sure," she said. She turned to Stone and said, "Up against the wall, creep, and spread 'em." She turned to Dino. "Isn't that the way the NYPD does it?"

Stone assumed the position, and Corey quickly found the Walther and the S&W snub-nose. She didn't take the magazines.

"Thanks," Dino said. "You proved a point for me. You can give him back his guns, now."

"You've got something in the crotch, haven't you?" she asked.

Stone nodded.

"You're too squeamish, Corey," McGonigle said.

"You wouldn't have found it, either, McGonigle," Stone said.

"You're exactly right," Corey said. "Next

time I put my hands on you, I'm going for your crotch," she said to Stone.

"Promises, promises."

Stone's cell phone began to vibrate. He held up a hand for silence, grabbed a pad and pencil and answered it.

"Yes?"

"Good afternoon, Stone," Billy Bob said. "I'm looking forward to getting together in a little while."

"Oh, me, too," Stone said. "It's been too long."

"I assume you're at home."

"Right."

"When we've finished talking and you've hung up, I want you to go to your front door, where you'll find a small package. Inside is a handheld radio. Exactly ten minutes from now I want you to turn on the radio and back out of your garage in your own car. After that, you'll receive instructions. Got it?"

"Yes."

"Bye-bye." Billy Bob hung up.

"Corey," Stone said, "there's a package on my front doorstep; will you bring it to me, please?"

"Sure." Corey left the room.

"What are your instructions?" McGonigle asked.

Stone waited until Corey had returned, then he opened the box. "I leave in nine minutes in my car," he said. "I get my instructions on this."

McGonigle was on his cell phone. "Lance, we've had the call. Stone is to leave the house in his car in eight and a half minutes; he'll get his instructions on a handheld radio that was left on his doorstep. I'm looking at it, and there is no tuning knob, and it doesn't have a brand name, so it will have a single frequency, and it will probably be off any of the commercial spectra. You're going to need a wideband scanner." McGonigle listened for a moment, then handed the phone to Stone. "He wants to speak to you."

Stone took the phone. "Yes, Lance?"

"Time is short; I'm scrambling the chopper now, and we'll be on you as quickly as we can. McGonigle is going to give you another radio, and you can use that to communicate with me on the chopper. We'll be scanning all frequencies to try to pick up your other radio, but it won't matter much. Just repeat all your instructions into our radio."

"Will do," Stone said.

"There'll be a sharpshooter on board. If you think it's worth the risk, just hit the dirt at any time, and pull Arrington down with you, if she's there, and he'll start firing. Don't get up until everybody is dead."

"Got it."

"Is Dino with you?"

"Yes."

"Let me speak to him."

Stone handed the phone to Dino.

Dino listened. "I got you," he said, and handed the phone back.

Stone took the phone back, and he could hear a helicopter's engine whining as it started up. "I'm ready."

"I hope so," Lance said. "Go and get into the car; you've got five minutes before you open the garage door."

"Goodbye, Lance."

"You're going to have to play your end by ear, Stone. Good luck." Lance hung up.

"He told me not to get my people involved," Dino said.

"I think it's best that way." Stone looked at his watch. "Four minutes."

"I'm going to go and make sure the garage door is working right," Dino said. "I'll leave that way. Good luck." He slapped Stone on the back and was gone.

Stone sat next to Peter on the kitchen table. "I have to leave again for a while," he said. "But I'll be back later, and if there's still daylight, I'll take you to Central Park."

"Okay," Peter said.

"Did I mention they have a zoo?"

"No, really? Do they have lions?"

"They sure do."

"Oh, boy!"

Stone kissed the boy. "Corey will take care of you. See you later."

"Bye-bye, Stone."

McGonigle handed Stone a small hand-held radio. "It's on, and it's on the correct frequency." Then he picked up Billy Bob's radio, removed the back, placed a chip about two inches square inside and closed it. "That will let Lance track you." He handed it to Stone.

Stone took the radio and walked through the house to his car. Dino had left the garage door open. He got in and started the engine. A minute to go.

At the appointed minute, he put the car into reverse and backed out of the garage, closing the door behind him with the remote control. Then he almost panicked. He had forgotten to turn on Billy Bob's radio. He switched it on, and immediately heard the voice.

"Stone? Are you there?"

Stone pressed the transmit button. "I'm here, Billy Bob."

"Get headed east. I'll give you more directions in a minute."

"Right." Stone got headed east. Stone didn't pray much, but he prayed now.

49

Stone turned off Third Avenue onto Forty-eighth Street and headed east.

"Take a left on First Avenue," Billy Bob said.

Stone turned left on First, then picked up Lance's radio. "I'm headed up First Avenue in my car," he said.

"Roger," Lance replied.

Stone drove on for another dozen blocks.

"Get on the FDR Drive, going north," Billy Bob said.

Stone made the turn and got onto the drive. "I'm on the FDR, heading north," he said into Lance's radio.

"Roger," Lance replied.

Traffic was light, and he moved well. He picked up a radio. "Lance, do you have me in sight?"

"Roger," Lance said. "We're in what looks like a news copter. We've got you in sight, so there's no need to report again. If we lose you, I'll call. Relax."

Stone tried to relax.

"Turn onto the Triborough Bridge," Billy Bob said, "and keep left."

Stone breezed through the tollbooth, because of the E-ZPass device on his windshield, and moved over to the left lane.

"Follow the signs to Randall's Island," Billy Bob said.

Randall's Island is in the East River; Stone had never been there. He drove down the ramp and approached an intersection.

"Turn right."

Stone turned right.

"Follow the road."

It was like having a talking GPS navigator in the car. He was driving past a series of baseball diamonds. He had never known they were there.

"After the traffic circle, turn into Field One Twenty-one," Billy Bob said.

Stone went around the traffic circle, came out and followed a sign to 121.

"Pull under the bleacher cover, get out of the car and leave the radio," Billy Bob said. "Leave your other radio, too."

Stone picked up Lance's radio. "I'm at baseball diamond number one twenty-one on Randall's Island. I have to leave your radio here. Billy Bob thinks I had another radio, so be prepared for some sort of surprise."

Stone stopped under the bleacher cover, at a place where equipment could drive onto the field for maintenance. He got out of the car and, immediately, a man stepped out of the shadows with a shotgun and pointed it at his head.

"Turn around and put your hands on the roof of the car," the man said.

Stone did as he was told. The man rested the barrel of the shotgun against the back of his head and began to pat him down. Right away, he found the Walther in the holster on Stone's belt. He found the magazines, too, dropped them and the pistol on the ground and kicked them under the car. Then he started down Stone's legs from the crotch. He wasn't shy about feeling everything, but he was doing it from behind, so he missed the Keltec .380 in Stone's Thunderwear. He found the S&W snubnose, though, and kicked that under the car, too.

Stone felt a handcuff snap onto his right wrist.

"Give me your left hand," the man said.

Stone did so, and his hands were cuffed together behind his back. The barrel of the shotgun against his head persuaded him not to object.

The man grabbed him by the collar and stood him up, facing the rear of the car.

"Now listen to me very carefully," the man said.

Stone looked over his shoulder and saw the trunk lid of his car slowly open.

"My instructions are to kill you, if you give me the slightest difficulty," the man said. He was standing with the short-barreled shotgun at port arms.

"Oh, I won't give you any trouble," Stone said. He saw Dino roll out of the trunk of his car, and he had never been so glad to see anybody. "But the guy behind you might."

"Yeah, sure," the man said.

Dino put a pistol to the back of the man's head and said, "Drop the shotgun."

The man dropped the shotgun.

"Oh, no," Stone said aloud.

"What da ya mean, 'oh, no,' " Dino said, and then somebody put another shotgun barrel against the back of his head.

"Oh, no, there's a guy with a shotgun behind you," Stone said.

"Swell," Dino replied. He dropped his pistol on the pavement.

Stone watched as the second man put Dino against the car and searched and handcuffed him as had been done to Stone.

"What do we do with this one?" one of the men said.

"I dunno; there were no orders about that."

"Call and find out."

The first man produced a radio. "Boss, we've got two of them here," he said.

"I told you it might happen," he said. "Sit them down and carry out the rest of the plan." The men put Stone and Dino on the ground, leaning against a light pole.

From somewhere out beyond the field, Stone heard a helicopter. "It's Lance," he whispered to Dino.

"It goddamned well better be," Dino whispered back.

Then another man appeared from the shadows. He was Stone's height and weight, with the same hair color.

"Let's go," one of the men said, grabbing the man by the arm.

Stone was baffled by this turn of events, but then he watched as the man with the shotgun marched the other man toward the center of the little ballpark. They stopped on the pitcher's mound, and seconds later, a green helicopter swooped in and set down in a cloud of dust. The man with the shotgun pretended to force the other man onto the chopper, then it lifted off and flew away to the east.

"I think you just left by helicopter," Dino said.

"Yes, and it wasn't Lance's."

The shotgunner ran back under the shelter and waited. Stone could see the helicopter head out in the direction of Long Island, and, a moment later, he saw another chopper in pursuit, one with "News 6" painted on its side in huge letters.

One of the shotgunners spoke into a radio. "Okay, we're good."

A moment later, a silver Lincoln Navigator screeched to a halt under the roof, and Billy Bob got out. "God, your people are stupid," he said.

Stone tried and failed to think of a snappy comeback.

"Put them in the luggage compartment and cuff 'em back to back," Billy Bob said.

The two men put first Stone, then Dino into the rear compartment of the Navigator, and Stone heard another pair of handcuffs snapping shut. He and Dino could lean against each other's backs, but they couldn't turn around. Somebody then pulled a shadelike cover over their heads and fastened it. A moment later, the Navigator drove away.

"All comfy back there, Stone, Dino?"

Neither of them replied, but Dino was swearing a blue streak under his breath.

"I hadn't expected you, Dino, but you're

welcome. I ought to be able to gain some sort of advantage by having a cop as my guest for a short while."

"Thanks for coming," Stone whispered to Dino.

"My pleasure," Dino replied.

"Now you boys settle down back there," Billy Bob said. "While your friends are chasing my rented chopper around Long Island, you and I have other fish to fry."

"Where's Arrington?" Stone asked.

"I didn't expect you to keep your end of the bargain, Stone, so I didn't keep mine. You'll see her later, though."

Stone tried to relax and count the car's turns, figure out where it was going. After five minutes of left and right and U-turns, he gave up.

50

Stone couldn't look at his watch, but he estimated they'd been traveling for nearly an hour when he heard the rattle of a metal garage door opening. The Navigator reversed, and the door came down again.

"Get 'em out," Billy Bob said to somebody. The rear door of the truck opened, the blind was rolled back and Stone and Dino were hustled out of the vehicle.

"Set 'em down in the corner," Billy Bob said.

Stone and Dino were pushed into a corner of the garage, which was lit only by daylight coming through small, high windows in the door. A moment later, the garage door opened again, and the Navigator drove out. Stone figured there was still a guard inside with them.

"Excuse me," he said to the wall, "do you think you could cuff us a different way? This is very uncomfortable."

There was no response.

Stone managed to turn toward the door and looked around the garage. "We're alone," Stone said.

"Now what?"

"I'm not sure," Stone said. "Since our hands are locked behind us, I can't get to the Keltec."

"And, even if you could, there's nobody to shoot."

From somewhere outside the garage came a faint woman's voice. "Get me out of here!" she said, and there was a banging noise.

"Is that Arrington?" Dino asked.

"I've never heard her voice under these conditions," Stone said, "but my best guess is yes." He yelled as loud as he could. "Arrington?"

"Stone?" she shouted back.

"Where are you?"

"How the hell should I know?" she screamed. "It's dark."

"Just hang on. I'll try and find you."

"I'd help, but they've got me handcuffed," she yelled back.

"You, too?"

"You mean *you're* handcuffed?"

"Yes, but I'm working on it."

Dino spoke up. "I don't want to interrupt, but I'd like to know how you're working on it."

"Good news," Stone said. "I have a handcuff key."

"Why?" Dino asked.

"I've been carrying one in my wallet since I was on the force, just for times like this."

"Well, that's just wonderful," Dino said. "Now could you unlock these cuffs?"

"There's a small problem," Stone said.

"What problem?"

"My wallet is in my left front pocket."

"Nobody carries his wallet in his left front pocket."

"I do. It's very small and just has credit cards and my driver's license, that sort of stuff, in it."

"Can you reach your left front pocket?"

"Well, no. That's the problem. Do you think you can reach it?"

"Let's find out," Dino said. "Sit still, and move your hands to your left."

Stone moved his hands to his left, while Dino worked his way as far as he could to Stone's side.

"I can't reach," Dino said. "I'm a good eight inches short, too. What now?"

Stone thought about that. "I don't know," he said finally. "I'm armed, and I can't reach the gun, and I have a handcuff key, and I can't reach that, either."

"You don't have to explain the situation to me," Dino said. "I get it."

"All right, *you* think of something."

"I'm thinking."

They both sat quietly, their backs against each other, and thought.

"I've got it," Dino said.

"Tell me."

"What we have to do is hang you up by your feet, and then your wallet will fall out of your pocket."

"Swell, Dino; how are we going to hang me up by my feet?"

"Jesus, do I have to think of *everything?* It's your turn to figure out something."

"Let's see if we can get to our feet," Stone said. "Press your back against mine, and let's work our feet back until we're upright."

"Worth a try," Dino said.

They pushed against each other and began taking tiny steps backward. They were halfway up, when Stone's feet slipped out from under him, and they both fell down, hitting the concrete floor hard.

"Shit, that hurt!" Stone said.

"Tell me about it. It's those faggoty Italian loafers you're always wearing," Dino said. "The soles are too slippery."

"I suppose you're wearing those black cop shoes with the thick, rubber soles?"

"Sure, I am, and I didn't slip, did I?"

"Let's try it again."

"And what's changed that's going to make it work this time?"

"We have to try. Billy Bob could come back at any moment."

"All right, let's go."

They started pushing up again, and this time, after a good minute of trying, they were on their feet.

"Man, that was hard," Dino said, puffing.

"You're in lousy shape, that's why," Stone said.

"Yeah, sure, like you actually use that exercise stuff in your basement?"

"Of course, I use it."

"Don't bullshit me, Stone. You're breathing just as hard as I am."

"All right, all right. Now what are we going to hang me from?"

They started to move in a circle, looking at the walls of the garage.

"There are tools in here," Dino said. "Shovels and stuff."

"Yeah, it looks like some sort of maintenance facility."

"You see anything useful?"

"Yes!" Stone almost yelled. "There's a hose coiled up and hung on a hook!" He moved toward a wall, and Dino followed him, walking backward.

Dino looked over his shoulder. "First, we

have to get the hose off the hook, so we can use it."

The hook was chest high. Stone tried nudging the coil of hose with his knee, but couldn't reach it. Finally, he bent over and pushed upward on the hose with his head. Most of it fell to the floor, leaving several coils on the hook. "I think that'll do it," Stone said. "The hook's available; I've just got to get a leg up that high."

"Try walking up the wall," Dino said. "I'll back up closer." He did so.

"Push hard against me," Stone said. He put a foot against the wall, then another. "It's working," Stone said. "About two feet higher. Push harder!"

Dino pushed, and Stone continued walking up the wall.

"We've got to move about a foot to the left," Stone said.

Dino worked in that direction, taking tiny steps.

"I think I can . . ." Stone got a leg over the hook and put his weight on it. "Okay, I've got a leg hooked. You've got to get lower, and as slowly as possible."

Dino eased himself down to a squatting position. "I don't know how long I can do this," he said.

Stone had all his weight on the one leg

over the hook, now. He began to shake his hips back and forth.

"What are you doing?" Dino demanded.

"I'm trying to shake out the wallet," Stone said. "It won't come out."

Dino began to jump up and down an inch or two from his squatting position.

"It fell out!" Stone yelled. "Now you have to stand up again, so I can get my leg off the hook."

Making loud groaning noises, Dino slowly pushed himself upright.

Using his other foot for purchase, Stone managed to get his leg off the hook, and the two of them fell to the floor in a heap. They lay there for a moment, panting.

"Where's your wallet?" Dino asked finally.

"It's around here somewhere. Feel for it with your feet."

They scurried around in the dimly lit garage, feeling for the wallet.

"I think I've got it," Dino said. "It's tucked up under my ass. Let me see if I can reach it. Move backwards a little."

Stone moved backward.

"Got it," Dino said. "I pushed it between us. Feel for it."

"I have it," Stone said.

"Well, get the fucking key out!"

Stone got the wallet open and shook it. A tiny metallic sound came back. "It's on the floor." He felt for it. "Got it!"

"Unlock any bracelet," Dino said. "Doesn't matter which one."

Stone got hold of Dino's wrist, found the bracelet and the keyhole and turned the key.

"Yes!" Dino shouted, holding up his free hand. He turned to Stone. "Give me the key."

Stone put it in Dino's hand, and a moment later, he had a free hand, and a moment after that, they were both free of the cuffs.

Stone unzipped his trousers and fished out the Keltec and its silencer. He screwed the tube onto the barrel, then popped the magazine and counted. "I've only got five rounds," he said. "The guy who searched me took the other two magazines."

"Then make them count," Dino said. "You got any qualms about putting one in somebody's head, say so, and I'll do it."

"None whatever," Stone said. "Now let's find the switch that opens this door."

"Before we do that," Dino said, "you've got to hoist me up so that I can get a look outside and see what we're up against."

Stone stuck the gun in his belt and made a

stirrup for Dino. Dino hopped up and had a look outside.

"Nothing," he said. "Nobody. Just a wall."

"You take that wall," Stone said, pointing. "I'll take this one. Look for the switch."

They both groped in the semidarkness.

"Got it," Dino said. "You ready?"

"Hit it," Stone said, his gun at the ready.

51

Dino hit the switch, and the door started up. Stone ducked under it and stepped outside, the gun pointing ahead of him. He checked both directions. "Clear," he said, and Dino came out.

"What is this place?" Dino asked.

They were in a kind of alley between two long rows of garages.

"I don't know," Stone said. "Let's find Arrington, then we'll worry about it. It sounded as though she was nearby, but not too near. You take the other row."

Stone and Dino began walking down both rows of garages, banging on the door and shouting Arrington's name.

"Here!" Dino yelled, two doors down.

"Dino? Stone?" Arrington shouted.

"We're right outside," Stone said.

"Well, get me out of here."

"First, we've got to figure out how to get inside. You said you were handcuffed. Are your feet free?"

"They're tied together, and I'm lying on my side," she shouted back.

"Can you get to your feet?"

"Maybe. What do I do then?"

Stone went over to the side of the garage door and tapped the silencer against it. "There's a button that opens the door, and it's probably right over here. If you can get to your feet, hop over this way and find the button."

"I'll try," Arrington called back. There followed some grunts and groans. "Okay, I'm on my feet, hopping your way." Her voice got closer.

"Do you see a button on the wall? It's about shoulder high."

"I see it."

"Press your forehead against it and push."

A moment later, the door started upward. Stone ducked under it and found Arrington, her head still pressed against the button. "You can stop pushing now; just hold it right there, and I'll get the cuffs off you." He unlocked the handcuffs while Dino untied her feet.

Arrington fell into Stone's arms. "Oh, God, I thought I would never see you again. I thought I'd never see anybody again." She hugged Dino. "How did you find me?"

"We were brought to you," Dino said. "You have any idea where we are?"

"No."

Stone pointed upward. "Seagulls; we're near water."

"That's very helpful, Stone," Dino said archly. "Come on, let's look around." He started down the alley, and Stone and Arrington followed.

They came to the end of the garages, and the alley joined a street.

"Look," Stone said, pointing. A sign said "Field 121." "We're back where we started; Randall's Island."

"All that driving was just to confuse us," Dino said.

"Where the hell is Randall's Island?" Arrington asked.

"In the East River," Stone replied. "Come on, let's find my car." He started across the street, and they followed. Then Stone caught a flash of silver at the end of the street, where it joined the traffic circle. "Quick," he yelled. "Under the stands."

They ran across the road and ducked under the grandstand of the ballpark. "Hit the dirt." They all got on the ground.

Billy Bob's silver Navigator turned into the street from the traffic circle and started toward them. It turned into the alley and drove toward the garages they had just left.

Stone was on his feet. "Come on, we've got to get to my car before they find out we're gone!" They started running down the street toward where Stone had left his car. From somewhere behind them he heard car doors slamming. "They're back in the Navigator!" he puffed. They were still a hundred and fifty yards from the car, he reckoned. Arrington fell, and they stopped to help her. "Hit the deck!" Stone said.

They were all on the ground again as the Navigator turned the corner and drove past them.

"They're seeing if your car is still there," Dino said. "When they find it, they'll know we're still here and on foot."

The Navigator turned into the ball field.

"Come on," Stone said, running toward his car.

"We can't go *toward* them," Arrington said, grabbing his arm.

"We've got to get to the car. I've only got five rounds in this thing, but there are two guns under the car. Anyway, when they find it, they'll start driving around, looking for us." He heard car doors slam again. "Hit the dirt!" They all did.

A moment later, the Navigator backed out of the ball field and drove slowly away from them. Obviously, they were searching.

"Come on, but stay as far under the

stands as you can," Stone said. They kept low and ran toward the Mercedes.

Stone could see the rear end of his car, now, and he saw the brake lights of the Navigator come on, then the reversing lights. "Go for it!" Stone yelled, and he sprinted, leaving Arrington behind. "Make for the car!" he yelled over his shoulder.

He made the car, but the Navigator was reversing toward them, and he had no time to get inside. Dino arrived at the car, and Arrington was close behind.

"You left me!" she said.

"One of us had to get here," Stone said.

Dino was on the ground, looking under the car. "It's too low," he said. "I can't get under it."

"Keep the car between us and the Navigator," Stone said. "It's good protection."

The Navigator stopped, the two front doors opened and the two men with shotguns got out, looking around.

"Arrington," Stone whispered, "stay close to me." He looked around, but Arrington was gone. Dino was huddled close, on his other side. "Where's Arrington?" Stone asked.

"She was right here," Dino whispered back. "Here come the shotguns."

"They're behind the car," one of the men

shouted, and the two brought the shotguns to their shoulders.

"What are you waiting for?" Dino asked. "Shoot somebody!"

"They're too far away," Stone said.

"You're just chickenshit! You just don't want to shoot somebody!"

"Give it a moment," Stone said. He heard a shotgun being racked. He looked up, and one of the men was ten feet away. Stone took his shot. The side of the man's head exploded, and he went down. As Stone ducked, he heard a shotgun go off and the sound of pellets striking his car.

"One down, one to go," Dino said.

"If I stick my head up again, he'll blow it off."

"Come out from behind the car," the man yelled.

A millisecond after he yelled, Stone heard a gunshot, and the man cried out in pain. He stuck his head up, and the man was gone. He stood up further and saw him on the ground, holding onto a bleeding foot.

The man saw him, too, and brought the shotgun around.

Stone fired, striking him in the shoulder, but he was still trying to aim. Another shot exploded, and the man stopped moving.

Stone looked under the car. "Arrington?"

"Did I get him?" she asked.

"You did. Stay where you are, and throw Dino a gun." Stone began to run toward the Navigator. He could see nothing through the darkened windows, but if one rolled down, he was going to start shooting.

The Navigator roared away, and Stone fired twice at it. The rear window shattered, but the second shot went astray. Stone turned and walked back toward his car, spent.

Dino was pulling Arrington from under the car. She stood up, and they all looked at each other, dirty and skint, and they began laughing.

"Okay," Dino said, finally, "it's time for the cops. Fuck Lance."

"Right," Stone said. There was, after all, the matter of the two dead men with shotguns.

52

Stone tried Lance's radio but got no answer. He got the car started and headed back for the Triborough Bridge, while dialing Lance's cell phone. No answer, so Stone left a message.

"Lance, it's over; Dino and I are out, and we've got Arrington. We're headed back to my house. There are two dead men back at Field One Twenty-one, and Dino has put out an APB for a silver Lincoln Navigator with no rear window, probably driven by Billy Bob. Call me." He hung up.

"Where's Billy Bob headed?" Dino asked.

"I don't know. Maybe to Martin Block's building in Queens. Lance has that covered. To tell you the truth, I don't really give a damn. We've got Arrington back; that's all that matters."

"Now you're talking," Arrington said.

"And what was all this in aid of?"

"Billy Bob wants to kill me."

"So, why didn't he?"

"Beats me, but I'm not going to quarrel with the fact."

"He was planning to," Arrington said. "It was about some fellow with a German name?"

"Mitteldorfer," Stone said.

"Not a friend of either of us," Dino chipped in.

"They were in prison together," Arrington said. "Until Billy Bob escaped."

"Jesus, yet another crime of his," Stone said.

"That means the whole world of law enforcement wants him," Dino replied.

"I couldn't care less, not anymore," Stone said.

"So you don't care about Billy Bob anymore?" Dino asked. "You don't want him?"

"Let Lance worry about Billy Bob; I'm done with him."

"Maybe he isn't done with you, did you think about that?"

"He'd be a fool to keep trying to kill me," Stone said. "He's got to worry about surviving, now. Anyway, Lance is going to scoop him up in Queens."

"You hope."

"I hope? Why are you being such a pessimist?"

"So far, when it comes to Billy Bob, I haven't found anything to be optimistic about."

Stone hit the remote-control button and swung into his garage, closing the door behind him.

"Where's Peter?" Arrington asked as they got out of the car.

"He's in the kitchen with McGonigle and Corey."

"Where's his nanny?"

"I'm sorry to tell you this, but she was a victim of Billy Bob or his people."

Arrington put her face in her hands. "She was a sweet girl; God, I hope this is over."

"I hope so, too."

Arrington started running. "I want to see Peter," she said.

"I promised to take him to the Central Park Zoo," Stone yelled after her. He went into his office to let Joan know he was back and to try to call Lance again. Dino went with him.

Joan was at her desk. " 'Morning," she said.

"I'm back. Will you get me Lance Cabot on his cell phone?"

"Sure."

Stone heard the scream from his office. He and Dino started running toward the kitchen. When they came into the room Arrington was still screaming, as much in anger as in fear. McGonigle lay on his face in a pool of blood. Stone checked for a pulse and found none. Corey was on the other side of the kitchen table, lying on her back, with a bad-looking chest wound. Dino was bent over her.

"She's still alive," he said. He got on his phone and called for help.

Arrington had stopped screaming, but she was pointing at the kitchen table. On its top, someone had written, apparently in Corey's blood, "IT'S NOT OVER."

Stone took Arrington in his arms. "We're going to fix this," he said. "We're going to find Peter."

Joan buzzed him. "I've got Lance on the phone."

Stone picked up the extension. "Where are you?"

"Sitting on Block's place in Queens."

"We just got back to my house: McGonigle is dead, and Corey is in bad shape with a gunshot wound to the chest. Peter has been taken."

"I'll be there as fast as I can," Lance said.

"Don't take Block's building; Billy Bob may go there with Peter."

"I got your message about the APB. That may not be helpful."

"Why?"

But Lance had hung up.

* * *

The paramedics had left with Corey and sedated Arrington by the time Lance arrived, and the coroner and a team of detectives were dealing with McGonigle's body and the crime scene in the kitchen. Stone had put Arrington to bed, and he and Dino were sitting in his study when Lance came upstairs.

"I saw McGonigle," Lance said. "Where have they taken Corey?"

"To Bellevue," Stone replied.

Lance called somebody on his cell phone. "Corey is at Bellevue Hospital with a chest wound," he said. "Find the best thoracic surgeon in New York, kidnap him, if you have to, and get him to her immediately." He snapped the phone shut. "All right, Stone," he said, "why did you call the cops?"

"Lance," Dino said, "*I* called the cops. I *am* the cops. You blew catching Billy Bob, and we now have a trail of dead bodies that can't be ignored. This is obviously bigger than your resources, and we needed an APB to find the Navigator."

"Then there's Peter," Stone said. "We need the biggest possible net out there."

Lance sat down. "This has all gone horribly wrong," he said. "We chased that fucking helicopter all the way out Long Island Sound to Montauk and halfway back, before we had to stop to refuel and lost it. I thought you were aboard."

"That's what Billy Bob arranged for you to think," Stone said. "I told you there would be some sort of switch. Has anything at all happened at Block's place?"

Lance shook his head. "I sent Sandy back in there to buy some more stuff, and he reports that all was normal. Block is working in his office, and nobody seems suspicious."

"Billy Bob is going to be in touch with him at some point. As far as we know, Block is all he's got in New York."

"We've tapped the phone lines; now all we can do is wait."

They sat silently for a while.

"Waiting is not fun," Stone said.

53

Dino's cell phone rang first. "Bacchetti. Yeah . . . yeah . . . yeah . . . shit! Keep me posted." Dino stood up. "A patrol car spotted the Navigator trying to get into the Lincoln Tunnel, tried to stop him, but couldn't. A pursuit is under way as we speak."

Then Lance's phone rang. "Yes? Where? Good. Hold it there, and . . . wait a minute." He looked at Dino. "Which way is Billy Bob headed?"

"He was on Forty-second Street, headed east."

Lance turned back to his phone. "Stand by there, and start questioning the pilot." He snapped the phone shut.

"What?" Stone asked.

"My people caught up with Billy Bob's chopper at the East Side Heliport five minutes ago."

Dino's phone rang again. "Bacchetti." He listened, then covered the phone. "Billy Bob turned into a parking garage off Times Square, and he's being pursued upward, level by level."

"Why would he corner himself like that?" Stone asked.

"What kind of building is it?" Lance wanted to know.

Dino went back to the cell phone. "What kind of building?" He covered the phone again. "Office tower, big one; the first six floors are parking."

"I know what he's doing," Lance said.

"What?" Stone asked.

But Lance was already on his cell phone. "Look inside the chopper," he said. "Is there a handheld radio there?" He waited impatiently. "Right," he said. "Get the radio to the pilot; if Billy Bob calls him, make him answer, even if you have to put a gun to his head. I'm on my way."

Dino was back on his cell phone. "Billy Bob made a run for the elevators and made it. He's handcuffed to Peter, and he's carrying a large, metal suitcase."

"I *knew* it," Lance said. "Stone, you come with me. Dino, you join your people in Times Square."

"Okay," Dino said.

"And I want you to empty Times Square immediately."

"Jesus, I don't have the authority to do that," Dino said.

"Find somebody who does. Tell them that

Billy Bob very probably has a suitcase containing thirty-six very powerful grenades and a rifle launcher. Are you getting the picture?"

"Holy shit," Dino said.

"Stone, let's get going."

Dino was calling for his own car as Stone and Lance ran for the garage.

When Stone had made the street, he turned to Lance. "Now, tell me what is going on."

"Billy Bob is headed for the top of that office tower," Lance said. "He's probably already there by now, and from the top of that building he can . . ."

"Threaten Times Square with the grenades," Stone said, completing his sentence. "It's what you predicted a while back."

"I meant it as an illustration, not a prediction," Lance said. "My people have Billy Bob's helicopter at the East Side Heliport, and his driver, too. That's got to be Billy Bob's way out. I seriously doubt if he has *two* choppers at his disposal."

"What's your plan?"

"*Plan?* I don't have a plan; no plan will work. All we can do is react to what Billy Bob does and try to predict his next move. Right now he's on top of a tall building with Arrington's child and all those grenades. As crazy as he may be, nothing so far has indicated that he's suicidal. He expects to get out of there, and how else but by helicopter?"

They turned into the heliport and abandoned Stone's car in some executive's parking space. Stone brought Billy Bob's radio. He followed Lance into the building, and they were waved into a back office by one of his people.

The helicopter pilot, dressed neatly in his uniform of black trousers and white shirt with epaulets was sitting in an office chair, surrounded by Lance's people. "I'm telling you that's all I know about it," he was saying.

"Tell *me*," Lance said.

"Are you in charge here?" the pilot demanded.

"Tell me, and do it now."

"This guy, Stanford, chartered our chopper; he's been our customer in the past. He said he wanted to run through some routines for a movie he's producing. I was to snatch the guy off a Little League baseball field on Randall's Island, then fly out to Montauk and back doing a lot of maneuvers. I did it, and that's all I know. I haven't even been permitted to call my office."

Lance nodded. "Has his helicopter been refueled?" he asked one of his people.

"Yes, sir," the man replied. He handed

Lance a handheld radio. "This is what Billy Bob gave the pilot."

"I've got another one," Stone said, holding it up.

"Where's our equipment?" Lance asked his man.

"Van, outside."

"Get me the rifle and some loaded magazines."

"Yes, sir." The man left.

"What are we doing?" Stone asked.

"We're waiting for instructions," Lance replied.

"Instructions?"

"From Billy Bob."

The man came back with a large case and a box of magazines.

"Let's wait in the chopper," Lance said.

"Where are you going with my chopper?" the pilot asked.

"Wherever your client tells you to. You're still flying it."

"Who are you people?"

Lance shoved an ID wallet under his nose. "Read it carefully," he said.

"Okay, I got it."

"The man you call Stanford is an enemy of your country. We have to deal with him. You're the only person who can get us to him."

"All right," the man said. "Let's go."

Stone's cell phone vibrated. "Yes?"

"It's Dino. Tell Lance I got to the police commissioner, and he's given the order to close Times Square."

Stone relayed the information to Lance.

"Thank God for that," Lance said.

"Where are you, Dino?" Stone asked. Stone turned on the speakerphone.

"I'm in a subway entrance in the street below the building. There's a SWAT team ready to take that roof."

"Don't do it, Dino," Lance said. "If you try, Billy Bob is going to start lobbing grenades into Times Square, and you don't want that. Are you in touch with the commissioner?"

"He's on his way here, now; I can reach him by phone."

"Good. Tell him to keep police and television helicopters away from that building, too."

"Okay, but what are you going to do?"

"I'll let you know in a few minutes."

"Okay, Dino?" Stone asked.

"Yeah, I'll wait for word."

Stone hung up. "Why don't we get this chopper started and get over there?"

"Because we have to wait to be asked. If we show up without an invitation he'll regard us as hostile and start shooting."

"And why do you think we'll be invited?"

"How else is he going to get out of there?" Lance asked.

54

Stone sat in the left copilot's seat of the helicopter and looked back at Lance, who had contrived a harness and some straps to keep him in the back of the helicopter. He was checking over a heavy rifle with a telescopic sight. The pilot sat nervously in the right front seat, waiting for instructions.

Suddenly, the radio in Stone's hand came to life.

"*Chopper One*, this is Stanford."

Stone handed the radio to the pilot.

"Stanford, *Chopper One*," the pilot said.

"What's your location?"

"East Side Heliport."

"Are you refueled?"

"Yes, sir."

"Here are your instructions: Take off and fly down the river to Forty-second Street, then up Eighth Avenue to Forty-third, then down Forty-third to the Briggs Building. Do you know it?"

"Yes, sir, there's a heliport on top."

"Right. Set down there, and I'll get aboard with a passenger."

"What's our destination from there, sir?"

"I'll tell you when I'm aboard."

"Yes, sir, I'm on my way; starting engine now."

"See you shortly."

The pilot looked back at Lance.

"Let's go," Lance said. He was practicing opening the sliding passenger door on the pilot's side of the helicopter. "When you set down, I want this door pointing at Stanford," Lance said. "I don't care what the wind sock says, this door has to face him. Got it?"

"Yes, sir." The pilot started through his checklist and a moment later, they were lifting off the heliport.

Stone put on a headset so that he could talk with Lance and the pilot over the noise of the engine. The pilot plugged Billy Bob's handheld radio into a socket on his headset, so they could all hear it over the intercom.

The helicopter rose and turned toward the East River, gaining altitude rapidly. At a thousand feet the pilot headed down the river, and when he was abreast of Forty-second Street he turned right and followed it west across Manhattan. Stone had flown in helicopters before, but never in the cockpit, and he watched as the pilot maneuvered the chopper. For controls there was a stick and two rudder pedals, as on a conventional airplane, then there was a lever Stone knew was called the "collective," which, apparently, had something to do with the propeller on the tail cone. Stone's understanding was that it kept the chopper from spinning with the big rotors.

Stone looked back at Lance, who was on his feet, the big rifle slung over a shoulder, looking ready. "Lance?" he said.

"Yes?"

"You will remember that Billy Bob is handcuffed to Peter, won't you?"

Lance did not reply.

"Lance?"

"Shut up, and be ready to follow me out of the helicopter," Lance said.

"Any other instructions?" Stone asked.

"Yes, don't let Billy Bob shoot either one of us."

"Pilot," Lance said. "I want you to land very slowly, more slowly than you're accustomed to, understand?"

"Yes, sir," the pilot replied.

They were passing Times Square. Stone craned his neck and saw that the NYPD had emptied it of traffic, that the only vehicles in the streets were black-and-white cars. He was amazed to see how quickly this had happened, but he knew the department had a procedure for clearing Times Square, as part of its response to terrorist threats.

"Eighth Avenue," the pilot called out.

"Slow down," Lance said. "I want him to have plenty of time to see you coming."

The pilot eased back the throttle, and the nose of the chopper came up to allow it to maintain altitude.

"You see the building?" Lance asked.

"Yes, sir," the pilot replied. "I'm aiming for the big *H* on the roof. Wind's from the north, less than ten knots, according to the wind sock on the roof."

"Remember, land with the right side of the aircraft pointing at Stanford, regardless of where the wind is."

"Yes, sir."

Stone heard a magazine driven home and the rifle having its action worked.

"Remember Peter," he said into his microphone.

No reply from Lance.

"I don't see anybody on the roof," the pilot said.

"Neither do I," Stone replied.

"Neither do I," Lance said.

"If I don't see him, how do you want me to set down?" the pilot asked.

"Land into the wind."

"Roger."

Stone could see other helicopters in the distance, but they were all keeping well clear of Times Square. He wondered what arms Billy Bob had with him, besides the grenades. He supposed he was going to find out in a moment.

The helicopter turned south, flying a downwind leg to the building, and Stone's side of the aircraft was now facing the building, perhaps a hundred feet below. He still saw no one on the roof. The chopper turned its base leg, to the east, then turned for its final approach, upwind to the north. The entire rooftop was laid out before them, empty.

The pilot brought the machine slowly down, and as they cleared the edge of the roof they were only about fifteen feet off the deck.

Stone glanced back at Lance. He was braced, the rifle ready in his right hand, his left on the door handle.

Ten feet, then five. Then Stone saw somebody.

55

The somebody Stone saw was a man dressed in black with a helmet, full body armor and an automatic weapon. Then a dozen more of them stepped from behind air-conditioning units, ventilators and other objects on the roof. Stone caught sight of the back of one of them, and emblazoned across it were the letters "FBI."

They surrounded the helicopter the moment it touched down, and one of them stood in front of the machine, his arms raised and crossed, which meant "Cut your engine." The pilot did so.

Somebody threw open the sliding rear door of the helicopter to find Lance, strapped in place, with his rifle at port arms. Men were all over him, taking the rifle and cutting the straps. Lance was replaced by an FBI agent, who pointed his machine gun at Stone and the pilot.

"Out!" he screamed. "Out right now!!!"

Stone and the pilot were assisted violently from the helicopter, thrown facedown on the roof, searched and handcuffed. Then

Stone looked up and saw a familiar face, under a mass of blond hair. “Tiff!” he yelled.

“You!” she yelled back. “What are *you* doing here? Get him on his feet!” she shouted to the agents.

They stood Stone up. “Gee, aren’t you glad to see me?” Stone asked.

“Throw him off the building!” she shouted to nobody in particular. Nobody moved, for which Stone was grateful.

“I asked you what you’re doing here,” she said to Stone.

“Uncuff me and don’t throw me off the building, and I’ll tell you,” Stone said.

Two agents marched Lance up to where they were standing.

“I believe you’ve met Lance Cabot, of the Central Intelligence Agency?” Stone said.

“So nice to see you again,” Lance said drily. “How do you do?”

“How do I fucking do?” Tiff screamed. “I do terrible! What are you people doing on this roof?”

“We are here to detain one Billy Bob Barnstormer,” Lance said, “a man of many aliases. What, may I ask, are *you* doing here?”

“I am the goddamned United States Attorney for the Southern District of New

York, and I am here to oversee the capture of the same man. Where is he?"

"My information was that he was on this roof and desired helicopter transportation," Lance said, "which I was planning to provide, after I had shot him."

"Tiff," Stone said, "would you kindly uncuff us, and maybe we can help."

"Oh, all right," she said, exasperatedly, "take the cuffs off them."

Stone, Lance and the pilot were uncuffed.

"Now," Tiff said, "tell me why you're here."

"I'm very sorry," Lance said. "I didn't realize you were hard of hearing. WE ARE HERE AT THE INVITATION OF BILLY BOB, TO TAKE HIM OFF THIS ROOF. DID YOU GET THAT?"

"Stop shouting at me, you . . . you *spook!*" she shouted at him.

"Tiff," Stone said, "Lance has told you repeatedly why we're here. We've been pursuing Billy Bob for some time, now. How did you and your band of merry men happen to be here on this roof?"

"We were in a meeting downstairs," she said, "when all hell seemed to break loose in Times Square. I called the police commissioner, and he advised me that Billy Bob was on or on his way to the roof."

"And everybody just happened to have handy one of those fetching black outfits with the body armor?"

"The fucking New York office of the FBI is in this building!" she screamed. "Now where is Billy Bob?"

"Well, he's clearly not on the roof," Stone said.

Lance spoke up. "Where are the NYPD?" he asked.

"In the fucking garage!" she shouted.

"Then, may I suggest a thorough search of the building, with the NYPD working their way up and your agents working their way down? If Billy Bob is in the building, perhaps you'll encounter him."

"SEARCH THE GODDAMNED BUILDING!!" Tiffany screamed, waving her arms at the agents.

"Tiff," Stone said, taking her arm and steering her toward the door, "if you don't calm down, you're going to have a stroke. Take a few deep breaths."

She stopped yelling and began breathing deeply. "Thank you," she said, finally. "That's better."

"Now, why don't you just phone the police commissioner and request that he start his people up, floor by floor," Stone said, as soothingly as he could.

"Stop talking to me as if I were a child," she said, whipping out her cell phone.

"You're getting excited again," Stone said. "Now, how can Lance and I help?"

"You can stay on the roof and out of the way," she said.

Lance walked over. "Are you aware of what Billy Bob is carrying?" he asked.

"I heard he had a small boy and a suitcase," Tiff replied.

"Do you know what is in the suitcase?"

"No."

"It contains thirty-six extremely powerful new grenades developed by the army, and a rifle launcher. If he is allowed to start firing them, many people will die."

Tiff looked appalled. "Nobody told me that."

"Perhaps you should mention that to your agents?" Lance said.

She grabbed an agent. "Guard that door, and see that these three people stay on the roof," she said, then she disappeared through the door.

"That," Lance said, "is a madwoman."

"Well, yes," Stone said.

"It frightens me to think that she is in charge here."

"I think she just wants to kill Billy Bob personally," Stone said.

"You don't mean to tell me she's armed!"

"I don't think she'll need a gun; she'll just claw him to death."

"How did this go wrong?" Lance asked.

"I don't know. Perhaps it was something to do with the FBI being housed in this building?"

"But why didn't Billy Bob make it to the roof?"

"I don't know, but I think we should hang on to his radio; it's in the helicopter." Stone retrieved both his and the pilot's. "What do we do now?"

Lance was on his phone. "I'm calling my director," he said. "Perhaps he can free us from this rooftop prison." He walked away and began speaking into the phone.

Stone walked over to the edge of the roof and looked over the chest-high parapet into Times Square. The only things moving down there were police cars and policemen. His cell phone vibrated. "Yes?"

"It's Dino. Were you in that chopper that landed on the roof?"

"Yes. We were greeted by the insane U.S. Attorney and her mob of jackbooted thugs. Right now, we're prisoners on the roof, but Lance is talking with Langley about changing that. Where are you?"

"I'm on the ground floor of the garage,

and I've had instructions from the commissioner to start a search of the building. It has sixty-one floors, by the way."

"Yes, Lance suggested that — quite sensibly, I thought. The FBI are working their way down, floor by floor. My guess is, the search shouldn't take more than a month."

"That was my estimate, too."

Then the radio in Stone's hand came to life. "Chopper One," Billy Bob said. "This is Stanford. Do you read?"

Stone waved the pilot over. "Answer Stanford; find out where he is."

"Yes, sir," the pilot said into the radio. "I'm on the roof; where are you?"

Stone looked around for Lance, but he had disappeared, presumably behind some of the equipment on the roof.

"Here are your instructions," Billy Bob said.

56

Stone looked around for Lance, but he was nowhere in sight. Billy Bob's voice came back on the radio.

"I want you to start your engine and prepare to take off when I instruct you to do so."

Stone looked over at the FBI agent guarding the door from the roof. The man was lying on his side, his helmet was next to him with a hole in it, and blood was pooling around his head. "Tell him yes," Stone said.

"Yes, sir, will do," the pilot said.

"Go and start the engine," Stone said, "but don't take off until I'm aboard."

"Yes, sir," the pilot said and strode toward the helicopter.

Stone ran around the roof, looking behind equipment, but Lance was nowhere to be found. He gave up and sprinted for the helicopter. Its rotor was already turning.

Stone dove into the back of the helicopter. He was on the floor between two facing rows of seats. He looked aft, found a baggage compartment and rolled over the rear seats into that area. There was a small window in the compartment, and he looked out both sides, wondering what was going to happen. He was looking west when Billy Bob's head rose above the building's parapet, followed a moment later by Peter's head. Billy Bob was holding the boy in his arms.

As Stone watched, Billy Bob swung a large case over the parapet and dropped it onto the rooftop, then he got a leg over and dropped Peter, who landed on his feet. They were still handcuffed together, and Billy Bob had an assault rifle fitted with a suppressor/silencer slung over one shoulder. Stone was still being amazed by Billy Bob's feat of levitation when it occurred to him that there must be a window-washer's platform on that side of the building, one of those things that went up and down like an elevator to allow workers to clean the windows on each floor. The fucking FBI, he thought, had not bothered to look over the parapet when they searched the roof.

Billy Bob strode toward the chopper, dragging Peter, who was struggling to keep up. Stone unholstered his 9mm, but he knew that, because of Peter, he would not have a shot, until Billy Bob got into the helicopter. Stone ducked behind the seat to avoid being seen.

He felt a bump when Billy Bob dumped his case and climbed into the machine, but he could not see between the seats, only over them, and he did not want to risk popping up at a time when Billy Bob might be facing him. Also, he didn't know Peter's position.

"Take off now!" Billy Bob shouted over the whine of the engine, and the chopper immediately leaped off the roof.

The motion cost Stone his balance, and he toppled sideways. By the time he regained his knees they were moving forward. Stone knew they were beyond the help of anyone in the building, and that the NYPD helicopters had been told to stand off.

"Fly right up the middle of Broadway!" Billy Bob shouted, "and stay just above rooftop level!" He must have encountered some resistance from the pilot, because he began shouting again. "Do it, or I'll blow your fucking head off!"

Stone popped his head up for a split second, then ducked. Billy Bob had been standing, facing forward, while Peter sat on the floor, still handcuffed. The sliding door on the right was open.

"Now you be still!" Billy Bob shouted, apparently at Peter. "I'm going to unlock the handcuff, and you don't want to fall out, do you?"

Stone flicked off the safety on his pistol and waited a reasonable time for the cuff to be unlocked, then he sat up and pointed his pistol forward. Peter was free, and Billy Bob was still facing the pilot, the assault rifle pointed at the man's head. Stone climbed over the seat and swung the barrel of his pistol at the back of Billy Bob's head, hard. A gunshot could be heard over the noise of the engine, and Stone thought his pistol had gone off, but, as Billy Bob collapsed at his feet, he saw that the back of the pilot's head was gone. Billy Bob's weapon had fired a round when he was struck.

The helicopter began a slow, descending left turn, and Stone made a leap for the copilot's seat. "Hang on, Peter!" he yelled, grabbing the boy's hand and dragging him forward. Stone made the copilot's seat and grabbed the stick, trying to get the chopper level, but then he saw the top of a building coming at him. He yanked back on the stick and cleared the building by a foot, then continued climbing, feeling the airspeed bleed off. They were going to stall any second.

Stone pushed the pilot's body out of the

way and found the throttle, pushing it forward. The chopper climbed, and he breathed a sigh of relief, until he realized that Peter was no longer next to him. He looked over his shoulder and saw the boy tugging at the inert Billy Bob, one of whose legs was dangling out the open door.

"Come back to me, Peter!" he shouted, and in that moment of looking back, he lost control of the helicopter. It banked sharply to the left, and Stone desperately tried to correct. The chopper had turned a full three hundred and sixty degrees before he could level it again and glance back. The good news was both Billy Bob and Peter had been thrown against the left side of the helicopter, away from the open door. "Come to me, Peter!" he shouted.

"No," the boy shouted back. "He'll fall out, if I let him go."

"No, he won't. Come to me!"

Peter shook his head and clung to Billy Bob.

Stone looked at the chopper's instrument panel, trying to find something that looked like an autopilot. He found nothing but the usual flight instruments, like the ones on his own airplane. He was headed north again, toward Central Park. At least that was open space, he thought. He might have some chance of setting the thing down. He looked back at Peter.

"Listen to me!" he shouted. "He's all right, he won't fall out. I want you to climb over the backseat and stay there while I land. Sit down and don't move!"

The boy looked at the rear seats, then at Billy Bob, then at Stone. He nodded.

Stone tried to keep the chopper level while Peter inched his way aft. He glanced back to see the boy disappear behind the rear seats. "Thank God," he said, then he turned his attention back to flying.

It didn't feel like an airplane, exactly, but it had a stick, rudder pedals and a throttle, like an airplane. He hoped to God he wasn't going to need the collective handle, because he didn't really know what would happen if he used it. They were crossing Fifty-seventh Street now, and the bare trees of Central Park beckoned.

Then he heard Peter scream, "Stone!!!" He looked back to find Billy Bob on his knees, his head bleeding and his assault rifle pointed at Stone. What was worse, he could see that a grenade had been attached to the rifle.

"Shoot me, and you die!" Stone shouted.

"Do what I say, or we *all* die," Billy Bob shouted back. "The boy, too!"

57

Stone tried to think of something, but he could only concentrate on keeping the helicopter in the air.

Billy Bob slipped on a headset and handed Stone one. "We're going back to Times Square," he said.

Stone put on the headset. "I've never flown a helicopter before. I don't know if I can make that kind of turn without dumping this thing."

"Well, you seem to be doing okay," Billy Bob replied. "Let's give it a whirl. Say, where's the boy?"

"I lost him trying to turn this thing. He was trying to keep you inside, and he went out."

"And I had grown so fond of the little shit," Billy Bob said. "To think he gave his all for me. Hey, why aren't you turning?" He nudged the back of Stone's head with the assault rifle.

Stone started a right-hand turn, keeping it shallow. He was making a wide arc to the east, now, and they were over Fifth Avenue before he was headed south.

"You know," Billy Bob said, "there are an awful lot of cops around Times Square, and they probably have snipers set up by now. Maybe a nicer spot would be Rockefeller Center, and you're right on course."

"Oh, shit," Stone muttered.

"I can put a grenade right into the skating rink," Billy Bob said. "The area will be jammed with tourists this time of year."

"Why are you doing this?" Stone asked. "What's in it for you?"

"I know I'm not getting out of this alive," Billy Bob said. "I may as well make a splash."

"Look, I can fly this thing to Teterboro right now. Don't you have an airplane out there?"

"Not anymore, Stone."

"Then hijack one. There are always a dozen jets on the ramp with their engines running, waiting for passengers to arrive. Take one and get the hell out of here."

"And where would I go?"

"Iceland doesn't have an extradition treaty with the United States." This wasn't true, but maybe Billy Bob didn't know that.

"Iceland doesn't have an extradition treaty? I've never heard that."

"Few people know about it, but it's true."

"Bullshit. I don't believe that for a moment."

"Then . . ." Stone was about to make another suggestion, but he was interrupted by the sound of the engine sputtering and dying. The helicopter began to descend.

"What the hell is wrong?" Billy Bob shouted.

"I don't know," Stone replied. He was scanning the instrument panel, looking for a warning light or some other reason. His eyes stopped on the fuel gauges: One of them showed full, the other empty. He found a lever and shoved it sideways, changing tanks. The engine came back to life, as if it had never been starved for fuel.

"Good work, Stone."

But now they were low over Fifth Avenue. Stone eased the throttle forward, and the chopper began to climb again. "What's wrong with Mexico?" he asked.

"Too far. They'd shoot me down before I could get there."

"Then go offshore and head for South America. They can't shoot you down over international waters." This was a lie, too.

"You know, you might have something there."

"So, we'll head for Teterboro?"

"Yeah, but not yet; first I want to lob a couple of these grenades into Rockefeller Center, see how they perform. Call it a test."

"You do that, and they'll never stop looking for you, Billy Bob. Come on, you've got money offshore, right? Head south and lie low. Find some nice spot and buy a house and a few girls. Eventually, they'll get tired of looking."

"You make it sound so inviting," Billy Bob said.

"It'll never happen if you fire those grenades," Stone said. "The cops will blow us out of the sky; they'll be finding pieces of us around midtown for days. But, right now, they're standing off. We can make Teterboro."

"That's a very tempting thought, Stone," Billy Bob said.

"Turning right for Teterboro," Stone said. He eased the chopper into a right turn. Then he felt the gun barrel at the back of his head again.

"I don't think so," Billy Bob said.

"Come on, why not?"

"Because I'm tired, Stone. I've run out my string, and this is going to be my last day on the planet. Yours, too. You know, I'm really sorry about the boy; he was a sweet kid."

Stone leveled out heading west. He wasn't going to be complicit in this. If he and Peter were going to die today, then they weren't going to take hundreds of others with them.

If a grenade had to go off, then the Hudson River, he decided, was the best place for it to happen. He didn't think Billy Bob would have time to fire one and reload from the case before he could dump the helicopter into the icy river.

"Hey, you're headed in the wrong direction," Billy Bob said.

"No, I think you really want to go to Teterboro; that's the best deal." They had crossed Sixth Avenue, now, and Seventh was coming up fast. Five more crosstown blocks, and he'd make the water. Stone pushed the throttle farther forward and adjusted the trim to keep the chopper level, so it would pick up speed. He watched the airspeed climb from eighty-five to a hundred knots.

Billy Bob rapped him sharply on the head with the barrel of the assault rifle. "You're not paying attention," he said.

Stone felt a warm trickle of blood run down his scalp to his neck. "There's something I've got to do before we go back to Rockefeller Center," Stone said.

"What do you mean, there's something *you've* got to do?" Billy Bob demanded. "This is *my* party, and we'll go where I say."

"Yeah, well you're going to have to say it to that police helicopter on our tail. Those things are equipped with rocket launchers, you know, but if we can get across the Hudson, they can't touch us. They'll have to scramble Jersey State Police choppers on the other side, and that will take time." He was coming up on Twelfth Avenue, now, and the river was just ahead.

"What police chopper?" Billy Bob asked. "I don't see it."

"It's dead behind us, and gaining," Stone said. "But we can make Jersey, and we'll be okay." The chopper crossed the banks of the Hudson at a thousand feet, and then Billy Bob did something that Stone would always be grateful for.

He stepped back, transferred the assault rifle to his left hand, grabbed a handgrip bolted to the airframe and stuck his head into the slipstream, leaning out and looking behind them for the police helicopter.

Stone yanked back on the throttle, whipped the stick to the right and the chopper went into an impossibly steep right turn. He looked back to see Billy Bob hanging out of the helicopter, still gripping the rifle, hanging on to the handgrip for dear life. Stone kicked the right rudder, and the chopper's roll became even steeper. It was more than Billy Bob's grip could handle. His grip failed, and Stone watched him begin his plunge toward the icy Hudson a thousand feet below.

But Stone had no time to relish the moment, because the helicopter continued to roll. Stone could see the George Washington Bridge, in the distance, and it was upside down. Stone had a sensation of falling from the sky, and he closed his eyes. Then a huge explosion rocked the helicopter, and Stone knew Billy Bob had tested his grenade.

58

The heat from the explosion caused a huge thermal, and the helicopter rode it upward, threatening to roll again. Stone got hold of himself and got hold of the stick. The airspeed had bled off to sixty knots, and he was afraid of stalling again. He shoved the throttle forward, and held the stick centered between his legs, hoping aerodynamics would do the rest. But now there was something new — a thumping vibration that rhythmically shook the chopper.

The instrument panel was a vibrating blur, so he looked outside to orient himself. He was flying up the river toward the George Washington Bridge, and he didn't have enough altitude to clear it. He pushed the stick down, and a moment later, the bridge passed over him. He eased back the stick, trying to gain altitude without advancing the throttle. He thought he must have lost a rotor tip in the explosion, and he didn't want to put any more strain on the machine.

Finally, he was at the top of the Palisades, the high cliffs overlooking the Hudson, then he managed to gain another couple of hundred feet. He remembered that Teterboro was southwest of the bridge, and he eased the chopper into a shallow left turn. The vibration increased, but soon, he was on the right heading. Then he saw a big business jet a few miles ahead, making an approach, and he followed its line of flight toward the runway. He had the airfield in sight.

He found a radio in the panel, but he couldn't for the life of him remember the frequency for Teterboro tower, so he tuned in 121.5 mhz, the emergency frequency, and pressed the push-to-talk switch. "Mayday, Mayday, Mayday," he said. "Helicopter approaching Teterboro from the northeast for emergency landing. Teterboro tower, if you can hear me, clear the way, because I've never landed a helicopter, and I think I have a broken rotor tip."

"Stone?" A familiar voice.

"Dino?"

"Right behind you, pal."

"Helicopter, Teterboro tower," an urgent voice said. "We have you in sight; cleared to land anyplace you want to put her down. Suggest runway one niner, if able."

"I'll do the best I can," Stone replied. "Dino?"

"Shut up and fly the chopper," Dino said.

Stone took his advice. He began trying to slow the helicopter; he was too hot, and he pulled back on the throttle and held his altitude to bleed off airspeed, the way he would do in an airplane. He could see the runway, now, and he was about two hundred feet above it. He pulled the throttle back to idle, and the thing began dropping like a rock. He added power, but he was still high and hot. He chopped the throttle again and yanked back on the stick. The sky filled the windshield, and with his peripheral vision he could see the ground coming up fast. He passed over the runway, losing altitude, in a nose-up position.

The helicopter struck tail first, and still Stone held the stick back. Then it slammed into the ground, and strangely, there was water everywhere. Stone, who was not wearing a seat belt, was thrown forward, striking his head on the windshield. The last thing he heard was the noise of the rotor chewing up the ground, then everything went quiet.

The voice came from a distance: "Stone?" A small voice. "Stone?" Somebody shook him and pulled him back into his seat. Stone opened his eyes and looked around.

"Peter?"

"Here I am, Stone."

"Are you all right?"

"Yeah, and I did what you said."

"What?"

"I got behind the seat and stayed there. It was sort of like a ride at the carnival in Charlottesville, but not as much fun."

The air was filled with approaching sirens, and Stone was aware that a helicopter was landing a few yards away. He looked out the window and saw that they had come to rest in shallow water, a swampy area between a runway and a taxiway. Twenty yards away he saw his own airplane, parked with others in the infield. Then he passed out.

His dreams were not good: They were a montage of Billy Bob, Arrington, Peter and Tiffany Baldwin, who always seemed to be screaming at him. Then, slowly, they faded and he found himself in a darkened room. Sunlight peeked from behind venetian blinds. Someone was holding his hand.

"Stone?" A woman's voice.

"Go away, Tiff," he said wearily. He had had enough of her.

"It's Arrington."

Stone turned his head and looked at her. "It is, isn't it?" he said, relieved.

"You're all right; you just had a couple of

bumps on the head. You lost a little hair, and you have a few stitches, and your head is sort of swollen, but you'll be just fine. All you have to do is rest."

"I'm hungry," Stone said. "Am I on drugs?"

"The doctor gave you something when they stitched your head up yesterday. He wanted you to rest."

"Yesterday? And now it's today?"

"That's how it works, Stone: yesterday, then today."

"Can I have a bacon cheeseburger?"

"I'm not sure that's on the menu, but I'll get you something." She picked up the call buzzer and pressed it. A moment later a nurse came in, followed by Dino and Lance.

"Okay, Lance," he said. "Now you can court-martial me."

Everybody began laughing.

59

Lance and Dino took him home that afternoon, in Arrington's chauffeured Bentley.

"Where's Arrington?" Stone asked, as they got into the car.

"She and Peter had something to do," Dino said. "She didn't say what."

"Let me tell you where we are," Lance said. "We recovered thirty-five grenades from the helicopter you crashed."

"Crashed? I thought that was a pretty good landing, considering."

"Controlled crash was how the FAA described it," Dino said. "The helicopter is a total loss."

"That's what insurance is for."

"Billy Bob managed to fire one grenade while he was falling from the helicopter," Lance said.

"Nearly blew the police chopper I was riding in out of the sky," Dino said.

"The explosion broke a lot of windows along the New York bank of the Hudson, but nobody was seriously injured," Lance said. "We rolled up Martin Block's operation in Queens, and he's singing like a bird. The feds have put a stop to three or four cons Billy Bob was running out of Block's building, and they found all his bank records there, so they're going after his offshore cash as we speak."

"Where did he get all the two-dollar bills?" Stone asked.

"Billy Bob bought them at a sharp discount from the grandson of one of the robbers," Lance said. "He met the kid at Sing-Sing, where he did a five-year stretch for financial fraud. Got out a couple of years ago. That's also where he met your old friend Mitteldorfer, who asked Billy Bob, as a favor, to first ruin you, then kill you, after he got out. Mitteldorfer made him a lot of money with investment advice while he was inside, so he was happy to oblige."

"Mitteldorfer sure knows how to hold a grudge," Dino said, shaking his head. "I've asked the people up there to put him in solitary for as close to forever as the rules will allow."

"Mitteldorfer will think the company is good," Stone said.

"Tiffany Baldwin is annoyed with you for killing Billy Bob," Lance said.

"The ungrateful bitch," Dino muttered.

"She was so looking forward to prosecuting him," Lance said. "At least she'll have the pleasure of announcing all his operations that she's rolling up. The Attorney General will like that."

"And what does the Agency get out of it all?" Stone asked.

"We got thirty-five of thirty-six of the stolen grenades back, plus we nailed the guy in New Mexico who sold them to Billy Bob. Unfortunately, the stolen grenade-launching rifle is at the bottom of the Hudson. We've got divers looking for it."

"How's Corey?"

"Antsy, because she can't work for a couple of weeks," Lance said, "but she's on the mend."

"I'm sorry about McGonigle."

"It wasn't your fault; these things happen in my line of work."

"Is that how you think of it? As a 'line of work'?"

"It's as good a description as any. Oh, by the way, Holly Barker is joining us; I'm expecting her signed contract tomorrow. She drove a hard bargain, though."

"I'll bet she wouldn't leave the dog behind."

"Good guess. Daisy will be joining the team, too."

The car pulled up in front of Stone's

house, and he got out. "Lance, what happened to you on the rooftop when Billy Bob showed up?"

"Oh, I happened to see the FBI man take a bullet, so I lay low. By the time it was safe for me to come out, you were already in the chopper, and I felt I shouldn't shoot it down."

"Thanks," Stone said drily. "You fellows want to come in for a drink?"

"Thank you, no," Lance said. "I have a very long report to write."

"Me, too," Dino said. "You feel up to dinner at Elaine's tonight?"

"Sure," Stone said. "See you at nine." He turned to go, but the chauffeur spoke.

"Excuse me, Mr. Barrington, but Mrs. Calder asked me to give you this." He handed Stone a sealed envelope.

Stone went inside and upstairs to his bedroom; he wanted a nap before dinnertime. He sat on his bed and opened the envelope. Inside was a single sheet of heavy, cream-colored stationery.

My Dear Stone,

First, I want to thank you for protecting Peter. I would have gone crazy, if anything had happened to him. Thank you, too, for taking such good care of me, something you have always done so well.

I'm afraid that New York is just a little too exciting for Peter and me right now, so we've headed back to Virginia. Peter misses his pony, and I miss the peace. Of course, I'll miss you, too.

I don't think you'd transplant very well to Albemarle County, so I won't even suggest that. But perhaps you'd like to come for a visit now and then. I think your son would like that.

Love,
Arrington

Stone lay back on the bed and tried not to cry.

Author's Note

I am happy to hear from readers, but you should know that if you write to me in care of my publisher, three to six months will pass before I receive your letter, and when it finally arrives it will be one among many, and I will not be able to reply.

However, if you have access to the Internet, you may visit my Web site at www.stuartwoods.com, where there is a button for sending me e-mail. So far, I have been able to reply to all of my e-mail, and I will continue to try to do so.

If you send me an e-mail and do not receive a reply, it is because you are among an alarming number of people who have entered their e-mail address incorrectly in their mail software. I have many of my replies returned as undeliverable.

Remember: e-mail, reply; snail mail, no reply.

When you e-mail, please do not send attachments, as I *never* open these. They can take twenty minutes to download, and they often contain viruses.

Please do not place me on your mailing lists for funny stories, prayers, political causes, charitable fund-raising, petitions or sentimental claptrap. I get enough of that from people I already know. Generally speaking, when I get e-mail addressed to a large number of people, I immediately delete it without reading it.

Please do not send me your ideas for a book, as I have a policy of writing only what I myself invent. If you send me story ideas, I will immediately delete them without reading them. If you have a good idea for a book, write it yourself, but I will not be able to advise you on how to get it published. Buy a copy of *Writer's Market* at any bookstore; that will tell you how.

Anyone with a request concerning events or appearances may e-mail it to me or send it to: Publicity Department, G. P. Putnam's Sons, 375 Hudson Street, New York, NY 10014.

Those ambitious folk who wish to buy film, dramatic or television rights to my books should contact Matthew Snyder, Creative Artists Agency, 9830 Wilshire Boulevard, Beverly Hills, CA 90212-1825.

Those who wish to conduct business of a more literary nature should contact Anne

Sibbald, Janklow & Nesbit, 445 Park Avenue, New York, NY 10022.

If you want to know if I will be signing books in your city, please visit my Web site, www.stuartwoods.com, where the tour schedule will be published a month or so in advance. If you wish me to do a book signing in your locality, ask your favorite bookseller to contact his Putnam representative or the G. P. Putnam's Sons publicity department with the request.

If you find typographical or editorial errors in my book and feel an irresistible urge to tell someone, please write to David Highfill at Putnam, address above. Do not e-mail your discoveries to me, as I will already have learned about them from others.

A list of all my published works appears in the front of this book. All the novels are still in print in paperback and can be found at or ordered from any bookstore. If you wish to obtain hardcover copies of earlier novels or the two nonfiction books, a good used-book store or one of the online bookstores can help you find them. Otherwise, you will have to go to a great many garage sales.